DATE DUE			

Also by JULIAN F. THOMPSON

point

SIMON PURE

Julian F. Thompson

SCHOLASTIC INC.
New York Toronto London Auckland Sydney

Scholastic Books are available at special discounts for quantity purchases for use as premiums, promotional items, retail sales through specialty market outlets, etc. For details contact: Special Sales Manager, Scholastic Inc., 730 Broadway, New York, NY 10003.

ISBN 0–590–41823–8

Copyright © 1987 by Julian F. Thompson. All rights reserved. Published by Scholastic Inc. POINT is a registered trademark of Scholastic Inc.

12 11 10 9 8 7 6 5 4 3 2 1   8   8 9/8 0 1 2 3/9
Printed in the U.S.A   01

This book was made for Perry, Marilyn, Jean, and Ellen, in gratefulness for their perception, faith, wise counsel, understanding, tolerance, and friendship. And for Polly, whose loving kindness shone on it each day.

Author's Preface

Some of the events in this book may have taken place at Riddle University within the last few years. For various legal, aesthetic, and personal reasons, the names of the college president and his family; of various professors, administrators, and alumni; and of all the students in the book have been changed from their real ones to these others. Also, in spite of anything that's said or implied here, there's no existing documented proof of any relationship between any elected or appointed member of the federal government and anyone described in these pages. Supposedly.

And one other thing. If any reader, a graduate of . . . (no point naming names, *you* know who are), is tempted to unload some line like, "Just what you'd expect, at Riddle," or, "Thank God I didn't let my kid go *there*," think twice. What happened in this book might also have occurred at . . . where you went. Or where you're going. And in another printing it just might.

1

Acceptance Date

"Our notification date is April the fifteenth, of course," said R. Montford Layton, dean of admissions, Riddle University. He had his hand on Simon's shoulder, walking toward his office door, as he said that. But then — step 2 — he took it off and offered it, belt-high, for firm, let's-make-a-deal-type shaking.

He also gave the boy his special smile, certain he'd be understood. If they were good enough to merit such a smile, they were always smart enough to "get" it ("women and minorities excepted," he was "sad to say").

Simon surely did, so — what the heck — he grinned delightedly and boyishly (that's 1) and dropped his eyes (step 2). It didn't cost him anything, and he was grateful, he supposed. Riddle would be sending out its letters of acceptance and rejection on the same day as Harvard, Stanford, and his other backup schools. If it took *his* letter three days to get from Riddle to his parents' house outside of Peacemeal, Vermont — as it almost surely would — he'd get the news, officially, on April the eighteenth.

Simon wasn't impressed by the Postal Service any more than he was by himself; he figured neither getting mail in three days' time from a place three hundred miles away nor being all that smart were things he caused to happen. But he *did* like the idea of getting into college on the day he turned fifteen. That year, he wanted college for his birthday.

2

Simon Storm

Here's a little background on the guy — what Dean Layton might call his "curriculum vitae," barely touching the top of his head as he said those words, as if testing for a fracture, or wet paint. Or what Henry Portcullis, president of Riddle University, *did* call "the poop on him," while requesting same from his old college roomie, Simon's father, Jared Storm.

Since the middle of first grade (Peacemeal Regional didn't have a kindergarten yet) Simon Storm had come into school no more than three days a week, and then for just a while. He'd sit in on a class or two and try to look stimulated and thoughtful, and "be polite," the way his mother'd taught him to. Afterward, he'd get to play outside on a field, or in the gym, with kids his own age. That part always went real well. Quick and graceful, even-tempered and unselfish, he got right into sports and games and teamwork, and excelled. As he grew older, coaches there at Peacemeal, talking to each other, likened him to Bambi and bemoaned his progress through the system. ("I swear to Christ, that kid skips grades like most of them skip *school* . . . " with heads in side-to-side, regretful motion.)

But the kids in his schoolrooms thought he maybe was a *re*-tard of some sort, because the teachers never called on him, and he would never volunteer an answer, right *or* wrong. And when they'd question him about what grade he was in, or if he had himself some crayons or a notebook, or where he spent his time when he was out of school, he'd only shrug and smile and mumble something vague. As far as he was concerned, it was better to do that and be thought of as a *re*-tard than attempt some sort of explanation. That would be (he thought) like explaining to people with an allergy to bee stings that he spent most days teasing hornets. Simon Storm, you see, was busy learning stuff.

Almost every day his mother would drive him to sessions with men and women she or his father had known for years, or had dug up somehow. They were a mixed, eccentric, brilliant bag: a poet resident at Goddard, a physicist who was the former scientific adviser to the Joint Chiefs, a pastured economic forecaster, the entire staff of a holistic health center (which included a woman who was studying how heavy metal — lead *or* Twisted Sister — acted on the human embryo).

Because his mom — Maria Storm — had been a brain researcher since before she'd owned a car, he'd absorbed a combination of global and analytical approaches to learning, as well as speed-reading techniques that transformed him into a bibliophilic Carl Lewis by the age of ten. In other words, the kid was one fast, multipurpose sponge. By the day he got his letter of acceptance from Riddle, the 5,479th of his life, he'd not only read and sucked the vital juices from as many books as his average agemate had watched hours of TV, but he'd also learned to fast-forward the videotape of *Flashdance*, and eye-peel all the skin off it in under seven minutes flat.

From time to time and for the record, Simon would go into school and take exams, which were administered by the principal himself in the big supplies closet behind his office. But then, in his last year at Peacemeal Regional (and to many kids' amazement), Simon came out and took the SATs right there in the school gym, with a whole lot of other, older people — and then the Achievement Tests as well (with four girls and a Cambodian) in the faculty conference room.

Simon thought they were stupid — not the other kids, the tests. The other kids also thought they were stupid — not the tests but, sadly, their own selves. A rotten time was had by all, in other words — though nothing that different home environments, higher teacher salaries, Stanley Kaplan, or (in Simon's case) a more contemporary value system mightn't have changed, I guess.

Scoring in the 99th–100th percentile, nationally, on tests constructed by the ETS, did not give Simon any pleasure. He could do it, but it wasn't fun. What he imagined would be all sorts of fun, but which he almost certainly couldn't do, for quite a number of substantial and intimidating reasons, was scoring on (or was it "with"?) Jennifer Beals, the star of *Flashdance*, or anyone even remotely like her.

3

Women

It was, of course, perfectly possible that there would be a Jennifer Beals equivalent in his class at Riddle. She had gone to Yale, he knew, and most people who went to Riddle had probably also been accepted there, and vice versa.

But it wouldn't matter, Simon Storm was sure of that. There could be twenty — a hundred — Jennifer Beals look-alikes and act-alikes at Riddle, and it wouldn't change his status one iota. Except to make him that much more conscious of it, probably. He suspected there wasn't a single other kid in the universe so badly made — so *out of phase* — for meaningful relationships as he was.

Here's the way the situation seemed, to him. Through no fault of his own, he happened to have (was *cursed with*, as he sometimes — almost — thought of it) this ability to read and understand (remember, organize) a lot of information. And also — face it — to be capable of using what he learned to reach conclusions, understandings — some of them unusual, original, creative even. Partly as a result of these abilities, he'd got a handle on the so-called "facts of life" at five, and had gained a pretty good appreciation of the meaning of "mature love" before he turned nine. By the age of twelve he'd attained the capacity to reproduce the species and, based on his research, believed he'd very much enjoy *that* process.

The problem with all this was that it put him miles ahead of girls his own age — which was more or less the opposite of (so-called) "normal." It wasn't so much a matter of hormones as it was of sensibility. There were certain girls in his age group, or even younger, who were definitely "hot to trot" (as the boys of Peacemeal put it), some of whom were said to have already taken a few laps at that gait with wild and crazy older guys like Jerry Archambo. But as far as Simon was concerned, these girls were almost like another planetsworth of people, when it came to interests, knowledge, attitudes, and style. They were just so *different*, hard to understand; for instance, almost all of them smoked cigarettes. For (maybe) that, and other reasons, he wasn't lovable to them, himself, at all; if anything, he was a jerk-off. Truthfully, he didn't covet them as friends.

Where Jennifer Beals made clear and total sense to him, girls his age were very near . . . impenetrable.

At the same time, Simon knew that *older* girls who looked at him saw nothing but "a kid." Acceptable — but only as a kind of mascot, up to maybe eight o'clock at night. *They* could get a lot of dates with men much older than themselves, but did that make them willing to extend such courtesies to guys a little younger? Not in this guh-*laxy*, Maxie.

Simon Storm was a sociosexual island, if he did say so, unto himself. John Donne had not been talking kids.

4

Other Thoughts

Women weren't the only things on his mind at the age of fifteen — not by a long shot. Sex must have a really great agent, or something, the way it always seems to get first mention whenever a series of things that it's one of is being talked about.

Like, with human *drives*:

"Well," whatever simp or simpette that's doing the talking says, "there probably isn't any question but that the *sex* drive is responsible for more great art (bad advertising, peculiar food experiments) than any other human urge or impulse. . . ."

But Simon also thought, with great regularity, about other milestones and decisions in his life to come:

— what he'd do next summer
— whether he'd get bald
— what the chances were of the "nuclear winter" ever taking place
— what the chances were of the "nuclear winter" taking place before next summer
— what he'd do when he grew up, out of all

11

the things that seemed as if they might be
fun
— how he'd look when he was old enough to
grow a beard and/or mustache
— when was the earliest he might hope for a
car
— where on a girl's body he'd actually put his
hand *first*, if he ever was invited or permit-
ted to (I know, I know)
— whether he would ever write a book, or own
a country inn
— how he'd get along, in college
— what really mattered, anyway.

Please don't hold his not thinking about getting
into college against the guy. *You* probably wouldn't
have any trouble getting a date with Jennifer Beals.
Or you could *be* her, for all I know.

Or maybe you're a skier and think a nuclear winter sounds "just fab."

5

Old Roomies

Jared Storm was slouched in a big old wing chair with the phone on the floor beside him. He took another strengthening *soupçon* of Black & White (no ice, a little soda, in a pistol-grip coffee mug), swished it here and there around his back teeth, and listened to his old roomie, fourteenth president of Riddle University, enthuse.

". . . damn fantastic . . . utterly delightful . . . didn't have a clue. . . ."

That's just the froth, of course; Henry Portcullis (called, since junior high school, "Gate" or "Gates" or "Gatesy" or "the Gater") was on a real high bubble, going on and on. He almost didn't have another setting; in college, Jared Storm used to watch him, in amazement, while he studied, bouncing up and down. Now, he imagined him sitting at a different desk, both elbows on it, leaning forward, gesturing as he so often did, like mad. Three hundred miles away, but Jared *knew* that big, expressive hand was pumping back and forth: open, fingers slightly bent, as if it held a football no one else could see.

It wasn't any lack of affection for the Gater, or

of enthusiasm for the event, that had kept Jared off the phone to Riddle — even after Simon's ". . . very pleased to offer you a place . . ." letter had arrived. More, it was the way he was: low-key and deferential, very much averse to brag. Henry'd called him, though, when *he* found out.

". . . figured that it *couldn't* be. . . . Dean Monty Layton, right away . . . folder, and by golly . . . *fifteen* whole years old! . . . Hey, Barn," Henry Portcullis dropped his voice and calmed it. "What's the poop on this guy Simon, anyway? He must *look* exactly like Maria, too — right? Those aren't Daddy's numbers in that folder, babe. But will he love ol' mothuh Riddle, too? Or great-grandma, that'd be in his case, right?"

The questions caught Jared by surprise, in the middle of another sip of Scotch. Instead of answering, he tipped his head back and gargled with the mouthful. Whisky was a damn good antiseptic, he had read one time — why not get your money's worth? A lot of Henry's questions were just rhetorical, anyway.

". . . absolutely great . . ." the guy was going on. "But still" — he heard another tone, concern, in Gatesy's voice — "can a fifteen-year-old be expected to handle what we — the Lord's anointed — call 'the residential life' at Riddle?" He laughed. "Can anyone?"

Jared shrugged a time or two as he considered — *re*considered — the question. He was sort of glad the Gater'd brought that subject up. Not because he'd have an answer — no one could — but just because he'd been around the situation; he was *there*. They'd made him president of Riddle three years

14

after Simon was born; Henry was fresh from pressing suntanned flesh and taking on experience as ass't. to the pres at Santa Cruz. There'd been a certain amount of snickering in the Ivies about Riddle going for a nonintellectual as its fourteenth president (although the United States had done more or less the same, by way of Franklin Pierce, a Bowdoin man), not to mention such a lad. Some alums called it a blatant sellout/bribe to trendy, youth-freak counterculture, while others predicted senior and distinguished members of the Riddle faculty would rise in scholarly rebellion. Of course that didn't happen. As the ol' Gater well knew, professors like nothing better than being left alone to profess to smart kids in comfortable and well-equipped surroundings, unless it's having their salaries raised to heights above — oh, well above — the ones at M.I.T., or any of the huge state schools out west. And he was just the boy to cause all that to happen.

Henry Portcullis was a realist who wore enthusiastic, bouncy crepe-soled shoes. Students in the early seventies saw him as potentially "aware" and "sympathetic"; older Riddle people (like alumni optimists) hoped he might be the buffer between themselves and something alien and threatening. And so, when they perceived he was a *bridge* (in fact), they paid the toll with pleasure, reaching for their checkbooks almost at the sight of him. As president, Gates Portcullis raised money the way a bigot raises hackles, and partly as a result of his abilities, Riddle bopped through the last years of student unrest with less on-campus graffiti and more substantive (but not radical) program changes and enlargements than any equivalent college in the country. For more and more ambitious families all over America, Riddle was "the answer" (I'm sure you know the question), and in a way it was that fact, known even in Peacemeal, that worried Jared Storm.

"Well, as far as *he's* concerned," Jared finally said, "everybody seems to like him well enough up here, if that means anything. He gets along with all the different ages, and even people from New Jersey. So the thing that cautions me, to tell you the truth, is not so much his getting on with them as what he'll think of . . . well, his fellow Sphinxes." The Riddle animal was, unsurprisingly, a sphinx — but the Greek variety with a woman's head and bust, plus the lion's body, and wings. It really made the perfect monster-mascot for a coed school, which Riddle always had been, unlike you-know-where and what's-its-name. And anything mythological is faintly classy, right? "From what I read," continued Jared, "the clientele has changed a lot down there — style-wise, I mean — since you and I hitched up the wild-oat wagon."

He said that last thing just to stir up Henry, who knew full well he'd spent his childhood shooting baskets in a driveway five long blocks from Bronxville center — rather than woodchucks back of Molly Stark's privy, or whatever. Henry knew it because he'd never beaten Jared, one-on-one, starting at the age of twelve on that same driveway.

"Yeah, wild-oat wagon," Henry said. "As I remember: Chrysler Newport, wasn't it? But anyway. . . ." He said the students of the eighties *were* a good deal different than the ones they'd gone to school with, or themselves at eighteen-nineteen-twenty. ". . . more pragmatic, that's for sure." He laughed. "Now there's a word I learned at Riddle. And they look a whole lot better, too, I guess." Jared thought he might have sighed. "They're okay," he continued quickly. "What is it they say? Whatever goes around, comes around? Something like that." He chuckled, maybe half a tad nervously, though Jared couldn't be sure of that. Ever since divestiture, the phone had seemed a lot less clear, less user-friendly, somehow.

In any case, Jared Storm didn't think that further questions on that subject were in order. Henry didn't *know*, it turned out, any more than he did. Everything was different everywhere; that figured. Si would find out soon enough, and certainly the boy was up for it. And in many ways a lot more poised and self-aware than he had been, at age *eight*een, when he had gone to Riddle. Besides, he had another thing he had to ask the Gater.

"Say, Room," he said, "one last thing. This freshman adviser business. Si got a poop sheet from the registrar's that said that you were his. His freshman adviser. Is that, like, SOP? I can't remember Dr. Raintree having advisees in our day, did he? I mean, we wouldn't want Si to get any sort of — you know — special treatment. The sort of thing some other kids might . . . well, pick up on. Be a little jealous of," he thought to add.

Of course he might have guessed. Typically, Gater'd changed the whole adviser system in his second year as prez. Said he'd wanted to get the bureaucrats involved with *kids*, in nitty-gritty kinds of ways. So he and all the deans and other officers now took ten frosh apiece, each year.

But, in spite of random selection, it was still possible, Henry said to Jared, to "jiggle the handle" a little. He chuckled when he said it. And added that Betsy, his good wife, demanded it in this case; she said that was the sort of thing being president was good for. So, did Jared mind? Did Simon? They could always make a switch, no sweat.

Jared said heck, no — he was glad and grateful. And that Simon didn't mind at all, provided . . . *you* know.

"As a matter of fact," Jared went on, extemporizing, "he said he'd told me lots of times he'd like to get to know my friends. That he wished I'd bring them home more often." He laughed, swigging down the last of the Black & White, and Henry laughed and said, "My God, he *sounds* like you."

Henry also added that this way it'd be a cinch for him and Bets to have old Si to dinner, or for him to drop in other times. That was the way it *worked*, he said. And he said that Kate, their daughter, had endorsed that plan, as well. Kate was fourteen "nowadays," said Henry, "and a drippin' double handful — gold doubloons, of course."

And very shortly after that they both hung up.

Simon never heard anything about the very last part of their conversation. His father forgot to give him any information on the makeup of the family Portcullis.

6
Selective Forgetting

The poet John Ciardi once wrote a neat little one about how he, as a parent, could "listen selectively." Parents forget selectively, too, I've noticed, and some of them, if caught, blame it on the Scotch.

That's certainly no reason to take up drinking, but I just thought I'd mention it.

7

Letters

Department of Psychology
Frabbit Hall, Riddle University
August 19, 1986

Mr. Simon Storm
RFD
Peacemeal, VT 05666

Dear Mr. Storm:

I have your name and vital statistics from the
Registrar's Office. I won't tell you that I'm not
impressed. Up until the time I looked in your
folder, I thought *I* had the most off-the-wall upbringing in the history of American child care.

Just *kidding*! I only wanted to get your attention. Promise.

Anyway . . . *my* name is Hansen Grebe, and I
am (here's dazzlement) the Nora Reston Adjunct
Professor of Psychology here at Riddle. And,
worse yet, I want something. I'd like to get you
involved in a research project of mine.

Here's the deal. Awash in other people's
money, I'm hoping to discover how ordinary,
functioning, garden-variety, gifted adolescents organize their life experiences. Really (as they say).

20

More: So far, almost all the important studies of your age group have focused on pathology or deviance, using groups of "special" adolescents; mine is after "normalcy," so-called. What thoughts, activities, and (how'd you guess?) emotions/moods do teenaged people choose/experience and (as the actress said to the bishop) how often? The literature is devoid of hard, empirical data on this subject; I propose collecting just such data — *at the source.*

Specifically: Every volunteer participant in the study (50–100 males and females, some students at the U., some in local schools) will be supplied with a small, annoying electronic device — a "beeper," that's right. And for the duration of the study — i.e., every other week for the entire fall term — participants will "get the beep" at odd and random moments during the day, up to a maximum of five (gasp!) times in the course of any twenty-four-hour period. At the tone, participants will record their ongoing thoughts, and/or feelings, and/or activities, either by checking answers on a short questionnaire or by writing a very brief narrative statement. Signals will occur only between the hours of 8 A.M. and 10 P.M., except for Friday and Saturday nights, when they may be given up to 1 or 2 A.M. (depending on my mood, condition, luck, *et cetera*). No recording (of thoughts/feelings/activities) should require more than two minutes of a participant's time.

Let me stress a couple of points (as the bishop said to the actress). First of all: I guarantee *absolute anonymity* to all participants. I, and I alone (no graduate students or other additives), will receive and examine and tally your responses, which will be identified only by a code name chosen by you. I will never know which "handle" (if you will) goes with which participant. *But* — second stress point — if, in spite of this

21

safeguard, you are not prepared to be *completely frank and honest* in your responses, please (please, please) do NOT accept this invitation. Here's something to remember: Science makes no value judgments; science is *completely* shockproof. Besides, after twenty-odd [sic] years in the field, I suspect I've either done, watched movies of, or led discussion groups about almost anything that anyone this side of Plastic Man can do, think up, imagine, or aspire to — no matter how disgusting or divine. So there.

Just let me know — okay? — as soon as you can. If you say, "I will," there's going to be a packet of materials in your campus mailbox two weeks from today, the first day of registration for the fall term. Included in that package, and thanks to the unbridled (indeed, uncontrollable) generosity of the foundation providing the grant for this project, there will be (ahem!) a crisp, new twenty-dollar bank note. And another such bill will be forthcoming at the beginning of each week, for the duration of the study. So much for heart balm, or whatever.

Please don't hold anything in this letter against what should be a very significant and historic research project. I probably carry on this way just to convince people (myself?) that I'm. . . . Oh, well, let's not go into that. In any case, I hope you join the study. Really (2).

Best wishes,

Hansen W. Grebe, PhD

It was the first time in Simon's life that anyone had addressed him as "Mr. Storm," or offered him a job that paid anything like $17.14 an hour. (A maximum of 35 beeps a week times 2 minutes reporting time equals 70 minutes, or 1⅙ hours, divided into $20 = \$17.14$. He did it in his head, of course.) And, of course, every other week he'd be getting \$20 for no hours of work at all. Besides, he liked the sound of Dr. Grebe. So, unsurprisingly, he sent the following:

RFD
Peacemeal, VT 05666
August 23, 1986

Dear Professor Grebe,

Okay, I'll do it.

Regards,

Simon Storm, Class of '90

8

Convocation

From the 1986 Riddle University Catalogue, page 45:

FRESHMAN WEEK

In an effort to promote class unity, provide effective counseling and orientation services, encourage familiarity with the extracurricular offerings of the university (as well as its geography), and facilitate the formation of friendships within the class, a Freshman Week was established in 1972 and rapidly became a Riddle tradition. All freshmen are expected to check in with their hall advisers by 5 P.M. on September 1, and at that time will receive a complete schedule of the week's activities. All university facilities will be open and available for student use, beginning on that day.

Translation:

Sophomores, juniors, and seniors interested in hitting on attractive freshman women, or in otherwise profiting from the naiveté of members of both sexes in the class of '90, would be crazy not to be on campus by sun-up on September the first, when the

24

station wagons start to come a-rolling. Recom-
mended equipment: cold six-packs of imported beer
and well-established lofty looks, which now and
then give way to battle-weary yet empathic smiles.

Reality:

Add to the above the facts that many students had to find a job (or, anyway, appear to look for one), and that others were involved in fall athletic practices, and that still more were anxious to write *finis* to their bummer-summers, and you'll have the reasons that almost all Riddle students, every year, roared back to campus and were in their rooms by the day after the end of August. College, without the inconvenience of classes, or the annoyance of assigned work, is just about as pleasant a situation as anyone is liable to encounter, this side of . . . well, a trunk stuffed full of tax-free bearer bonds, for instance.

9

Bliss

The rooming/living situation at Riddle U. is somewhat different than it is at all those other seats of higher learning that like to think that they compete with it. At Riddle, everyone but married students and one other, even smaller group is required to be involved in campus "residential life" (as H. Portcullis called it), at least to the extent of having — make that "paying for" — a room on campus. That other, even smaller group consists of those who, after one year's residence (at least), present a note from their therapists to the dean of students' office, attesting they — the students — "need" to live off-campus. (One year — Simon's second — a junior by the name of Bartnose handed in a note in Mandarin Chinese, and written by his acupuncturist, he said. The dean admired the calligraphy, and had it framed and hung above his desk, but Bartnose stayed on campus.)

So Riddle students almost all reside in dorms, called "halls"; there are no Greek societies, or clubs, or colleges. The halls, these days, are almost all coed, some of them by alternating floors, or corridors, others just by rooms, or studies. There are no officially coed bathrooms, though, and there are three small halls that still are single sex — one for men and two for women. Freshmen are assigned to halls by administrative whim as much as anything, although incoming students who strongly request single-sex housing are accommodated if possible.

After freshman year people get to choose the hall they'd like to live in. Whether they get their choice or not is another matter, depending on *its* popularity and *their* seniority. In the mistaken belief that it'd be a lot quieter "anywhere else," some students pack their stuff in cardboard boxes every spring, and move to other less convenient and attractive halls. The noise level usually isn't all that different, but the moving practice doesn't hurt the ones who end up at DuPont, or (rarely, lately) in the State Department.

When Jared Storm and Henry Portcullis were undergrads and roomies, they'd lived their freshman year in Bailey Hall, and after that in Lapham, where they'd lucked into a good two-room suite with a fireplace. In those Paleolithic times, Bliss was thought of as a zoo, the home of dinosaurs and other strange, prehuman creatures (all male, back then) who whiled away their time by making water bombs and getting snoggered weekday nights. In fact, the expression "blissed-out" was probably first used at Riddle around 1960 to mean not something *good* (as now) but: "being expelled from the university for excessive course failures, coming as a result of indulging in too many of the extracurricular activities common to the denizens of John Bliss Hall."

As a result of this historical perspective, Jared

was a little bit concerned when Simon was assigned room 211 in Bliss, although he knew full well that nothing stayed the same for very long at Riddle, or anywhere else, outside of Peacemeal, maybe. In any event, he didn't say anything to Simon about his room assignment other than, "A single? Lucky you. Plus Bliss has just a *prime* location."

Driving down to Riddle on September 1, he decided he'd be real laid-back, the model dad, never an embarrassment. He'd put the Speed Stick to his personality (he vowed) and not do things like rocking back and forth with his arms folded, gassing outside Bliss with other dads, or telling the hall adviser how they'd plastered up the door of Blinky Wainwright's room in May of '59, and how the Blinker told the proctors someone stole his room while he was off at Vassar for the weekend. Jared was so quiet Simon even gave him a few looks, as a matter of fact, and told him and Maria over a lunch at Pizza Perfect that he realized this was liable to be pretty hard on all of them for a while, and were they sure they didn't want to stay and watch him . . . well, *unpack*, or something?

But true to his resolve, Jared said he'd planned to hit the road by two o'clock, and he thought they'd better stay on schedule. He didn't bother to inform his son the road, at first, would be New Prospect Street, as far as the president's house, where he'd have a couple for the interstate with Betsy P., which'd mean Maria'd end up driving home. Good plan.

So Simon checked in with the hall adviser, Barry Seraphim, by himself, at two-fifteen P.M. and received both a printed copy of the schedule of the

28

week's activities and a verbal invitation to attend "a little hall get-together" at eight o'clock that night. *Then* he went back to his room to unpack, solo.

The room itself was not at all intimidating. First of all, it was a single, which he'd asked for, not wanting to impose his singularity (in terms of age) on someone else. And secondly, the room looked — in size and shape — a lot like his room at home. It would have been a cinch, in fact, to place the basic pieces of furniture in the same general relationship to each other that they were in back in Peacemeal. But that would never do, he thought. His room at home was nice, but not exciting, or expressive of this new, emerging *college* self of his, this participant in historic research projects, this potentially (or should that be "eventually"?) attractive younger *man*.

So instead of having the bed on the long wall on the left side of the room, he jammed it under the window, where it looked more like a couch, a piece of casual (or even vaguely *carnal*) furniture. And he put the ratty old (but plenty soft and squooshy) chair from home near the head of the bed, with just a little table between the two, and the stereo on the floor across the way, pointed at this little "comfort zone" he'd made. The cracked leather hassock from the attic was temporarily placed in front of the chair. Hopefully, it wouldn't interfere with the sounds; if it did, he'd have to move it, period. His father's huge old Riddle banner would go on the wall across the way from the chair, sort of, maybe right over the desk and down from the dresser. He was glad it was obviously an *old* banner, a veteran of many

29

days and nights at Riddle — a banner that said, "Hey, I've seen it all." *He* was all the bright green, brand-new stuff room 211 needed.

Actually, it was almost easy to imagine himself sprawled on the bed or slouched in the chair, just bullshitting with a friend. It was somewhat harder, at that point, to imagine the friend. Would eighteen- or nineteen- or twenty-year-old guys be caught dead in the room of a fifteen-year-old? Maybe not for a while — until they came to realize he didn't wet the bed, or play with a G.I. Joe, or listen to Mister Rogers or Duran Duran. And that he *could* talk sports or jazz — or even politics, religion, or the meaning of life. Talking about girls, though . . . that'd be a problem. But not — he reminded himself — as big a problem as talking *with* girls might prove to be. Mildly hard as it was to imagine another guy just hanging around his room and rapping, it was fifty times that hard to think about a *girl* in there with him. Maybe leaning in the doorway, asking to borrow some shampoo or a copy of *The Waste Land*, but lying on the bed, with her head propped up on one hand — and her slender waist upcurving gently to her solid melon hips, encased in tight, tight faded jeans, or maybe sweat pants? Almost inconceivable.

He got his father's banner tacked in place and paused. He had another decorating thing to think about, decide on.

Before he'd left home, he'd had this idea. The background for it was as follows: As soon as other Riddle students realized they had a fifteen-year-old in their midst, they'd think he was a megabrain, a genius of some sort. And then they'd pretty likely think he'd be stuck-up about it. So what he'd want to do was show them that he wasn't, right away, somehow — that he wasn't Mister P. (Precocious) Know-It-All. At all. That he was just a regular guy of a (slightly) different age, that's all.

And so he'd gotten out his Polaroid and gone to the high school baseball field and taken a good close-up shot of that particular white square canvas pillow that batters hitting triples safely reach. Then he'd gotten his friend Alfie Mason to take a similar close-up (this one in his room, at home) of his . . . (gulp) his bare behind — and another of the same area with his pants pulled up in the very likely case he chickened out of using the first one. The idea was that he'd put the two photographs up on the wall of his room at college, where everyone would notice them, with MY ASS printed under the one that *wasn't* it, and THIRD BASE printed under the other. If that didn't show people he was humble, he didn't know what would. (Alfie didn't get it, but so what?)

Even at home he'd sort of doubted that he'd dare to use the pantsless picture, even though one day that past summer Jenny Diver, fourteen going on twenty, had hollered, "Great buns, Simon," after he'd walked by her cloud of cigarette smoke and her friends (who whistled) in his tank suit on the beach beside Lake Dunmore, at the state park there. And now that he was actually at Riddle, the whole *idea* for the joke seemed sort of . . . suspect. It was even possible, he realized, that the saying "He doesn't know his ass from third base" was unique to his father, or the Peacemeal area, or (worse yet) hopelessly old-fashioned, from the sixties.

He sat down on the bed to think, decide, the pictures in his hand. As if on cue, there came a knocking on his door. He crossed the room to open it.

10

Amanda Dollop

"Simon Storm?" the knocker asked. *She* asked. *Jennifer Beals* asked.

Except, of course, she wasn't Jennifer Beals any more than this was Yale, or he was destiny's tot, or the Giants win the pennant.

He nodded.

"Hi. I'm Amanda Dollop, your R.A." She offered him a chance to shake on that, and he accepted. He also remembered to look her in the eye; by chance he chose her left one, which was wide and brown with thick black lashes.

"Mind if I come in?" she said.

He shook his head, trying to pull some words, ideas together in a way that they became a sentence — a trick he thought he'd mastered years before. He couldn't think of anything. Stepping back, he gave her space to walk through, anyway. This wasn't like him. He'd babbled easily with anarchists, an astronaut's ex-wife, a Nobelist, and Joan Baez. What on earth was his *problem*?

"Barry said you'd gotten in," she said.

She'd walked into the middle of the room, which meant she'd had to turn to say that to him. So, in just a few seconds' time he'd managed to see her from the front, the back, and, pivoting, in profile. In all cases, she was wearing (just) a boat-necked cotton sweater (white and orange stripes, with sleeves pushed up), and defining drawstring shorts (bright white). Gold chain around her neck, white tennies. She seemed to have both very tan (where he could see) and well-proportioned . . . everythings.

Now she cocked her head a trifle and pushed back her short, curly, black hair, although it hadn't been in the way of anything. It wasn't that she *resembled* Jennifer Beals particularly, but that she made him think of her, he realized. Which in turn made him think of . . . freedom, waterfalls, his own log cabin, roller coasters, rocket ships, and lime juice. He simply had to speak, say *something*.

"Barry Seraphim's the hall adviser," Simon said at last. She nodded at this information, lips apart, so Simon gave her more. "I just checked in with him."

Later on, Simon challenged himself to make up two dumber sentences than those — other things he might have said that would have been more asinine or obvious. He couldn't. It wasn't any excuse, but for some stupid reason he'd been certain that the resident assistant (R.A.) to the hall adviser would be male and would look something like the actor Jeff Goldblum. The way a graduate student is meant to look, in other words: tall, with glasses, Jewish. An ugly piece of stereotyping on his part — in still other, truer words. But he could have turned even that dumb thought to his advantage if he'd said, "You don't look anything like Jeff Goldblum" to her. That would have been not only mildly witty

34

and attractively self-deprecating but also slightly *personal*, as well. Mature. Collegiate. As a sentence it could *baby-sit* for "Barry Seraphim's the hall adviser."

"So how do you like your room?" she asked him.

"Unbelievably," said Simon, just letting the word burst out of himself, before he'd even thought of it, it seemed like. He had this urge to praise, to compliment, to love everything about Riddle — let her know that. It was really thoughtful of her to ask him about the room.

"Great," she said. "Well, I just wanted to say hello and clue you in on a couple of things, all right?" For the first time, he noticed she was carrying a clipboard. "May I?" She sank into the squooshy chair before he could reply; it breathed: a little, grateful, dusty exhalation. "Okay, now look. . . ."

Simon perched on the edge of the bed and did so. He was starting to calm down. This wasn't such a big deal, he tried to tell himself, just business between a freshman at a Most Competitive college and his resident assistant, the person who, all year long, would be there for him to go to, to consult on anything he needed to . . . consult on. Particularly (as it said in the catalogue) on things a "peer" would know about, *by reason of experience*. She looked like a competent and experienced person, all right. There was just something about her.

". . . don't, whatever you do, buy the radiator," she was saying. "It comes with the room and belongs to the college. You might get some guy — an upperclassman — coming by with a monkey wrench and telling you it's his, and that he's going to disconnect the thing and take it to his *new* room, down in Dudley. That's unless — he'll say — you haven't bought one yet, in which case he could save you *both* some time and trouble, right? Just tell him thanks but no thanks and he'll go away. It's sort of a game for a lot of the juniors and seniors. They try to earn their munch money for the entire Freshman Week by different little scams like that. They call it 'eating off' the freshmen. Especially the women." She made a face, but a good sport's sort of face.

"There'll be a lot of legitimate salesmen coming by, too," she said, "but they'll all be wearing tags that look like this." She unclipped an official student agency badge from her board: a laminated plastic affair with a place for the salesperson's photograph; plus the university seal; and a sphinx, rampant, in the background. Simon had never seen the college . . . beast in just that attitude before.

"Though I doubt that anyone who knew that you were *you* would. . . ." Amanda Dollop left that sentence hanging while she shifted weight a little, leaned in his direction, smiled. "You don't mind if I ask you something, do you?"

He shrugged, smiled back, and shook his head.

"Guess not," he said. He could trust his resident assistant if he could trust any student or graduate student in the whole university, probably. It'd be nice to tell her the absolute truth about whatever it was she wanted to know. Even if she hit him with a real heater, like, "Why *lime* juice, anyway?"

"Well, truthfully, how does it *feel*?" she said.

He blinked, not wanting to jump in with a truthful answer to the wrong question. She smiled, and

36

by way of clarification (he guessed) took one hand and stirred the air beside her head, three times, before she flopped her fingers toward his lap (it seemed to him). On his lap was the hand that held, face-up, the photographs he'd brought from home — the one mislabeled as "Third Base" right on the very top.

He felt his face get hot. She couldn't possibly be asking how his heinie felt, could she? That wouldn't make a lot of sense. How does *anyone's* ass feel, when you come right down to it? To himself, that is.

His mind raced. If it wasn't that, what could she mean by "it," then? Not sexual intercourse, surely, although from what he'd read in the papers that was a pretty common "it" at most colleges (as an act, without attachments), particularly in the Northeast and California. But he didn't think that was the sort of thing people — even at college — ask someone who they've just met, particularly a fifteen-year-old someone who they're meant to be assisting or advising, or whatever, and who'd (therefore) be a lot less likely to know than they would.

No, he decided (and all this in less than five seconds), she probably just meant, "How does *college* feel to a person your age?" He'd answer that one, but using words that would also be the answer — truthfully — to lots of other questions.

"I don't know." He shrugged again. "I'm not sure yet."

She nodded forcefully, up and down a few emphatic times.

"Of *course*," she said. "I remember what it was

like *my* first few days: a blur. I was *seven*teen, myself. But then, the second week, two big things happened. I'll never forget. The first one was: They
took us into the anatomy lab, just as a part of our
tour of the buildings, and I didn't pass out, or even
feel like ralphing, or anything, right? I looked at
those cadavers and I told myself — and I *believed*
myself — they weren't people; they were projects,
cases, things. That was my first real, total clarity at
Riddle. And from that moment on" — her eyes were
wide, in recollection, huge brown eyes with the
longest, thickest lashes Si had ever seen — "I *knew*
that I was going to be a doctor. And later that same
day. . . ."

It was odd, Simon thought: He'd been going to
tell *her* the truth, trust *her* with something personal,
but before he could lay his mind on something good
along those lines, *she'd* actually come up with all
these recollections of her own — about as personal
as they came. Cadavers and all that.

". . . walking through the house staff parking lot,
I looked around and saw those Porsches and those
Beamers" — her face lighted up, her eyes were clear
again, her smile was wide and full, and wet — "and
knew I *wanted* it." She shook her head, in wonder
at the moment, and the feeling, still, apparently.

"You're" — Simon cleared his throat— "you're
a medical student, then?" It was easier to let her
talk, if she wanted to, and besides, the more she
talked, the more they'd be getting to know each
other, in a way. Be making friends. He wanted to
keep her there, in his chair, just . . . bullshitting.
He thought it was sort of neat that she was a medical
student. That confirmed his guess that she was a

38

really *caring* type of person. Plus, a medical student would be really cool about any . . . physical stuff he might possibly need some advice about, at some point. Not that he ever *would*, most likely. Or, being truthful: not that he would ever dare to ask.

"Well, yes, kind of," she said. "I'm in the fourth year of this seven-year program they have here. It's a pre-med/med degree. You start from right out of high school, and in seven years you're a doctor. It's fantastic. The way they work it, you have a chance to take a lot of courses most pre-meds would never get within a mile of, because of all the science requirements — a lot of which you just forget, or they do over in a slightly different form in med school. Riddle's really great that way — how they let a person take what they really *need*, instead of a lot of repetitions, or pie-in-the-sky. You see a *lot* of double majors here, and even triples, sometimes. I made a bet with myself that you're going to go for a triple of some sort: maybe something-something-and-advanced-computer-science, right?" She laughed. "Every year the freshmen know tons more about computers."

"You know," he said, feeling even more relaxed, "it's interesting you said that. Computer science is really tempting, like a new frontier. But at the same time, I don't know . . . you know what I mean? I live in a little town in Vermont, in a pretty rural section of the state. Everything is just so peaceful and, like, *simple* there, and that's *great*. But I'm not sure, given everything that's going on, and all the *possibilities*, that I could ever. . . ." He shook his head. "*You* know what I mean. You're going to be a doctor. You obviously feel the same way."

He'd dropped his eyes, somewhat embarrassed, though not really — but not wanting to babble platitudes at this oh-so-modern sphinx: a woman with the heart of Mother Teresa and the body of a Solid Gold dancer. If she, a future doctor, didn't understand the dangers of this present age as well as Einstein did, when he said, quote, "The unleashed power of the atom has changed everything, save our modes of thinking, and we thus drift toward unparalleled catastrophe," who could? Doctors, a lot of them, were among the really upfront people in speaking out about the consequences of even the smallest nuclear confrontation. It was one of the things Simon had been looking forward to the most, about coming to college (although he'd never said anything about it, to anyone): being in the midst of a lot of people who were primed to put some energy into solutions to the world's pressing problems. It was only changes in our human intelligence, in our angle of vision, in the way people *thought* (just as Einstein implied) that would save the planet, Simon believed. Here at Riddle, for the first time, he'd be able to organize, expand the talents he'd been given, and justify not just his own but maybe all creation. He was, of course (and lucky for him), much, much too smart to have ever said *that* to anyone.

"*Exactly.*" Amanda Dollop was nodding at him again, and smiling again, but now with her eyes narrowed, as if in thought. "I was thinking the exact same thing the other day. It's up to me to make things happen, and I'm going to. When I was a kid" — she laughed and made a rapid gesture with one hand — "much younger than you, a *baby*, I used to have, like, dreams. Getting married to Alan

Alda. You know, the world's kindest and most fun doctor — in those days I always had my *husband* being the doctor — and I'd be busy with my house, and a couple of cute kids, and a lot of animals around, and stuff. But now I know that's wishful thinking, or romanticizing, or whatever you want to call it. Like sheer stupidity, maybe. Putting myself at the mercy of events and feelings I can't possibly control. I *hate* that idea." Her voice had gotten louder. She looked past Simon's head and out the window, her full lips drawn together.

"To hell with that," she said. "Of course, it still might happen." She shrugged and smiled a different kind of smile, a smaller one, eyes lowered, and spoke a lot more softly. "And if it happens, it happens. But meanwhile — Mandy's got the ball." She took a deep breath and let it out, and didn't raise her eyes till Simon spoke.

"Well," he said, as much to fill the silence as anything, "I'm sure that once I've been here for a while, and had a chance to take some courses in the different departments, I won't have any trouble picking out a major. And I think it's neat" — his heart pounded a little as he said this — "that I've got you and other people I can go to for advice on stuff like that."

Amanda Dollop got up.

"Well, you sure do," she said. "And just for openers, let me put this one little bug in your ear. Think about business. Seriously. Maybe not the business school *per se*, necessarily — though it is one of the best in the country — but at least as a part of any multiple major you decide on. A *lot* of kids are doing that, *especially* the really bright ones. Even in my program everybody takes a business course or two, and from what I hear there may be some *required* for the first-year class next fall. The age of the ignorant doctor is just about over, I kid you not." She started toward the door.

Simon was a little slow in getting to his feet; probably a bug in someone's ear is always a distraction, a surprise. Business courses? She was saying he should go for *business* courses? He shook his head a little as he rose and followed her.

"Why go up without a safety net? Take chances you don't have to?" she went on. "Fall through the cracks, as the saying goes. And by the way" — she pointed at the pictures in his hand, and no mistaking this time, and she grinned — "*nice* bunzerinos. Much better than the batch I've had to look at in my practice physicals at school. If you're thinking of advertising, take my advice: Don't sell yourself too cheap."

Simon blushed. He'd forgotten he was holding the things.

"Oh, it isn't that — it's just sort of a joke," he said. He wasn't sure he'd followed what she'd said. "Look." He showed her all three pictures. Her being a medical student, it wasn't all *that* embarrassing; in fact, he was rather enjoying himself. "They're just something I had in my room at home. Actually, it was kind of my father's idea. He likes to tell me I don't know my ass from third base." He forced a little laugh. "He's kind of weird."

She batted him on the head, but softly, and left her hand there to tousle his hair a little in the process. And she laughed, too.

"Well, I'm sure you do — know the difference,

that is — and unless I'm very much mistaken," she continued, "so'll a lot of young sphinxettes, before you're finished here. So — don't forget — check all the salesmen's badges, and I'll see you at the meeting: eight o'clock, at the main common room, right?"

She waved, and sashayed out the door.

Simon turned around and walked back to his bed, but this time he lay down on it, his hands behind his head, and stared, unseeing, out the window, at the wonderful world of Riddle.

11
Mail

If Jared and Maria Storm had chanced to observe Simon getting off his bed in 211 Bliss and starting toward the mail room, they almost certainly would have said (except, why bother?) that he was the exact same kid they'd wished a fond good-bye to earlier that afternoon. Obviously. And so he was, if what we're speaking of has anything to do with height (five ten), and weight (one forty-five), and face (smooth, unspotted, gray-eyed, but with thick, dark eyebrows and an eager, clean-cut mouth). Or even, for that matter, stride (buoyant to the point of friskiness), or style (slightly faded, sock-free), or scent (a little like a golf course in the summertime).

But no matter what they might have thought, Simon, in that little while at college, had already changed, internally. Underneath his breastbone (as he hastened down the hallway) was a smile: I'm going to like it here (it said); I know I am.

And *that* meant that while Amanda Dollop, meeting him, had thought, "Cute kid, but such a baby," other students, strangers in that hall (like Asmussen, for instance, or Clee Clymer) noticed him and only (merely) had the feeling that the freshmen got a little younger-looking every year, it seemed like.

Simon noticed Clee right back: She was Amanda Dollop's roommate and had a combination of the lightest blonde hair and the darkest bronze tan that Si had ever seen. Both of these features and, indeed, the rest of Clee, required the expenditure of an enormous amount of her time and money, but almost any sighted person would have said she got a deal. Asmussen, by way of contrast, was almost unnoticeable; in looks, dress, personality, and intelligence he was your basic C-minus. In desperation, and because his parents (both of them from San Francisco) had never seen fit to give ("impose on") him a name (besides the last one of his richer granddad), he'd decided just that fall to call himself Maurice (or, sometimes, "Rico"), and start up an unusual student agency, one that'd really make people sit up, or even start up, and take notice. But more on that when Simon gets to meet him, later on. In case you're wondering, the only reason Asmussen got into Riddle in the first place was that he was a member of such a rare minority, the first-name-less. During his freshman and sophomore years he'd let people call him whatever they wanted to, most commonly, "Yeah, *you*," and "The jerk with no first name."

In the mail room in the basement of Bliss Hall, Si found his box and got its combination lock to work, eventually (you had to bang the door three times and blow your nose between the first and second numbers). Inside, there were two letters and a little package, quite a haul. He sat down on the floor, his back against the green cement block wall.

Going by the three other people in the room — all of whom looked poised and popular — that was the way to read your mail, at Riddle.

One of the letters, and the package, bore the return address of the department of psychology, and he opened that letter first. It was a lot shorter than the other one he'd gotten from Grebe:

Dear Mr. Storm,

I'm delighted you've agreed to take part in our project; welcome to the murky world of research. Under separate cover, I'm sending you the "beeper" that I spoke of in my last, a number of question-and-answer sheets, and that meretricious $20 bill.

Please, from the moment you open the package, let that small, outspoken gadget, little Bob Beeper, become as Castor to your Pollux or, better, Chang to your Eng — that is to say, your constant and inseparable companion. The fun will start almost as soon as you're in harness (as the bishop said to the actress).

I'd also appreciate it if you would drop by my office sometime, or phone for an appointment. As they say over at admissions, your folder "reads like Evian on the Kalahari." And I like to meet the subjects of my object, so to speak.

Best wishes,

Hansen Grebe

P.S. I don't care if you use an answer sheet or not, when the beeper goes off. If you don't use it, just make sure your narrative includes what you were doing, with whom, and how you were feeling. And that the time, date, and your code name are on the top of whatever scrap of paper you *do* use. For obvious reasons, it's important to have your code name on everything you do for the study.

Next week, I'll send a supply of large, self-addressed, stamped envelopes, along with your "salary." Please mail me each week's collection of sheets and/or narratives every other Monday morning.

Over and out.

Cap'n G.

The package, which Simon opened next, yielded (from the top) that crisp and promised portrait of A. Jackson (which went right in his wallet); the small, rectangular black plastic box (he clipped it on his belt, for the time being); and a number of the sheets he could use — instead of writing a short paragraph about his activity, and company, and mood — whenever the beeper did its thing. The sheets were multiple-choice, and though there was a lot of stuff on them, they wouldn't take long to complete, Simon realized, once a person got familiar with their curiosities.

Here's what the darn things looked like:

ADOLESCENT STUDY — Grebe

Date and Time _____ Code Name _____

General Instructions Be sure that in all cases your answers reflect your activity and attitudes just *before* the beeper went off. We don't need to be told that you are *now* filling out this answer sheet, and that you're totally enraged by being interrupted while doing and feeling whatever it was, at the time of the big beep. You're getting paid for this, remember.

I. Is what you're doing in the area of:

a. STUDY	i. WATCHING
b. PLAY	j. DAYDREAMING
c. EXERCISE	k. SLEEPING
d. EATING	l. CHANGING YOUR
e. WORKING	CONSCIOUSNESS
f. SHOPPING	m. SEX
g. SOCIALIZING	n. OTHER (specify)
h. LISTENING	_____

Check more than one, if that's the case. Same thing below.

a. If STUDY, are you
1. reading 2. writing 3. memorizing 4. pondering 5. staring blankly and uncomprehendingly 6. cheating 7. alone.
b. If PLAY, are you
1. holding a musical instrument 2. playing a game (e.g., cards, Monopoly, Trivial Pursuit, etc.) 3. toying with someone else 4. playing by (not with) yourself 5. cheating.
c. If EXERCISE, are you
1. breathing hard 2. part of a team 3. wet 4. miserable 5. cheating 6. alone.

d. If EATING, are you
    1. having a regular meal 2. having a snack
    3. gorging yourself before throwing up
    4. cheating on your diet 5. alone.

e. If WORKING, are you
    1. underpaid 2. overpaid 3. doing this of
    your own free will 4. planning to invest
    a portion of your earnings in America
    5. crazy.

f. If SHOPPING, are you
    1. looking for something specific
    2. looking for anything 3. doing this to
    make someone very, very happy 4. like
    yourself.

g. If SOCIALIZING, are you
    1. with one other person 2. with two to
    four people 3. with more than four peo-
    ple 4. a part of the interaction 5. wishing
    you were somewhere else.

h. If LISTENING, would you call what you're
hearing
    1. rock & roll 2. jazz 3. classical 4. voices
    5. crap.
    And are you 1. alone or 2. with one or
    more people.

i. If WATCHING, is it
    1. TV 2. a movie 3. a play 4. the human
    drama 5. it.
    And are you 1. alone or 2. with one or
    more people.

j. If DAYDREAMING, are you (were you)
    1. sitting 2. lying down 3. recalling
    4. imagining 5. hallucinating 6. plotting
    and scheming.

And are you 1. alone or 2. with one or more people.

k. If SLEEPING, are you (were you)
      1. in bed 2. sitting in a chair 3. on a bed or couch 4. on the floor 5. in the nude.
      And are you 1. alone or 2. with one or more people.

l. If CHANGING YOUR CONSCIOUSNESS, are you
      1. smoking 2. sniffing 3. snorting 4. shooting 5. swallowing 6. sipping, slopping down, etc.
      And are you 1. alone or 2. with one or more people.

m. If SEX, better you should just write down exactly what you were doing and with/to what variety of creature or thing: _____
_____.
(You may use a separate sheet, if necessary.)

n. If OTHER, specify: _____
_____.

II. How were you *feeling* at the time of the beep? Check all that apply.

a. anxious	h. impotent
b. confident	i. turned-on
c. guilty	j. turned-off
d. carefree	k. angry
e. depressed	l. blah
f. joyful	m. hopeful
g. powerful	n. pessimistic

o. alert
p. bummed-out
q. in control

r. manipulated
s. tense
t. relaxed

III. When the beeper sounded, were any of the people you were with (if any) your parents? If so, how many?

Or other blood relatives?
If so, how many of *those*?

The other letter Simon got was a bit of a surprise: not entirely unexpected, but hardly something he had counted on. After he read it, he decided it was much more welcome than not. The weight of history was on the side of his enjoying adults who his parents knew as friends.

Here's the way that letter read:

Dear Simon,

Welcome to Riddle. I still remember my first day here, vividly. Henry went to the office, and our cat expressed herself in the exact center of the mahogany dining room table that first belonged to Thos. P. Riddle, Esq. 1718–82. But I also discovered the chocolate-crunch ice cream at the Dairy Bar. It is, beyond any doubt, the most successful consequence of any research project ever undertaken at the college.

Anyway — we were wondering if you'd like to come to dinner. Nothing fancy or formal — just you and us — and it *is* a standard way for freshmen to meet their official advisers, which, as you know, Henry is yours of, or however you say it.

51

Six-thirty, if you can make it; just show up. If you don't we'll try you again soon.

Warmly,

Betsy Portcullis

Of course Simon noticed right away she'd neglected to mention a day. He thought that was pretty neat of her, whether it was done accidentally *or* on purpose.

12

Dorm Meeting

Unlike most dorms in other colleges, the halls at Riddle all had common rooms: large areas intended and designed for meetings, social life, and even study. In point of historical fact, however, the question "If you feel like making noise, why don't you go down to the common room?" has probably been asked more often in the suites and corridors of Riddle U. than any obscenity-free other — although "How can you be so gross?" has also done extremely well, in recent years.

During the late 1940s the wood paneling on the walls of most of the hall common rooms was temporarily removed, so that soundproofing materials could be put in place behind it, and also on the ceiling, while the carpenters were at it. With the addition of thick, padded, indoor-outdoor carpeting, and heavy fire doors, the halls ended up with rooms that any bedlam would have envied. They were, it was discovered, so disgustingly sound-absorbent that it wasn't even any fun to break things in them, and halls had to hold dances on the staircases and in the corridors, or at least have the band set up out there, or sometimes in the bathrooms.

"Enamel rock," as that was called, was acoustically fantastic, but a lot of other problems came up in the bathrooms, and sometimes got on the speakers, or the band members' shoes, which affected the music after a while. Ambiance aside, the Riddle gym was best for dancing, probably.

When Simon arrived at the Bliss common room, close to eight o'clock, it was so stuffed with people that all the casement windows had been opened, just to let a little unbreathed air in. So it was a very real relief when he saw a hand go wigwag back and forth, and probably at him — Amanda Dollop's hand, no less. To make completely sure, he pointed at his chest and raised his eyebrows; she smiled and nodded, patting the floor between herself and the blonde woman with the amazing tan who Si had seen before. He waded through the crowd in their direction.

"Hey," Amanda said. And then, "Shove over, Clicker," to her roommate. "Simon, this is Clee. Clee, Simon."

He sank down on the floor between them, suddenly self-conscious. He could feel their soft, warm hips against his own. He imagined that everyone in the room who'd seen him come in and get called over by Amanda would be thinking this, about her and Clee: They can't be serious.

Simon smiled weakly at the two of them and muttered, "Quite a crowd in here." Then he marked his mental scorecard: an award of one-point-five for his insightfulness. Second-graders, nationwide, would average about a three, he guessed.

Barry Seraphim was standing by the fireplace, sort of hanging from the mantel by one hand, as he leaned to talk to some people on the floor near his feet. Unlike Amanda, he looked perfect for his part, for "hall adviser." He was a tall young man, but shiny-bald, with a fringe of rusty hair around the sides and back of his head, and a full neat beard of the same material, but darker. He wore rimless glasses and a blue-and-white seersucker jacket over a dark blue T-shirt and white duck pants. And an almost constant smile.

Amanda moved her lips toward Simon's ear.

"You know Barry, of course," she whispered, and her breath made a tickle, make that *tingle*, in his ear. "I'll clue you in on names. It never hurts to know who someone is."

He nodded his thanks, and turned up his attentiveness. Behind him, on the couch the three of them were leaning back against, a female student was conversing with a friend.

"So here I am with this thing of jelly in my hand, and this clerk comes up behind me, and she goes, 'May I ask you what you're doing, Miss?' Real snotty, right? And I go, 'What does it look like? I'm tasting this stuff so I know whether I want to buy it or not.' I go, 'You'd think they'd put the flavor on the tube.'

"And she goes, 'Well, you're not *meant* to eat that product, actually, you know,' like I was some kind of a mental, or something. So I just put the cap back on and handed her the whole sha-*mess*: the tube, the box, the applicator, everything. 'Here,' I said, 'if you don't like it . . .' and I left. I mean, where do they get those clerks in there, d'you think?"

The friend giggled. "What *did* it taste like, anyway?"

"Guava-grape," the first one said. "And Jamie just about breaks out from grape. He absolutely can't stand it. Even with peanut butter he wants strawberry preserves. What he likes is Harry and David's Wild 'N Rare. In the little cans, like?"

Simon sat there staring straight ahead. He imagined that the girls on the couch were now looking at his ears, both of which felt brilliant red, about the color of *cherry* preserves, but probably Smuckers, or Grand Union. When the second one giggled again, and then the first one did, too, he was sure they were doing that. Probably the second one had pointed at his ears and mouthed some sentence for her friend, maybe, "Check this bay-bee out." He wished the meeting would begin.

"Okay," said Barry Seraphim, almost in answer, "if we could just get going, now." A vein popped out on the side of his neck. Barry Seraphim was shouting, but his voice still sounded muffled, in that room.

"First of all," he said, "I'd like to welcome everyone, officially, to Freshman Week. I had no idea there'd be so many first-year students in the hall this year" — he let his eyes sweep slowly, left to right, across the room — "who look so much like people who were here *last* year. And even *sound* a lot the same. Why, if I didn't know that *no* one ever came to Freshman Week except for freshmen, I might swear — "

"Oh, no!" was yelped from somewhere in the back, in a falsetto.

Barry Seraphim's grin got even broader. *"Kidding!"* he exclaimed. "It's great to see you all, of course, old friends as well as new. We're all in this — this Bliss — together, right? And I just hope you're all as glad to be here as I am to see you."

"*Most* unlikely, Barry," came from a man who occupied one half a love seat by the fireplace. A lot of people laughed. The guy had sharp, handsome features and what appeared to be a plastic cocktail stirrer in the corner of his mouth, sticking out like a thermometer.

"Phil Hedd," Amanda whispered carefully, distinctly. "A finance major. He'll go platinum before he's thirty." Next to Hedd was another guy who stared straight ahead, and whose lips would move every few seconds, as if he was reminding himself of something he didn't want to forget.

"Thank you, Phil," said Barry Seraphim, with one of his broadest smiles. "I guess this year has now officially begun." He paused. "And the more so when I say this next to you: stereos. . . ."

For the next five minutes Barry described the Blissful atmosphere he felt that they'd achieved the year before, in the hall. It all sounded pretty commonsensical to Simon, having to do with noise, and mess, and other people's property, including the university's. Every so often, there'd be an interruption from the floor, like someone yelling, "We gonna have a lost-lunch counter this year, Barry?" And everybody'd laugh and look around and holler, "Yeah — Clive-baby," and point and clap when they had found the person they were looking for. Freshmen simply sat, dumbfounded, as they were meant to do, and listened to it all.

"Now here's an item" — Barry Seraphim switched

gears — "there might be different points of view about. Some people down in Dodd came up with these. . . ."

He reached out to the mantelpiece and picked up, from the top of a stack, a small cardboard sign with a string running from one top corner to the other — the kind of sign you can hang over a doorknob. On this particular model, there wasn't any writing, just a drawing of a large white open hand with its thumb sticking up, inside a red circle that had a black diagonal line running upper-left to lower-right, right through the hand.

"What we have here is a 'No Soliciting' sign," said Barry. "It'd mean that whoever's in the room doesn't want to see a salesman — or a candidate, in season. So, what do you think?"

Simon, for one, thought he was totally unprepared for the howls of outrage — almost anguish — that came next, over and above a little clapping and one "Sound idea." It appeared that many of the men who lived in Bliss Hall — and who effectively drowned out the women who were trying to speak — would face a lifetime of personal indebtedness if their access to their fellow students was limited in any way.

While all the shouting was going on, one man over on the far side of the room held up a large piece of cardboard, tacked on a broom handle. Painted on the cardboard in large capital letters was this question: MAY I SAY SOMETHING, PLEASE?

Barry Seraphim semaphored for quiet and pointed at the guy who held the thing. "Yes?" he said. "Maurice?"

"That's Asmussen," Amanda whispered. "A bit

of a dork. He doesn't have a first name, if you can believe it. Last year, he told people to call him whatever they felt like. You can *imagine*. . . ."

The guy was standing, taking fast puffs on a cigarette. He had a pair of mirrored glacier glasses on, with red frames.

"First of all," he said, "I'd like to say hi and *bienvenido* to the frosh. My name's Rico, and I look forward to meeting you all. Now, about this sign business — here's the way I look at it. I sell a product, and a service, that I *know* you'll want to check out. Think about. Have access to. Even if you don't buy into it, I think you'll agree that I've done you a favor by coming by your room at all. So, the right thing for me to do, ethically speaking, if I give even the smallest shit about *you*, is rip that damn sign off your door and stick it in my pocket. And just say, 'Sign? What sign?' if anybody asks. You follow me?"

He sat down quickly. A lot of people went, "Whoa!" stretching out the word, and shaking one floppy, open hand, from the wrist, in front of their chests. One girl yelled, "Tell 'em, Rico-*baby*!" Phil Hedd joined in the "Whoa's," but the guy next to him still just sat there staring, with his lips a-move.

"The guy next to Phil Hedd," Simon whispered to Amanda. "Is there something the matter with him?"

She looked and said, "Oh, no. I think he's just using the confidence-builder we learned at a seminar last spring. What you do is say your name — his is Brad Hammond — over and over to yourself. It's meant to help reinforce your own identity to yourself, to increase your commitment to who it is you are. And that improves your chances of being successful, of course. I think it's pretty neat. And he's got a great name, don't you think? *Brad Hammond*?"

"For what?" whispered Simon.

"Success." She smiled. "What else?" She up-turned a palm in his direction. *"Ralph Lauren,"* she said.

As proof, he guessed. Simon simply nodded. Until he knew Amanda Dollop much better, that seemed like the best idea.

Meanwhile, other people had taken the floor, some to denounce to signs and others, mostly women, to support their circulation. A lot of voices spoke at once, and somebody started singing a Cyndi Lauper song.

"Wait!" A tall, tan guy with an impressive mass of shiny black hair had sprung to his feet. His hair was unaffected by that move. Clothes-wise, he had on a red-and-white pinstripe dress shirt, with a white collar and cuffs, as well as slim black trousers.

"Hold on a minute, Barry," he said, although the hall adviser hadn't said anything for quite a while.

"Grant Kahn," Amanda whispered. *"Very* influential person. His father's Kahn Brothers, Grant."

Sure he is, said Simon to himself, and his brother's Grantfather Khan. He'd definitely have to keep an eye on Amanda.

"I'm not looking for favors," Grant Kahn said, "but if we aren't going to let the rules of the marketplace prevail here in Bliss, we might as well change its name to Nader Hall and turn it into a co-op. I mean . . . *really*. How big a problem has this been? Does the captain head for port because the cabin boy turns green? Do you call off the Super Bowl because they don't like blow-pong in New Zealand? I'm here to hope to hell you don't!"

When he sat down, no one said anything right away, and Simon, peering around the room, saw that most people were looking serious and thoughtful, and a lot of them were nodding, even many women.

"Okay, then," Barry said, after a while. He shrugged. "It looks as if the consensus is: The less we *faire* the better. And so be it." He cleared his throat.

"I have got one more thing on my agenda, though," he said. "This comes from Doctor Minor, up at SHO. (*'Student Health Organization,'* Amanda slipped in Simon's ear.) It isn't pleasant talk, but still — it's something that we have to face. Two somethings, actually. Number one is *stress* and number two's *depression*. How we recognize and deal with both these facts of life, whether in ourselves or others."

With that, the hall adviser went on to speak of deadlines, grades, failed romance, competition, loneliness, recourse to drugs and alcohol, bizarre behavior, neglect of clothes and personal hygiene, bingeing and vomiting, nervous tics and mannerisms, and social isolation. The soundproofing in the room absorbed all that and the place became even more unnaturally quiet than it was when it was empty. A lot of the people were looking at the indoor-outdoor carpeting.

At first, Simon felt a little . . . embarrassed, listening to all the terrible things that seemed to be expected of his hallmates. He couldn't connect any of that with himself — unless, of course, this was just a part of some elaborate joke being played on all the freshmen. Sort of one step beyond being sold a radiator: the famous mental-illness zinger that now took the place of paddling and other forms of hazing. With that possibility in mind, he tried to manage an expression for his face that included all of these: good-humored, sympathetic, yet un-taken-in; tolerant and wise, but also fresh, enthusiastic, and accepting of his place. The trouble was, that seemed to call for two, or maybe three more faces than he'd gotten on his birthday. He turned to check Amanda's look. She cupped a hand and whispered something that he almost didn't catch, she spoke so softly. But he was pretty sure it was, "A kid jumped off of Lapham tower, just last spring." Hearing that, believing it, Simon decided one face was enough. He made it — simply, serious — and joined the starers-at-the-carpeting. It was a mix of greens and browns and yellows, a rather nubby and conflicted weave.

When Barry Seraphim was through speaking, a few other people took "this opportunity" to "share" some things they'd felt, found out, or noticed. Simon listened to them, too. He believed what he was hearing, now, but thought that it was . . . dumb. To feel these different ways and do these different things about it. But then — like almost right away — he thought that maybe *he* was dumb, that he was missing something. He'd never felt too young for anything before, but now he didn't know. He noticed that, on this one subject, everyone spoke as equals, men and women both, and everyone on the basis of firsthand experience. That was good, but it also meant, to Simon, that if he was going to enjoy college properly, he might have to feel a lot worse than he was used to feeling. Here was a whole other subject of conversation — in addition to sex — on which he had, right now, pretty much zilch to offer.

Eventually, everyone got talked out, and it was generally affirmed that Bliss-ites would keep a close, but not intrusive, eye on one another, and that various levels of amateur and professional help would be sought and/or reported to, as necessary.

Finally, Barry Seraphim introduced the three other R.A.'s and Amanda Dollop to the multitudes, making them all stand up as he pronounced their names. There was applause, and in Amanda's case a lot of whistles, too, which caused some women to suggest a series of mouth-control talks aimed at the reduction and eventual elimination of voice-based sexual missiles in the hall. And *that* brought on both "Whoa's" *and* clapping, plus one shout of, "That's a pussy good idea."

As he was getting up, Simon snuck a look at the two girls who'd been sitting on the couch that he'd been leaning on. To his surprise, they looked more like his mother, clothes-wise, than . . . Sheila E., for instance. One of them even wore a string of pearls on top of her light blue, crew-necked, Shetland sweater; he wasn't sure *which* one, of course.

13

Phone Call

After the dorm meeting, Simon stood around in the corridor for a while, waiting for his turn on a phone. When it came, he dialed the number of the president's house. Betsy Portcullis answered on the second ring; it was then 9:30.

"Hi, *Simon*," she said, when he'd identified himself. "You eaten yet?" And when he laughed and said he had, she said, "How about tomorrow, then?"

"Great," said Simon. "And Mrs. Portcullis, it says in the handbook that I'm meant to have a meeting with my freshman adviser this week. Well, that's Mr. Portcullis, for me. What I wondered was, will my coming over to your house count as a meeting, or should I schedule another one with his office?"

She said, "I think I can fix it so that dinner counts. Frankly, Si," she said, carelessly, "I call most of the shots around this university, titles notwithstanding. You can ask anyone. Except what's-his-name, of course. Your father's friend. The guy I'm living with. So how about six-thirty?"

"Great," Si said again, "I'll be there."

"Oh," she said, "one other thing. Do you want to bring a date?"

"No," he said. "I don't think so."

"Good," she said. "That'll save me a call to your mother." She laughed and hung up.

By then, he *knew* that he was going to like her.

14

The Last Resort

"Of course I think about nuclear war," Simon told the guy. "A lot."

"Good man," said "Rico" Asmussen. He was lying on Simon's bed with his head propped up on one hand, and he'd kept his mirrored glasses on. "I figured that you would. You look like a sensitive guy."

It was just after ten in the morning. Simon had waked up at 6:15 on this, his first full day as a college student, a member of the class of 1990 at Riddle, but he'd decided to show a little maturity and stay in bed until a quarter to eight.

Breakfast went well. He'd come in alone and sat down next to a freshman wearing a "Don't blame me — I voted for Bill 'n Opus" T-shirt. All eight people at the table were males and members of his class, so adrenaline was flowing right along with orange juice and milk and sugar-frosted flakes. Conversation never lagged a moment. Breathlessly, almost, they went from pennant races on to tales of getting lost on campus on to different salesmen that had come to different rooms already. And then, finally, to how terrible the food was at all boarding schools, this one guy's mother's house, and from what somebody's neighbor said, Cornell. Simon was calling everyone at the table by his right name before the scrambled eggs and toast had even started going down, and the guy in the Bloom County T-shirt and his roommate said they'd stop by his room on their way to the eleven o'clock all-freshman meeting in Forsythe Hall.

After breakfast, Si'd gone over to the bookstore to accumulate a few essentials — Riddle stationery, notebooks, and a bookbag — and shortly after he'd gotten back to his room there came the knock-knock-a-knock-knock KNOCK-KNOCK that heralded Asmussen's arrival.

"Welcome, once again, to Riddle, guy. You may remember from last night: I'm Rico — Asmussen," he'd said. "The class of eighty-nine. It's great to see you, *hombre*."

Simon had started to offer a hand, but Asmussen hadn't come for shakes. Instead, he'd given Simon's left arm a comradely punch, and then had marched straight into the room, heading for the bed. Earlier, Si had wondered whether he should make the thing or not, and decided he'd better, just in case a girl came in. He was glad he had when Asmussen stretched out on it, sandals and all. "Rico" was also wearing, on a Mexican shirt, one of those official student agency salesman's badges, like the one Amanda'd shown him.

"Have a chair, *amigo*," the guest had said, from the bed, hospitably. "Like I said last night, we gotta talk, dammit. In a way, I wish we didn't, but we do. We have to." He pointed a finger at Simon. "Here's the first item on the menu," he said. "Everybody's menu. Nuclear war. Not anybody's favorite food, but out there, right? A *possibilitado*. You ever think about it, friend?"

It was then that Simon admitted he did, and Asmussen vouched for his sensitivity, at least in terms of appearance.

"As a matter of fact," Simon said, when "Rico" didn't keep on talking, "the people in Vermont — where I come from — sort of brought the nuclear freeze idea to national attention. You probably remember: how it came up in the town meetings and all."

"Town meetings — *right*!" said Asmussen. Simon wished he could see his eyes. "But let's say the Russians throw one down on top of the SAC base there, outside of Jettison City." He took his hand out from under his head and made a little tossing motion with it. "That'd make us — what? — sixty miles from Ground Zero. What's *your* next move, in that case?"

"My next *move*?" Simon said. He slipped on a smile. It didn't seem to fit right, so he took it off again. "I don't think I'd have one, really. I'd be a victim, a statistic. I'd have pretty much had it. And I probably couldn't *get* anywhere, like home or something, even if I wanted to. That's if you mean that kind of 'move.' "

"Quite *correcto*. Right as rain in Spain," said Asmussen. "Except good luck with even *rain*, these — " He sat up suddenly and dropped his feet on the floor. "But anyway — you'd have pretty much had it. And that's why you *could* need me: to take you to The Last Resort." He smiled.

"Which means that for a small fee," he continued,

in a very ordinary, conversational tone of voice, "I'm prepared to kill you, quickly and painlessly." He chuckled. "In the event of a nearby nuclear attack, of course." He leaned forward, elbows on knees. "Any time in the next three years, while college is in session, not counting summer term, for a premium of twenty bucks a year, you get the ultimate insurance and *a*ssurance. I never go anywhere on weekends, so that'd be all right. It'd be done right here in the privacy of your own room, probably within minutes after the blast. Less than an hour or your money back."

"You're kidding," Simon said.

"Well, yes," said Asmussen. "About the time part. But not the rest. Hey — I wish I were. You heard about the vote at Brown — on stockpiling the cyanide pill? And a couple of other places copycatted, right? But you can bet your ass that no college infirmary is really going to have a supply of the pills. Not for the *estudientes*, anyway. The parents wouldn't stand for it. Have their kids going around killing themselves, after they've laid out all those nonrefundable bucks for their tuitions and their rooms and boards? No *way*." He shook his head.

"Plus, a lot of people wouldn't *want* to do it themselves," he continued. "Maybe it's against their religion or something — suicide, that is. I think that Catholics are forbidden to do it to themselves, or maybe it's the Jewish. So there's a need out there, and I'm prepared to fill it, with the necessary skills. Look — I've been around guns almost all my life; my parents really encouraged me. What's more, I know anatomy, like the back of my hand — the brain and everything. My clients wouldn't even have to watch, you know? Hey, put the headphones on, be listening to music, looking at a magazine — I'd bring along a nice selection: *Penthouse*, *Arizona Highways*, *Gourmet* magazine, *Vogue* — and . . . blam, it's over. *Hello*, pearly gates — right there." Asmussen smiled. "Radiation sickness is a bummer, man. That's one bad trip you'd never miss, I promise you."

Simon stared at him. At first, he'd been thinking this was all a joke, an upperclass trick that got played on little freshmen every year, and later on was chortled over. But Amanda had called Asmussen a dork, and there wasn't anything about the guy that suggested . . . Eddie Murphy, say, or *anybody* funny. And, in a way, what Asmussen was suggesting wasn't all that different from . . . auto insurance, for instance, where you keep paying money every year and hope you don't collect the "benefits." And the guy *was* wearing the official salesman's badge, which meant — didn't it? — that whatever the person was selling had been deemed acceptable and workable by either the dean of students' office or the medical director's. Everything had to be either educationally, or socially, or medically okay, in other words. At the breakfast table that morning, someone had said the salesman for the SCS — the Student Contraceptive Service — had hit his room already with the "Condom-of-the-Month Club," and Simon had wondered, briefly, if that product was more an educational, or a social, or a medical necessity, at college. Sometimes the lines got sort of blurred, he guessed.

"Well," said Simon, finally. He knew he'd better start practicing rejections. "I don't know. It's something I'd want to think about. Maybe even talk over with. . . ." He was going to say "my parents," but switched to ". . . some other people." He could feel the thickness of Grebe's twenty-dollar bill bulking up his wallet, so he couldn't really say he didn't have the money.

"Hey, sure, go right ahead," the salesman said. "But just two things, before I go." He held up two fingers. "One, this is a limited-edition offer. The Last Resort is *not* just open to the public, understand. The service that I'm offering is much too personal. You deal with me, and me only, from beginning to end. Oh, I know" — he held up a palm — "it'd be easy enough for me to go out and hire a band of mad-dog psychopaths and make a mint on this. But that'd ruin everything; when I'm full, I'm full. That's number one.

"And two is: Don't be surprised if people don't want to admit they've signed up for the service. You know what I mean? I could give you names right now that you would love . . . to have as your associates in this, and your associa*tess*as, I should tell you. Already, my clients represent a broad *spectrum*" — he made an arc in the air in front of his face, with his open hand — "of the university population. Students, faculty, administration, and staff. But I don't give names, nor will I ever sell my list. Your secret will either die with you and/or with me." He suddenly whipped off his dark glasses, winked at Simon, and then jammed them back on his nose. "Think about it," he said, and he lay back down on Simon's bed, this time on his back, with his head down on the pillow.

Before Simon could come up with something else

71

to say, though, his beeper went off. Asmussen sat up immediately, looking left and right. Simon detached the little black box from his belt and shut the sound off.

"Sorry," he said. "I'm afraid I — "

Asmussen was already on his feet. Once again, he took off his glasses, this time just to stare at Simon.

"Sure," he said, and, "Boy, you're...." He shook his head. "That's amazing." He hurried toward the door, but stopped just as he reached it, and turned around. "I'll respect your decision either way, what with the oath and all. I really mean that, doc," he said. And he was gone.

Simon stood there blinking. He got out one of Grebe's forms, entered the date and time, and the code name that he'd chosen: GORODISH. Following directions, he rapidly checked off that he was "with one other person," and that he was feeling "tense" when the beeper went off. It was a few minutes, though, before he checked off "socializing." It certainly wasn't right, but he just couldn't think of any other word for what he had just done with Asmussen.

15

More Meetings

The all-freshmen meeting, held in the spacious auditorium in Forsythe Hall, gave Simon and his classmates their first self-satisfying taste of class-consciousness: a sense of having a place in history, of being . . . well, the latest link in a chain of classes stretching back, already, for 160 years, a chain that, God willing and the alumni giving, would stretch on and on for centuries to come. That was more or less what their official greeter told them, anyway, Ozimander Praline (if Simon heard the name aright) of the Riddle class of 1941, now one of the vice-presidents of the university and General Administrator of Graduate Affairs (GAGA).

With the official greeting given, Praline — or whatever — then led the freshmen in the singing of the "Riddle Song": "Riddle, my matrix, source which brings . . ." etc., which is sung to the tune of the *Great Doxology* and sometimes with the words "Riddle, my mattress coarsely springs . . ." in the place of the proper ones. Then he introduced the rock 'n' roll superstar Peter Mint (Riddle '78), who not only described the honor code of the university to Simon's class, but also confided how it had played a part in his decision to record only music that told the truth about America, good *and* bad.

After that, a series of other, lesser speakers had their turns: heads of cheerleading, of various athletic teams, of dramatic and musical organizations, of literary groups and salons, and the like — including the cochairpeople of the Alternative Lifestyle Student Organization (ALSO), one of whom said he liked to think of their class as "the first of the gay nineties." That made three people clap and a whole lot of other people swivel their heads around to see who was clapping.

Finally, President Portcullis gave the official address of welcome to the class, a chatty and collegial little number (twelve — minutes, that is — long), which managed, Simon thought, to be exciting, challenging, optimistic, nonspecific, and totally unpatronizing. The freshmen, men and women both, turned and smiled at one another as they clapped; for him, and what he'd said, and for themselves. The bones had been cast, the liver of the sheep examined — and it was roses, roses, roses, right across the line.

When the meeting was over — it lasted less than an hour — Simon took out his map of the campus and found his way to Frabbit Hall, the psychology building, and so to Professor Grebe's office door.

"Come," said a voice, in answer to his knock. He opened up the door and entered.

In the course of his eclectic education, Simon had been exposed to some unusual and gifted people and their workplaces. Almost as a rule, the offices of his mentors were not the traditional desk-with-facing-upholstered-chairs-and-Brueghel-right-behind-you-on-the-wall. But he'd never seen anything like this place.

To start with, there was a desk all right, which had, to go with it, a swivel chair, padded with what looked like down bed pillows covered in some shiny red material, possibly rayon. But sitting in the chair — or standing, actually — was a small robot, about a foot and a half high, that said: "Hi! How ya doing?" in the same deep voice that had answered his knock.

The rest of the room was almost even stranger.

There were bookcases, of course, and a lot of them *did* have books in them. But the books tended to have colorful dust jackets, or were paperbacks, and they were piled onto the shelves every which way, and often had other stuff on top of *them*. For instance: a stuffed lizard, hand puppets, two grip-strengtheners, some empty beer bottles with exotic foreign labels, a cellophane envelope containing different-colored stick-on stars, a Batman mask, a pink feather duster, an unplugged electric clock with DRINK NEHI on its face, and so on.

Some shelves had only records on them, and of course one of them had an amplifier and a turntable and a small TV set on it, and there was an electric bass, and speakers, and a pair of flippers on the floor, right by the desk. On the walls and on two closed doors, there were a bunch of signs and posters, and also one large mirror on which someone had written, apparently in lipstick, DOCTOR FREUD, DOCTOR FREUD, HOW I WISH THAT YOU'D BEEN DIFFERENTLY EMPLOYED. . . .

There were also two imitation leather chairs, shaped like human hands — but hands bent into right angles, of course, so that you'd sit in the palms and lean back against the fingers. The hand-chairs looked to have heavy metal bases, round, which connected to the backs of the palms; the thumbs seemed to serve as armrests.

"Is Doctor Grebe around, by any chance?" said Simon to the robot.

"Grebe is a fraud and an incompetent," answered the little round-topped, wheeled machine. "I'd suggest you put yourself in my hands" — it gestured toward the chairs — "or your cells on my glans, as the bishop said to the actress, and forget about that booby dabchick. Hey" — the robot's eyes blinked on and off in red-green-amber — "you're not by any chance the Wheel from Peacemeal, are you? The Storm that's known as Simon?"

Si had been starting to sit down while the robot was saying that, but as he did, he chanced to look at the mirror again. Reflected in it this time, from the place that he was standing, was the open door at the end of the office, and standing just on the other side of *it*, and talking into a cordless microphone in his hand, was a tall man with a striking head of thick, black hair.

The hair was much like black steel wool, very fine and kinky, maybe five inches long on the top of his head, where it was longest, and tapered to a neat, short trim around the ears. But instead of being worn in an ordinary, everyday Afro — like Gene Shalit's, say — this hair was parted in the middle and brushed left and right, away from the part. Because of its thickness, though, it couldn't come close to lying flat, or following the shape of the head from which it grew. At best, it sort of *leaned*, this way and that, as if there was a wind inside Grebe's head that blew not only steadily but in opposite directions.

Oh, yes — as Simon had assumed at once, this was Hansen Grebe.

"Right," said Simon, looking in the mirror, still. "I'm Simon Storm. And you're Professor Grebe?"

"To the best of my knowledge, I am," the man said, grinning, coming into the room. "And glad of it. Although a colleague here has consistently maintained that Secretary of Education Bennett had me, specifically, in mind when he said a lot of college students were being 'ripped off' nowadays. Nonsense. As a Grebe, I know a foul canard in any kind of clothing."

Simon smiled and nodded. The professor was a tall, slender man — now wearing a gray, hooded sweat suit — with a large nose; heavy, undisciplined eyebrows; and the kindest smiling eyes imaginable. He moved through the room's clutter with the grace of a dancer, or at least a tennis player, Simon thought, as Grebe slipped the microphone into the pouch pocket of his sweat shirt.

They shook hands, and Si did as the robot had suggested and sat down on one of the hand-shaped chairs. It was not only soft — surprisingly — but also quite supportive.

"Well," said Grebe. He put the robot on the floor and took the swivel chair himself. "Tell me what you think about the place, so far? You getting nicely settled in?" His eyebrows rose, on that.

"As the act . . ." he and Simon started saying, both together, and they laughed.

"So much for ice-breakers," Grebe said. "Now.

77

You got the beeper and the other stuff, okay? But wait — you'll join me in a Coca-Cola — kid?" He smiled; Simon nodded, and the professor went and got two bottles from the refrigerator inside his closet, uncapped them both, and handed one to Si, no glass.

They started with Grebe's research project, and how he felt about it, but soon they were whirling around some other fields of common interest, touching such bases as clairvoyance, what sort of person wears pajamas, propaganda, Caesar's wife, the so-called "peacekeeper," and various theories of human intelligence. Si found Grebe to be witty, informed, unpretentious, relaxed, and above all, curious (both meanings). Grebe would have said almost the same for Simon; he also thought he listened well.

"I agree with Howard Gardner, up in Boston," Grebe said, when they reached the last of their topics. "I'm completely convinced that the traditional tendency to distribute 'intelligence' into one of two pigeonholes — verbal and mathematical — is absurd. I applaud his identification of seven different styles, or categories, rather than two. But I'm not sure that seven's enough, myself." He cleared his throat.

"On the basis of my studies here the last few years," he said, "I'm postulating still another type. I'm calling it 'acquisitive intelligence' or, colloquially, 'git-wit.' What I'm speaking of, of course, is the kind of mental organization it takes to make a great deal of money: the enormous drive, competitiveness, and singularity of purpose that manifest themselves in tons of ways, including even the two-handed backhand. To call it just 'successful selfishness' is totally to miss the point, I think. Entrepreneurship of various sorts can have some fascinating depth, complexity to it. You find examples, lots of them, in fact, right here on campus."

"I guess *so*," said Simon. "That's one thing that's sort of surprised me about the people here — not that I've met that many — but how business-oriented a lot of them seem to be, at least in Bliss."

"By no means a local phenomenon," Grebe said. "That's the way it is all over. Business courses, economics courses, computer science — full to overflowing, with new classes being introduced every year. On the wall, leaning up against it, are such flowers as philosophy, religion, literature, history, foreign languages — except for Fortran, certainly — classical studies, and some others. Were it not for the good ol' distribution requirements, there'd be more tweed jackets with leather patches on the local breadlines than there are knit caps and army greatcoats. The trouble with those fields — the humanities in general, you might say — is that there's no *advantage* in them, see? The students' juices aren't set to flowing at the scent and sight and sound of them. Luckily for me, psychology has possibilities. Know thy neighbor, teach him, even mold him, baby. There's a nice belief abroad that we modern sorcerers — most of us wearing Greek fishermen's caps these days, instead of those pointy jobs — can show them how to make the rat run through the maze to . . . Macy's!"

Grebe wrinkled his nose at Simon.

"I don't take this seriously," he said, "but one hears certain rumors. Little birdie voices. Trills and portents of transmogrification."

"Of what to what?" asked Simon.

"Oh," said Grebe, "I really shouldn't say. But . . . with that mean caffeine now coursing through my system" — he turned his empty bottle upside down — "I feel like shouting from the rooftops, wild." He hitched forward in his chair.

"One hears" — he laid a finger alongside of his nose — "that there are those who'd like to see Portcullis out, and this traditional bastion of the liberal arts transformed into something called the First American Trade, Computer, and Technical College — a business school so specialized, high-powered, and advanced that its graduates would *start* at salaries comparable to those of first-string centers in the NBA." Grebe sat back to let that sink in, and then he added, "And that one of those pushing for the change has *this* on top of his stationery."

So saying, he grabbed a piece of scratch paper from the top of his desk and scribbled something on it. When through, he held the paper out to Simon, but he didn't let go while Si leaned out and read the words. Then, Hansen Grebe took matches from his desktop, lighted one, and set the slip on fire. Holding it this way and that, he stood and went into what Simon took to be a lavatory, closing the door behind him. In a moment, there were flushing sounds.

When he didn't come out after about eight minutes, Simon got up and knocked on the door and said, "Professor Grebe?" Then, louder, "Professor Grebe? Are you okay?"

From behind him on the floor, the robot answered: "I think the lying bastard's gone to lunch.

If I were you, I'd do the same. Come back again some other time, if you have the taste for it."

Simon laughed. That seemed like good advice, the lunch suggestion. His talk with Grebe had given him an appetite, for sure.

16

Café Portcullis

Leaving Grebe's office, Simon could hardly believe how *collegiate* he was feeling. That had to be the word for it, he told himself. What else, when questions filled his mind, like: What the hell is going on? and answers like: I doubt it.

He ate his lunch, hungrily but sociably, then went back to his room to write a promised postcard to his parents. Had they known what he was getting into? Maybe. They both had gone to college, one of them to Riddle. Yet the more things change, he knew, the more they stay the same. So, if things had been pretty much *status quo* since World War II, which surely could be argued, mightn't this be so: The *less* things change, the more *different* they are?

While he was trying to do the card, no fewer than four salespeople came by his room: two guys, one girl, and one potato chip. The last of those was first, and was in fact a dwarf disguised as a potato chip who called himself "The Munchkin" and said that he was only one of many in that line. All of them were taking orders for, and would deliver, almost anything that could fit in your mouth and came in bags, glass, foil, aluminum, or plastic with a lid. They'd do that seven days a week, at your command. The second was a fast-talking guy from A-See D-See Ceiling Posters. After a quick look around the room, he offered Simon photos of a very frank and carefree naked girl he called "Sariya," which, it turned out, was not her *nom d'amour* or *de travaille* but stood for "She's Always Ready if You Are." Thirdly, and his favorite, came a girl who proposed to write his parents and other, older relatives a series of innovative fund-raising letters, one every three or four weeks, for a mere fifteen percent of whatever they sent. As a business entity, she was known as GETIT — Graciously Extracting Tomorrow's Inheritance Today. Simon told her no, regretfully; the other two, as well. He just said he wasn't old enough to enter into a binding contract.

The fourth and final salesman of the afternoon was different. For one thing, he never said a word, and for another, he was in and out of the room in maybe forty seconds, tops. Afterward, Simon couldn't even remember for sure what the guy looked like.

When he walked in the door, he reached into the breast pocket of his nondescript jacket and pulled out a leather folder, which he flipped open to reveal his salesman's badge. But even in the flash he had to look at it, Simon saw the thing was not the same as what the other salesmen wore. This badge, in addition to the rampant sphinx, had a likeness of a woman, bending over, holding in her hand the torch of knowledge. And the sphinx, as Simon seemed to see it, had . . . *designs* on her.

As soon as the badge disappeared, the guy's hand dropped down into his side pocket and produced a business card. This he *gave* to Si, who read on it the following: HOW ABOUT A *POP*? with a little asterisk over the last P. Down in the righthand corner of the card, there was another asterisk and, in tiny letters: PREVIOUSLY OWNED PAPER.

Si painted on his good sport's, I-can-take-a-joke half smile and started to hand the card back, but the guy made a motion with his hand that said, quite clearly, "turn it over."

Si did as he was told, and read:

PREVIOUSLY OWNED PAPERS
(up to 100,000 words)

All subjects, all styles. Prices based on grades they got, and where, first time around, plus standard charge per word.

NONE EVER USED AT RIDDLE!

24-Hour Service, Free Delivery, call 899-2473
and leave a #.
Keep this card for emergencies.

And when Si looked up again, the guy was gone.

When he was finally able to finish the card to his parents, Simon grabbed his glove and headed for the softball mixer. Each of the R.A.'s was captain of a team, and Amanda Dollop, his, gave him a start at second base. It worked out great. In the field, he just devoured everything that he could get that glove on; at the plate, he lined a double over third the first time up, then popped a little blooper into right, which, running all the way, he stretched into a second double. That play, his upbeat 1980s brand of hustle, made his teammates (mostly male) behave as if they'd just invented him, and after he had come on in and scored, his captain shook his hand and swatted his rear end a good one. Yes, indeed. She also winked at him. Perhaps, he thought, that meant that she remembered seeing what she'd swatted, in the flesh. He spent the rest of the game wishing she'd score a run or make some spectacular play in the field so he could, just offhandedly, reciprocate. She didn't and he didn't; maybe just as well, he thought when he was back in his room. There was no mistaking Amanda Dollop's bottom for third or any other base and, in point of fact, he didn't really know if he could touch it, legally.

From time to time during the game Simon had brief flashbacks to his talk with Hansen Grebe. He'd met one other psychologist in his life, a woman at the holistic health center who widened her eyes a lot at things he said, as if she'd found the deeper and intended meaning in . . . oh, his views concerning gravel roads in springtime, say. ("Exactly," she had told him. "I understand *exactly* what you're getting at. Ruts and rutting *always* go together, don't they?")

Grebe didn't talk like that at all. He was a lot more fun. He also seemed to think — as Simon did, himself — that a mix of fact and fantasy was closer to the truth than all of either, certain times.

The question was: How much of which was in the things he'd said concerning Riddle and its president? For instance, Grebe had hinted — hell, he'd *said* — that Riddle's very name, its whole identity, might change. That if conspirators, unnamed, succeeded in their plans, the place would then become the First American Trade, Computer, and Technical College. FATCAT College? Hey, come on. Si couldn't swallow *that*. But yet, it seemed to be a fact that the place, or at least a lot of the students whom he'd met so far, were very . . . business-minded. In fact, up to that point it was fair to say he hadn't heard a literary allusion, or a single piece of political rhetoric, scrap of poetry, measure of *bel canto*, or cry of existential despair. Almost everyone was into that which could be weighed or measured, and marked with either stickers or a tag.

But overthrowing a duly elected, or at least *se-*lected, president was more than a commercial enterprise; that was politics. Meddling in the internal affairs of a duly accredited university. Was it even remotely possible that the person whose name Grebe had written on that piece of paper would countenance, in fact *promote*, a meddle of this magnitude?

Simon wasn't sure. One heard a lot of talk from government about it wanting to reduce, trim down to smaller size, get off the people's backs. Yet, at the same time, this same government believed — or so it seemed to Simon — that anything *it* said was right. And therefore not to be discussed or even looked at much. Riddle University, historically, had graduated more than its share of the nation's questioners, complainers, articulate uncoverers, and borers-from-within. That was one reason Si had wanted to attend it. Was it possible that Riddle, good *old* Riddle, was just the kind of place the government would like to hear say "uncle"?

That question was still rattling around in Simon's head when he pressed the doorbell of the presidential manse, just as the big hand got real near the little one, at six.

Betsy Portcullis "got" the door herself, and welcomed Si as if he'd come to sell her youthful skin forever in a peaceful world with puppies, guaranteed.

"Simon!" she said. "My God, it's been a while." She had her hands on his shoulders by then. "I'm really, really glad to see you." And she kissed him on both cheeks, as if she was the president of France, and laughed, and said, "I *love* your being here, at Riddle."

Being the sort of place it was, Riddle had to be one of the first universities to pay the presidential wife a solid salary — and leave it up to her just what she'd do besides lay in the gin and order fish and lean red meat for the trustees. In B. Portcullis this university had got itself a stuff-of-legends bargain, an oh-what's-this-behind-that-ripped-old-painting-I-just-purchased-for-the-frame? She was not only visible and ornamental, but also very useful, day by day. Women students — just for instance — found she gave them even better, cheaper, quicker answers than Ann Landers.

In style, the woman was a glider, which meant she never seemed to make an effort, trip, or be uncomfortable. She got, no matter what, nine hours' sleep a night, and never wore a watch. She'd practiced law, before they came to Riddle, and gotten to the point she played real well, against all comers. She would have loved her husband just as much — she'd told him this a hundred times — if he had been the village loafer, and never needed more than just one suitcase on a trip. That night, while flinging wide the portals, so to speak, for Si, she had on blue jeans and a red Hawaiian shirt.

"I'm glad I'm here myself," said Simon, in reply to her. "Silly as it sounds, I really had my heart set on it. Getting in, I mean."

"Come on upstairs," she said, sliding a hand under his arm. "We want to hear what you think of *every*thing. Tell me first — how was the speech today?" She pointed up the stairs. "*He* thought it went real well. In fact, he gave himself a perfect score for lip-synch." Simon laughed as they went up the staircase.

They settled in a living room with bright, exciting abstract paintings on the walls and large, soft chairs to sink in. Henry Portcullis, wearing a wine-colored velour top and khakis, had his left hand wrapped around a glass of Dubonnet, with lemon peel; he used his right to shake and then to chop the air beside him as he laid down social guidelines.

"Let's get clear in the name business once and for all," he said to Simon, smiling. "Anything but Uncle Hank and Aunt Elizabeth, okay? Whatever's comfortable for you. We say the same to all my advisees; it's up to them. What's in a name, anyway? The fact that you're a Storm and my old roommate's son is *totally* meaningless to me. But, Si" — he whined and knit his ample brow — "don't you think you'd rather have a nice big sunny suite than just that *rotten* little single?"

Simon smiled, almost ecstatically. The Portcullises were a great deal like his parents; they didn't have a special style or tone of voice they used with kids. He didn't know what names he'd call them —

probably just nothing for a while — but it was already obvious they expected him to speak his mind, and planned to do the same. A surprising feeling swept right over him. All of a sudden, he felt *safe*.

Still, he wasn't sure he'd mention Grebe, and what they'd talked about. It wasn't the sort of thing you'd want to bring up out of a clear blue sky, exactly. Maybe there'd be an opportunity later on, when they were all three settled, in one place, like after dinner; he'd probably just hang around awhile. In this time, though, before the meal, Betsy Portcullis had to keep gliding out of the room every few minutes, bringing back, each time, a new or stronger smell of something good to eat. Simon's stomach murmured.

At last she said, "It's ready, gentlemen," and then, to Si's considerable surprise, she turned her head and hollered down the hall, "Hey, Kate!"

Before Si'd even reached the door, the owner of the name was there; introductions were performed in transit to the table, more or less.

Kate Portcullis, aged fourteen, wished she looked more like Jennifer Beals than she did, but would have scoffed and whinnied scornfully at any such suggestion, even from a friend. She had short, curly brown hair, weighed ninety-eight pounds, and was wearing white gym shorts over lavender sweat pants, and an old army fatigue jacket over a huge red sweat shirt over a black oxford button-down. All that producing at least an illusion of . . . *bulk*, let's say. Before leaving her room, she'd pulled a headband on, just to check it out — like, the effect. One glance and it was circling thin air, in transit to the corner, hearing, "Sucks."

"Hey!" she said to Simon. She had a hoarse voice, as if she had a cold or had been doing lots of shouting. She loved the way she sounded. Both the tone and, by and large, the content. So she was a wise ass. . . .

"Hi," said Si, off-balance. He hadn't known there was one of these in the house, a girl who might be his own age. And who looked and sounded like a person who was into cigarettes. He felt like a Cambodian who's finally gotten to America to live and everybody thinks he'd like to meet this other refugee, this real nice Vietnamese.

"So you're the genius," she said next. "You have my sympathy." She was disgusted by how nice-looking he'd turned out to be.

"Why's that?" he said, trying to smile it off.

"Oh, I don't know," she said, with a shrug. "I probably oughtn't to say."

Si looked at her. Both of the replies that came into his mind seemed fraught with peril. "Well, don't then" sounded either snotty or like . . . someone *her* age, while "No, really. Tell me" opened up Pandora's box.

"Well, don't then," Henry Portcullis said. And then to Simon, "Take her word for it: If *she* says she oughtn't to say, she oughtn't. Most things that she oughtn't to say, she says anyway, and insists they ought to be said — "

"*Need* to be said," his daughter corrected him.

" — so when she says she oughtn't to say something, you're really talking about something that probably belongs in a lead cylinder, dropped down a shaft into the center of an abandoned salt mine," the president of the university concluded.

"That reminds me," Kate said to him, "did Mom tell you what one of your prize bozos yelled out of a car at Pam, yesterday? Right down on the corner of Main and Prospect? I mean — come *on*. Those people are *sick*. Where does Dean Layton *find* them, anyway? In some kind of a *zoo*? I think you ought to talk to him. But anyway, what I want to know is: Are they just harassing us, like being sexist pigs because we're girls and can't drag them out of the car and kick their ears off, or do they actually think we might want to *do* that stuff? What do *you* think?" she asked Si, passing him a plate of food.

"You're a college guy," she added, with one lip curled up. And then she laughed.

When Kate was talking to her father, Simon was trying to decide what exactly to make of her. She certainly seemed sharp enough — no dummy — but what was the story with this style of hers? he wondered. Maybe she was just a little defensive, being the only person there who was still in high school, if that. He should try to understand what she was feeling, show a little empathy, he told himself.

But when she said that last part, straight to him, with that sarcastic laugh, he knew he had a problem. He wondered: Could he rise above this pressing need he had to hate her?

He'd try. He'd laugh along — ho-ho, hah-hah-hah-hah — although his ears were burning, once again. So maybe he *wouldn't* know what the guy in the car's motivation was, exactly. So maybe he *wasn't* exactly a "college guy." It wasn't his fault. At least the people who went to the college were

91

mature enough not to make an issue of things like how old he was — to be a little considerate.

"Well, I think it's all a part of this age of explicitness we're having," Betsy Portcullis said, gliding in and intercepting. "Like in the movies, where it isn't enough anymore to just see the guy shoot and someone else fall down. Oh, no — you've got to see the hole the bullet makes, right through the skin, and different stuff come out of it, like blood and brains and bits of bone and — "

"*Muh*-ther!" Kate exclaimed. "Stop being gross. We're eating."

"Shoot," her father said. He chewed and swallowed. "You eat at the movies all the time. I've seen you." Simon smiled. "And it isn't only violence you get to look at in the flesh, it's all that other stuff. Why, you've actually seen young ladies and gentlemen doing things on the silver screen that me and my contemporaries — Simon's *father* and myself — didn't even know the *names* for, much less the geometry." He pursed his lips and touched them with his napkin. "I'd have to say that it's a whole new ball game!" he exclaimed, in simulated horror.

"Sure, Daddy, sure," Kate said. She was bubbling with laughter. "So what are you saying, anyway — that this makes it all right? For some moron at the college to ask a fourteen-year-old girl if she'd like to — " She laughed some more and rolled her eyes around. "See? I can't even say it."

"How old-fashioned," her father said, and he was laughing, too. "But no — I'm just agreeing with your mother. And adding that where some guys used to whistle at girls, now, maybe, they say more or less what the whistle used to mean. And yes, I also think it's partly a sexist thing, where they don't mean it *literally*, but just want to — I don't know, can you say *discomfort* the girl? But in any case, the age of euphemism is, for the most part, moribund. Except," he said to Simon, "at the Portcullis dinner table, apparently, thank God."

There was a silence. Kate Portcullis was nodding as she mopped the gravy on her plate with half a roll. Simon didn't have to blurt out, "I bet sometimes guys yell at girls because they're trying to make themselves look big, or in control, when it's really the exact opposite of the way they're feeling." But he did. And then added, "You know — nowadays. Given the world situation and all."

Later on, he wondered why he'd spoken at all. Was he just being natural, entering into a mildly interesting conversation? Or had he, possibly, been trying to make himself look big when it was pretty much the opposite of the way he was feeling?

Whichever, Kate Portcullis noticed.

"What?" she said. "So what am I meant to do, feel sorry for them? Is this the 'poor-baby' defense? My client didn't mean it, judge — but the fear of being vaporized has sent him off his gourd, poor baby."

"Well, I'm not saying anything about feeling sorry for them," Simon said. "It just seemed like a possibility." And then he said something that he was sure had never occurred to him before, and that he wasn't even sure he believed himself. "Guys here at Riddle are under a lot of pressure nowadays."

The Portcullises, senior, seemed to nod a bit at that one, possibly out of politeness, and because they didn't want a guest to feel uneasy, Si thought later. Their daughter, Kate, did not know such constraints, however.

"Huh?" she said. "At college? Here at Riddle? Nose hairs." He was pretty sure she said "nose hairs"; it *could* have been "no way," or even "nonsense." "Those stuck-up . . . louts? Tell me about it. What pressure are *you* under, for instance? You're a guy. You're here at Riddle."

"Well," said Simon, trying to keep his dignity. "In addition to the major things, like the next war and all that, I guess I'm concerned about how I'll fit in here. And what really matters to me, and where I'm going. Who I actually *am*, you could say."

He thought that was pretty frank and honest of him to say that. Maybe not completely frank and honest, in that it made no mention of relationships with women like J. Beals, but *pretty* frank and honest. It certainly wasn't the sort of response a person would make fun of.

"Duh," said Kate Portcullis. "Why don't you just ask around? People'll tell you. Or you could take one of those tests in *Seventeen* or *Cosmo*." She laughed outrageously again·and turned to her mother.

"Jennifer and I took one of them last month," she said. "Did I tell you? 'What kind of SAT score do you have these days?' it was called. Of course SAT stood for Sex Arousal Talent, instead of whatever it really does. I got a fifty-eight. But sixty was perfect." She laughed again.

"Don't misunderstand me" — she turned back to Simon — "I don't believe in any of that test and survey junk. Even the big deal so-called scientific ones you read about. And you know why I don't? People lie. Everybody lies. All they're doing is being exhibitionists, that's what I say: checking off their answers, telling Gallup what it is unmarried Catholics over thirty living in the Middle West and earning less than fifty thou a year fear more than anything. They want to look like big deals, so they say nuclear winter instead of the truth, which is probably pornographic messages on answering machines or birth control dog food, or something real basic like that. I swear, those people — "

At exactly that moment, Simon's beeper went off. It sounded strange, and he began to blush, Pavlovianly. Then he realized why it sounded strange, as if it had an echo: It did. Kate Portcullis, too, was wired into Grebe.

The rest of the evening there — what little there was of it — was pretty much a blur. Kate turned the color of a brake light, rose, and left the table. Si nodded and agreed with Betsy P. that yes, indeed, he was a part of Hansen Grebe's research, and wasn't it amazing — some coincidence — that Kate was, too. Although this could have been the opening that he'd been waiting for, to talk about the things that Grebe had said to him in person, he passed it up. The fact was: He was feeling funny, in an unfamiliar, grouchy sort of way. When he finished his dessert, he checked his watch and said he had to run — another meeting at the dorm. His father might have noticed Gates Portcullis throw a quick look down the table at his wife, and get a quick look back from her, but Simon didn't. He only heard his freshman adviser telling him — in the friendliest of tones — that maybe they could get together for a little while next Tuesday afternoon and get their business taken care of. Would he come by at four? Simon said (by rote and reflex) he'd be glad to.

17

Answer Sheets

When Kate Portcullis stomped back into her room, she grabbed the big manila envelope of adolescent study answer sheets and pulled one out so fast it fluttered. Muttering a string of words that started "Dumb bimbotic feebroid . . ." she filled in the date and the time; her code name, LADY JANE; and underlined the words "totally enraged" in the General Instructions on the top of the page. The words just somehow caught her eye, and they were there.

Then, with her lips still moving but the sound turned off, she decided that, at the time of the beeper, she was probably, technically, still EATING, and "having a regular meal," and feeling. . . . She paused, looking at the choices, trying to bring the moment back intact. Then she shrugged and very blackly checked the letter (i.): "turned-on."

Simon, who hadn't taken either pen or pad or answer sheet to dinner with him, had a longer time to reflect on the matter before he did his checking-off. He didn't really use it, though. Even walking home — it took him seven minutes, getting back to

Bliss — he mostly thought about a bigmouthed fool named Simon Storm.

But once back in his room, he dutifully sat down to earn his twenty dollars, or a fraction of it, anyway. At the time the beeper went off (he estimated that was quarter after seven) GORODISH was. . . . He stopped, considered, started to check EATING (d.). Then he thought that Kate Portcullis (what would *she* be known as — LILITH?) had probably put that. Maybe better if he went, once more, for SOCIALIZING (g.), "with two to four people." Then moving on to how he was *feeling* — he'd be absolutely honest — he chose the letters (a.) for "anxious," (s.) for "tense" and. . . .

What the heck, he thought. GORODISH didn't have to *explain* these things, or even understand them. So, the letter (i.) deserved some offhand, noncommittal, tiny *token* of a mention: maybe half a hurried, carefree, even *kinky* little check.

18

A-CHOIR

Even as Simon was sitting hunched over his answer sheet, trying to make a halfway decent contribution to the body of knowledge concerning (so-called) normal adolescence, otherwise knowledgeable bodies were still gathered at a table across the campus from the Portcullis home. It's just as well that Simon didn't know of their existence, as a group; he'd had his MDR of *Drang* — and more — already.

Their meeting — "dinner party" doesn't do it justice — had been called by the youthful ball-of-fire who was chairman of the Department of Economics at the university, Professor Greg Holt. He'd done that in the usual laid-back way by means of a tiny cryptic item in the "Meetings-Meetings-Meetings" column of the *Riddle News*. The wording of it was: "A-CHOIR: practice Thursday night, at seven."

Most logical and unsuspicious people who saw the announcement probably assumed that A-CHOIR was a choral group of some sort — perhaps one better than B-CHOIR, or made up of people with a minor interest in the key of A. It's even possible that some of them — certain aspiring baritones and

99

altos — might have wandered through the campus Thursday night, just listening for voices raised in song, hoping to try out for it.

But the fact of the matter was that A-CHOIR (pronounced correctly, it's: ACQUIRE) was the most exclusive secret society in the university (whose regulations specifically forbade such organizations), and had nothing to do with music whatsoever. Members of A-CHOIR — and membership in any year was limited to seven — were campus leaders, people who had made a real commitment to being Ambitious, Competitive, Hard-driving, Opportunitistic, Influential, and Resourceful. Professor Greg Holt, as faculty adviser/founder, helped them with the maintenance and further development of these qualities in themselves, as well as with what was, let's face it, a crusade to spread them, thick as possible, all over campus and, in time, the less-developed countries.

That fall, the returning members of A-CHOIR were: Phil Hedd, Grant Kahn, Amanda Dollop, Jeffrey Bung, Brad Hammond, and Clovis St. James. Clovis St. James was black, and also had a British accent and a foreign passport, and at times was pretty near — although delightfully — invisible; you already know what Amanda Dollop is. There was one vacancy.

Greg Holt had come to Riddle just three years before, he and his lovely wife, Renée, and their vivacious children, Jessica, now six, and Freddy, four. There would be no further additions to the family.

("That's it," Renée had said, when Freddy joined

the lineup, and that Christmas, from his stocking, Greg dug out a gift certificate, which was good for a free vasectomy, plus a sixteen-ounce Pepsi and an order of fries, in lieu of lollypop. Renée was quite a kidder, but she wasn't kidding anymore. So Greg just sighed and bit the bullet and went through with the operation — and yes, you bet he wore the pin they gave him to every class he taught, and mentioned what it was, with a boyish and opportunistic twinkle in his eye. Renée had chosen not to let him further sow; that didn't mean he couldn't reap, from time to time.)

The summer before they came to town, the Holts had bought a big old Victorian house of a size and shape suitable for a department chairman, which Greg was from the beginning. If you could believe it — and the search committee did — Holt was a scholar (see, see the list of articles in all the boring, boring journals), with gigs not only as a teacher (London, Basel, and Chicago), but also in the private sector (IBN — a typo, surely), and the public one (on the President's Commission for Aid to Needy Teenagers, which naturally, deservedly, was known as P-CANT). Meetings of A-CHOIR always were at Holt House, as he called it. Always had been, ever since he started it.

On meeting nights, Renée Holt and the children always ate early, but that didn't mean Professor Holt cooked dinner for "the gang," as he referred to them at home. Unh-unh. At Holt House there were roles, and very little overlapping; hence, as Greg and Renée agreed, efficiency and no confusion. In some respects — not all, but some — it made sense to run the home the way good businesses are

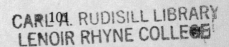

run, and so get peak production out of all the personnel. For instance, both adults made sure they programmed change, variety, in every day and recognized achievement in each other and rewarded it. As a result, morale was for the most part very high, and energy unflagging, even at the children's bedtime. By adults' bedtime, energy levels were sometimes down a tad, which Greg said was as a result of his operation. Renée's doctor said that couldn't possibly be so, but Greg argued that not being a man, she didn't have the facts at her fingertips. If the doctor had been a man, he told Renée, she would have known that there were certain postoperative . . . complications. Of course, if the doctor had been in Greg's classes, no matter what her sex, she would have also known the complications' names, which were Kathi, Robin, and Diane (or Dee-Dee).

In any case, on the nights A-CHOIR met, Renée would have usually prepared a dish — like boneless chicken breasts wrapped in bacon, in a sour cream and mushroom sauce — that'd be cooking happily in the oven when the guests arrived. The rice pilaf would be similarly engaged, but in a double boiler on the top of the stove, and the salad greens would be washed, dried, and bagged in the refrigerator, with the dressing freshly made on the counter, and the timer set for forty-five minutes. Greg and "the kids" could take the handsome copper and enamel baking dish, and ditto double boiler, from the oven and the stove top to the sideboard, Renée would have told him. Any of the group could toss the salad, and in the case of white wine, any of the men could work the corkscrew; if red was called for by the menu, Greg would have had it breathing for a while before the guests arrived, of course.

The timing of all this was a cinch, because the student members of the society were always punctual, for the best of all possible reasons. It was *smart* for them to be so. New members got the word from old: Dinner at the Holts' was like a *business meeting*; stuffing-face was incidental, only. *Product* was the thing, the only reason for this visit; *process*, one-time favorite of their age-group, was now important just as what Kraft did to cheese.

"Remember this," Grant Kahn had said to Jeffrey Bung, when Jeff was still the new boy on the block. "In a typical business drama, there are only two roles: One, The Guy Who Wants It Something Awful; and Two, The Man Who's Got Most Everything He Needs. The trick is to begin the meeting knowing you're a total One, but looking absolutely Two — and end it just the opposite. You follow me?"

Jeff had nodded; the guy was all synapses, Mr. Micro-chip.

"At our meetings," Kahn went on, "all of us students want the same things, basically. First, we're looking for factual, up to the minute, insider information about the world of jobs and businesses. Most of that will come from Greg, necessarily; he's turning all the valves along the pipeline at this point. He has something — plenty — that we want, but he also *wants* a little something in return. You'll hear what that is soon enough." Bung nodded some more, narrowing his eyes cagily.

"The second thing we come for," Grant continued, "is the feedback we can get, from Greg and from each other. Critiques about our total selves, as business entities — what's magnetic in the way we come across, and where the chrome could use a little polish. As a member of A-CHOIR, you're subject to a kind of intimate personal scrutiny money can't buy. Sometimes I think of it as a psychosocial rectal exam — that's how thorough and how *searching* what we do is."

"Wow," said Jeffrey Bung, squirming a little in his chair. "You wouldn't try to Kahn me, would you?"

"So," Grant Kahn concluded, ignoring that, but hating Jeffrey Bung as a *nouveau* little weisenheimer, "imagine the four minutes between seven-oh-one and seven-oh-five as . . . oh, let's say, the little green window in that hour. It's the time span we are framed in and come through, arrival-wise. And Bung-er, one last thing. You travel to the meeting by yourself. We never move around *en masse*, or car-pool, as if we were a . . . bowling team, or something. Besides, the travel time is good for focusing: getting all your weapons sighted-in."

Kahn made a pistol of his hand, pointed it at Jeffrey, and closing his left eye, peered down the finger/barrel.

"Got it," Jeffrey Bung had answered, getting Grant Kahn right between the legs with an imaginary kick, delivered at lightning speed by his crossed left leg, and the foot that wore the not-yet-purchased steel-toed shoe.

"Now, then. Can I get you a drink?"

Greg Holt always asked that question, and he didn't dilly-dally. By 7:02, in other words, the whistle had been blown, the first ball pitched, the starter's gun raised high and fired.

And sometimes — although not with this experienced sextet — the ball blew off the tee, the batter missed it by a mile, the swimmer/runner slipped and fell. Like with the answer Phil Hedd made (to give you an example), the first time *he* received the question.

"Absolutely. Thanks. Do you have any Scotch?" he'd said, with a broad grin on his face. This was long before he'd gotten started with the plastic cocktail stirrer in the corner of his mouth — which in itself was plenty controversial.

That answer, though, was simply rotten (he soon learned), all wrong. Too *eager*, number one: Was he some kind of an alcoholic with the "absolutely" stuff? And in the second place, and worse, his answer was an insult to his host. Here was (a part of) the Rule of Beverage: *Assume* Scotch. In fact (the rule went on), assume beer, blended bourbon, gin, rum, Scotch, and vodka — and vermouths, of course. Plus the following mixers: soda, ginger ale, tonic, cola, *and* two diet sodas, one of which *must* be a cola. And finally, two wines for before-dinner drinking, neither very good. Members of A-CHOIR learned never to do business with a person who, having asked, "Can I get you a drink?" lacked or *ran out of* any of the above. "Short on booze, never choose" was, in fact, one of Holt's Laws, a series of pithy sayings members were urged to memorize, and base their business dealings on.

On this particular night, though, the asking-for and getting all went smoothly, and by a quarter past seven the six students and one professor were all seated in the living room and sipping two white wines, one beer, one vodka tonic, one rum and cola, one Scotch rocks, and one tall diet something, with a twist.

"Well," said Greg Holt, cheerfully, setting everyone at edgy ease by his utterly relaxed intensity, "I can see who got the lifeguard job this summer. I'd call that top-ten tanning, Grant."

Everybody laughed at the absurdity of that: the possibility that he, Grant Kahn, would waste his summer on a beach while waves of market fluctuation washed up bloated whales of profit on the floor of the exchange. But still, G.K. was *very* dark, indeed.

Kahn bobbed his head, acknowledging the humor in the situation, and answered with a rueful smile. "My dad came down with Star-boat fever," he explained. "Which meant that every weekend both of us were on the sound from ten A.M. to dusk — and not just cruising, racing. He cleaned my clock, as usual, but we had fun. Though the glare off the water burned us to a crisp, as you can see." He put fingertips to his own cheek, as if expecting that it might be hot, still.

People nodded; explanation taken. Cornelius Kahn, Grant's father, was a legendary competitor. He won — and often princely sums of money — at everything he tried, "even spitting at cracks," it had said in *Newsweek*.

But Philips Hedd was sharp; he thought that maybe Holt had more in mind than irony or compliments.

"But isn't Grant a shade *too* tan?" he asked the room. "For a dark-complected person, like himself?" He looked at Kahn and smiled. "Don't take

106

this the wrong way, buddy, but I'm talking about the fine line that separates a BGG — your classic Bronze Greek God — from . . . frankly, *Swarthyman*. Couldn't you be setting yourself up for a bit of a buzz-reaction? The whoops-what-am-I-doing syndrome? Resulting in a small paralysis below the wrist, at contract-signing time?" He tossed out a reasonable white palm. "*You* know — the problem of the fear of mob connections, and all that."

Greg Holt paused before answering, so that Clovis St. James could slide in first, as if on cue, and say, "What a *frightful* possibility!" and, "Where's that leave a chap like me, d'you suppose?" and everyone could chuckle warmly, delighted by the total un-uptightness of the man.

"Good point," Holt said, letting the double-breasted blazer of invisibility settle down on Clovis's shoulders once again. "Of course, in Grant's case that wouldn't happen, because of the positive-name-recognition factor; anyone who didn't catch — or didn't know — *his* name would have the problem. But by and large, you're right. Businessmen have got to watch their faces, their whole *look* — hair, nose, eyelids, tan — every bit as much as *models* do. That's why you're seeing so many more skin coaches in the Apple than you used to. Once upon a time it was just a West Coast sort of thing, but all the New York health spas have 'em now, although the best ones are still in private practice, from what I understand."

Everybody nodded and the easy flow of talk went on, moving now to fashion, and the messages that everybody's present outfit — jewelry included — sent. Because she knew it was an okay thing to do,

Amanda Dollop got a little notebook out of her small, stylish, hand-painted shoulder bag and jotted down some things she wanted to remember. Brad Hammond saw her doing that, and thought that was just like a *girl*, and so he didn't, and later on forgot some real important stuff concerning bracelets on a guy.

During the meal, logically enough, the conversation had to do with current tastes in food and drink and styles of eating, such as: Was using chopsticks for spaghetti, while wearing white or beige, good fun or merely flashy exhibitionism? Jeffrey Bung raised an interesting hypothetical question having to do with eating strategy: Would it be a brilliant stroke or spell disaster, he asked, to order well-done American meat dishes — pork chops or the Yankee pot roast — while talking import/export with a Japanese?

After the main course and while dessert was being complimented, still, Holt got out the easel and a couple of charts for their usual review of corporate possibilities and good new business ideas. As usual, he'd rated the various "situations" on a scale that ranged from a high of five dollar signs ("prime") to a low of one ("lunch meat"). This time, members blinked in some surprise to see the Start-Up Special — a good business to get into *now* — which was manufacturing gourmet potato chips in the Sun Belt (four-and-a-half signs), but they nodded, grinning, at Holt's sense of humor when he flashed his Loozie-Doozie of the Decade: founding a small, progressive, private liberal arts college, anywhere in the world.

At the last stage of the meeting, when they were

back in the living room sipping demitasses, Greg Holt brought up their final bit of business, the matter of "the vacancy." The bylaws specified a membership of seven; Banks Beeman's graduation, just the month before (he'd had to clear that incomplete in English Comp at summer school), left them one man short, as everybody knew (even Amanda Dollop).

"Okay," said Greg Holt, grinning broadly at the company, "let's get it over with, good buddies." He cleared his throat with heavy mock ceremoniousness.

"In accordance with the bylaws, blah-blah-blah," he droned, "every member has the right to place a name in formal nomination, and so-on-so-forth-etcetera." His glance and smile then took a second lap around the room. "I assume there is a nominee?"

The members looked at one another. Greg Holt was not surprised to see them do so; he'd expected it, in fact. Although no one had ever told him — oh, hell no — he knew darn well that what the members always did was caucus, usually a day or two before the meeting, and at that caucus do the architecture on a deal whereby they'd trade off back and forth (girl friends, weekends, study outlines, other goods and services) until they got down to a single name that one of them would submit. The nominee would therefore — always — win by acclamation.

As far as Holt was concerned, this was a damn good process, which made for a strong and single-minded group, with the "mind" in question mucho like his own. Why shouldn't college kids (he reasoned) learn to "pack" a board? It fascinated him that this process had evolved — or should that be *appeared*? — at once, in the very first year of A-CHOIR. He hadn't even had to tell them how to do it; apparently that stuff was in their genes.

But this time, when the members looked at one another, there weren't any little knowing smiles. To the contrary, the glances Holt caught sight of were rather on the shifty side, and then — ye gods! — no less than *three* clean hands went up.

Holt's eyebrows followed, quickly.

"Ho-ho-ho," he Santa-ed. "And what have we here? Three great minds with but a single thought? Or the Democrats in 1984?" And then, because the bylaws said he had to, he sighed and said, "St. James?"

"I'd very much like to propose Mr. Esteban Sotomayor for membership in this society," said Clovis St. James, or at least Amanda Dollop thought he did. The room had never been more silent since the house was built.

"And you, Mister Bung?" said Holt.

"I nominate M.I. Bloom," said Jeffrey Bung, aggressively. People shifted in their seats at that one.

"Hmmm," said Greg Holt. "Grant?"

Kahn stood up. One thumb found a belt loop. "I take great pleasure in nominating a guy who's a close personal friend not just of mine but of every man on this planet who wants a better life for himself and his family, *Shep Hewitt*." And Phil Hedd and Brad Hammond both brought the palms of their right hands down, several times but almost noiselessly, on their crossed white-flanneled knees, even as they murmured, "Yes! Here, here."

"Well," said Greg Holt. "If there are no *further* nominations — "

"Wait," said Amanda Dollop, suddenly. Sidelong glances raced around the room. "I want to make a nomination, too. It *is* an unusual one, and I know some people think it's . . . silly. But I nominate Simon Storm to be a member of this society. I *know* he's only fifteen," she said to Phil Hedd, "and a brand-new freshman, and I have no idea what his business . . . orientation is. But he's probably the smartest kid who's ever come to Riddle, and I think it'd be really cool to have someone like that in A-CHOIR for the next four years, helping to steer its course through . . . through some pretty important years in this nation's history," she concluded, perhaps a trifle shrilly.

"Well," said Holt, again. "I *see*. Well, then." He got to his feet, and everyone else had the sense, right genes, or training, to spring up, as well. "I guess it's up to each of you," he went on, beginning to amble toward the front door, "to do whatever research on each of the candidates you feel is necessary and then, in two weeks' time, according to the bylaws, we can have our vote."

He smiled at everyone, but Amanda Dollop saw his lips were tight, tight, tight. She was delighted to be the first one out the door and hurrying down the path that'd take her to the pathology lab.

Sometimes it was a real relief to just examine tissue through a microscope — stuff that, though diseased, just lay there saying nothing, totally without ambition, plans, or expectations. Stuff that didn't even know . . . its *mass* from *furred lace*, she thought, and she was smiling.

19

Brand-Nouveau *Conspirators*

No sooner was Amanda Dollop out the door than the other six knocked off the departure small talk and scurried back into the living room, five of them shame-facedly, like brand-*nouveau* conspirators.

"Will someone please be good enough to tell me what in the name of T. Boone Pickens' basset hound is going on around here?" demanded Professor Greg Holt in one long breath (masking a sophisticated, metropolitan fury with some pseudo-simple country jocularity).

Everybody looked at everybody else, fingers curled as if to grasp a casting stone. Finally, four of them found voice together.

"It's *all* Amanda's fault," they said.

"Yes, eckshually, it *is*," said Clovis, half a beat behind the rest. As a boy, he'd seen more goats than any of the others, but not as many of the "scape" breed, maybe.

"I might have known," said Holt. He shook his head and swallowed. "Contrary Mary. I swear they're all the same. It's probably that time of month, or something. Tell me how it happened, boys." Once again, Holt's speaking voice was slightly softer, more

112

informal, with a rounded, rustic edge to it.

Everyone was happy to oblige. At first, they said, it looked as if Shep Hewitt was a cinch to fill the vacancy. He was the clear first choice of three of them, with not a blackball ("Sorry, Clovis") anywhere in sight. St. James and Bung had both thrown out the names of other people, but it was clear that these would never *win*, that they — that's Jeff and Clovis — were only dickering, for favors.

"Not exactly *favors*," Bung amended. "It was more that I was trying to construct a *climate* — establish, if you follow me, the groundwork for some future negotiations I wanted to enter into with Grant. It's the sort of ploy you told us about yourself," he said to Holt. "What you called" — he seemed to make adjustments on his wristwatch — " 'winning the fourth quarter while you're playing the first.' Isn't that right?"

Holt nodded and Bung leaned back, looking relieved.

"Then," Brad Hammond spoke, "Amanda started in with this Simon Storm business, and I swear, you could *not* shut her up. She was so damn sure of herself, so damned *stubborn*. This kid was not just brilliant, according to her, but he was also completely all-around, and nice, and humble — oh, God, but he was humble; it made you feel like beating on your chest and *howling*, just hearing her go on. And then she said how maybe it'd be a good idea for A-CHOIR to . . . well, *diversify* a little, and that maybe if corporate America could recruit more Simon Storms — nothing against us guys, of course — it'd be — "

"We *told* her what you said that time about taking brand-new freshmen in," said Hedd.

"And that perhaps we ought to check with you about the age thing. Like, how would it look if someone in A-CHOIR was still too young when he *graduated* to qualify for certain training programs? Or even hold a glass of white wine at a reception," Grant Kahn added.

"But nothing made any difference," Hammond said. "Even after I told her how *depressed* you might be if we didn't come in with just a single name, the way all the other A-CHOIR's had done in the past, she *still* said she was going to nominate this Simon Storm. So *that* seemed to get Clovis and Jeffrey here started up again, and — "

"Well, eckshually" — St. James had smiled before he interrupted — "I'd been serious all along about Esteban. The Sotomayors are multinational, of course, and I thought it might be edifying if our club were to include a Spanish-speaking person who, from what I read in *U.S. News*, has never paid a shilling's worth of taxes on an income that's *averaged* between five and — "

"M.I. Bloom," said Jeffrey Bung, not even looking at Clovis, "is by no means a frivolous selection. I believe that you, yourself, Professor Holt, once wrote the following on a blue book of his. . . ." He fiddled with his watch again. " 'Gilt-edged. Even Moody's couldn't rate this high enough.' Am I correct?"

Holt had to nod again, at that. Sometimes he wished the members of A-CHOIR would be a little less concerned with what he'd said or written. Bung, in particular, could stand to be more of a square peg — as long as holes were round, at least. Great entrepreneurship, in Holt's opinion, involved a certain nonconformity, a species of adventurousness, a willingness to go beyond authority and the boundaries of the field. These lads, for all their ability and all their acquisitiveness, seemed reluctant to take chances, to break new ground. They *wanted* to be told. By him. But what the hell (Professor Holt now shook his head, but just inside his mind, so they wouldn't see him do it), if that be tribute, he could make the most of it. Right now, he'd show them Mister Stretch, *Elasticman*, facing this brand-new and unexpected circumstance, and turning it to his advantage.

"Boys," he said, "I don't doubt for a minute that Bloom — I remember that exam of his — and Santodomingo or whatever the hell his name is, and of course *Shep Hewitt* would all be fine as members of A-CHOIR. And probably forty-fifty other folks that we could name. There's no shortage of able men on campus nowadays, thank the good Lord. But mebbe — just mebbe — we should write another program here. Put this Storm kid's name into the bin and turn the crank a time or two." He made a motion with one arm, as if he were working an old-fashioned telephone.

"We all know how stubborn girls can get — God bless 'em — *stub-or-run*," he said. "Once they get an idea between their ears, and especially if they think there's some kind of principle involved, they can make a Missourah mule look like some kind of yes-machine. Now the fact is, as you all know, we been thinkin' we have plans for our Amanda. Somehow, somewhere, sometime. All right, hell, say it: We may *need* her. More on that in a minute or two.

And we've always known that what we might need her for might demand a little *give* on her part, a little modification, shall we say, of certain of her habits . . . and positions. So it seems to me that possibly, in this instance, on this membership deal, we might want to appear to give a bit ourselves — give *in* to her, in fact. What we could maybe do is turn around and act as if we'd gotten real, real interested in her suggestion. We'd say it takes a little getting used to, *but* . . . maybe she's onto something. We'll say we want to study the idea, the boy — this Simon Storm — awhile. If the timing's as I think it'll be, we may be asking her to do a little bendin' " — Holt might have winked — "just about the time we're getting ready to do a bit of pushin' our own selves. You see what I mean?"

"Sort of like — " said Philips Hedd.

" — a deal?" said Jeffrey Bung.

"But maybe one of those 'you-first'-ers that you told us to look out for. The kind where Number One lets go on 'three,' like they agreed to, but Number Two holds on and says, 'On second thought . . .' " Grant Kahn threw in.

Greg Holt positively beamed.

"Exactly," he agreed. "And, hey — it's also possible the kid may be ideal for us. Don't rule it out; boy geniuses are in. So what we need to do is act unstressed and start a dialogue with him. . . ."

"I'll do it," Hedd said quickly.

". . . while also telling *her* about the second thought we had, right after she'd gone out the door."

"We can all do that," Brad Hammond said.

Grant Kahn smiled and raised his hand, and stirred the air with it.

"I'm going crazy, sir," he said. "Those 'plans' you mentioned? Does this mean you've heard from Washington?"

Holt's grin was different, this time. Much more the cat's, after a double portion of canary under glass.

"Indeed I have," he said.

20

The Handbook for University Reorganization™

The pamphlet had been made up with the situation at Riddle specifically in mind, and everyone agreed the secretary must have put some first-class talent to work on the project. Even the binder that enclosed each copy of the thing was redolent of class and caring; it was plastic, of course, but real good, heavy, limber stuff, the kind that almost *smells* like leather.

What the pages detailed, of course, was a series of strategies designed to help in the "redirection" and "pragmatizing" (English translation: *taking over*) of an American university, so as to render it "consistent and harmonious with, and useful to, the best interests of the nation." "Fewer questions and more answers" were to be confidently expected from the redirected college, according to the authors of this text.

The Handbook for University Reorganization™ (as it was officially titled) explained that the first step in any successful struggle for freedom (from the liberal permissivist administration that promoted irresponsible, intemperate, and undisciplined

118

experiments and inquiries) is to foul, and publicize the fouling of, the ivied nest. The best way to do this (and get the mess on all the news wires), it explained, was by creating an issue that'd suggest widespread corruption in the college, like a good solid cheating scandal, especially one ("N.B. Riddle") that involved an honor code.

"No sweatski," Phil Hedd said at once, the cocktail stirrer dancing from one corner of his mouth to the other as he spoke. "The honor pledge is mellow, but ethically it's like the dodo bird; situations are just so *different* than they used to be. Just off the top of my head, I can think of a bunch of different things we could blow the whistle on. Take-home tests'd be one. Devices of the kind that Jeffrey has right there's another. . . ."

He pointed at Bung's wristwatch, a microcomputer that told a great deal more than time. In Jeffrey's case, he'd programmed it to recall a lot of quotes from Holt and other business sources, but other people — everybody knew — had loaded up the things with facts and formulas pertaining to the course content of . . . oh, Politics 308: Emerging Political Philosophies of the Twentieth Century ("Pink Think") and Physics 99: Atomic Principles for Pacifists ("Nuke Puke"). And almost everything offered in the business/finance section of the catalogue.

". . . and then there's electronic grade-altering, by way of access to the main computer and your records," Hedd went on, "scalping the 'reserve' shelf at the library, everyday plagiarizing, of course — "

"Um," Holt interrupted. "We ought to — probably — just use *real* cases, don't you think? I mean, limit ourselves to stuff that's actually going on *here*, if possible?"

"Hey." Brad Hammond smiled. "You want to bet that everything that Phil's just said ain't real? Make my day, Professor. In the competitive departments, it's purely self-defense, that stuff; you gotta fight fire with fire. Probably a good fifty percent of the majors in your — our — department are 'users.' Once you're hooked, and see how easy it is, and what a great high you get when the grades come out. . . ."

"But for this I think we wouldn't target business guys," said Kahn. "Better to snag a couple of religious fanatics, if we could, Islamics, if available, plus some art history chicks — they're *always* doin' it — and a few choice specimens from poly-sci. Maybe even a baby-doc or two. Those animals'll *kill* for the right residency program."

"And if we target just the right kids," the already pragmatic Bung contributed, "we ought to see parental lawsuits all over the country, I'll bet, plus a certain amount of the old If-I-go-I'm-gonna-take-a-bunch-of-others-with-me syndrome."

Holt nodded, although feeling just a little bit . . . discomforted by the ease and good humor with which his boys described the *status quo* at Riddle. He'd known, *of course*, that some kids everywhere would always cheat — and always had — but he still preferred to think of this activity as an aberration at Riddle, rather than an everyday ho-hum-and-what's-for-lunch affair. After all, they weren't "out there," *yet*.

* * *

120

The next suggestion the pamphlet made (once the reputation of the university had been neatly smeared) was in the area of what it called "the neutralizing of major opposition leaders." It proposed that they — that's the "freedom-loving activists" like themselves — should take advantage of "the well-known liberal tendency to overvalue pleasures of the flesh."

Or, in plainer words, they should "uncover" nasty sorts of sex on campus, and connect them to unsympathetic, artsy-fartsy members of the faculty.

The expenditure of a few hundred dollars would be sufficient, the authors of the pamphlet felt, to purchase a number of charges of sexual harassment, of male and female students both, by male professors (only). So what if these charges were unprovable or even untrue (the experts said); they always left a satisfying stain and produced (at least) some resignations. And even better, sensation-value-wise, would be one or two good cases of genuine, documented sexual *involvement* on the part of faculty Casanovas — if possible "with poutingly-attractive young pubescent females," said the pamphlet with a leer.

It was in this last area, Professor Holt explained, that he hoped to use Amanda's . . . talents to "dig us up a can of worms, or maybe two."

There was this long-haired, freaky-weirdo psych prof (he told them), name of Grebe, who'd gotten a grant to do an adolescent study: to snoop around in the day-to-day and night-to-night "activities" of a whole bunch of teenaged kids.

Holt smiled, at that point.

"Now, I wouldn't know about you boys," he

said, "but when *I* was starting out in high school, most all my waking thoughts — and a bunch of my sleeping ones, come to think of it — were centered on one thing. Or better make that *all* the things that girls had underneath their 'itsy-bitsy, teeny-weeny, yellow polka dot bikinis.' " He cleared his throat. "Which of course was the name of a popular song they had back then." He cleared it again. "So my point is: This Grebe — a real big liberal artist, by the way, and a darling of the whole Portcullis crowd — is getting into some pretty juicy material there, if you take my meaning."

Everybody nodded, trying to decide whether to grin or look grim. Jeffrey Bung wondered if maybe a minor in psychology was still feasible at this point in his academic career; he'd always thought those people just got off on rats in mazes all the time.

"If we can get Amanda," Holt went on, "to throw some moves at Grebe — which might not be too strange a thing for her to do, seeing as how psychology and psychiatry are into pretty much the same garbage anyway — well then, the chances are she'd be able to find out if there *is* anything going on between Grebe and all that young quiff. And even if there isn't, she can probably make him end up looking like a dirty old voyeur or what have you, getting his jollies off the stuff the kids *are* doing, while also seducing an innocent female medical student at the same time."

That made real good sense to everyone. When they'd taken Amanda into A-CHOIR, they'd done so with the feeling that she'd come in handy, eventually. Not as a long-term holding, of course (who the hell wanted to put up with an emasculating

122

career-wench?), but perhaps as a speculation, an in-and-out-fast sort of deal, or even as a useful agent in the service of the club, in the style of Mata Hari. And besides, after they were through eating, at their meetings, she could go and bring the coffee in.

It also occurred to all of them but Clovis that in this instance there might be an opportunity for the whole gang to burst into Grebe's office with their Nikons and their Canons at the ready, and snap some photos of him and Amanda in . . . poses suitable for framing, you very well might say.

The third large item in the pamphlet's "things to definitely do" section was delightfully subtle and sophisticated, everybody thought, eventually. It involved the business of creating (from the ranks of the business faculty, of course) a "martyr" to their cause.

"I love the *concept* here," said Holt. "The idea is: You get someone fired for a perfectly legitimate reason, and then you twist the thing around and claim the *hidden* grounds — the real ones — were something altogether different."

"What?" said Hammond, looking seriously confused, uncertain of himself. "We're going to get someone we *like* fired?" He shook his head, and his lips, reflexively, began to form the words "Brad Hammond."

"Sure — well, *sort of* like," Professor Holt replied. "We can get him his job back later on, if we want to. But anyway" — he smiled cheerfully — "I have the perfect pigeon in mind already: Professor Mowbray. In Marketing and Trends Analysis? It's about his PhD."

"His PhD?" Grant Kahn looked skeptical. "Doctor Mowbray's PhD? There's something wrong with it?"

"You just might say," said Holt. "It's from Western Hawaii A&T, that's all. Say WHAT? Precisely. Western Hawaii's entire campus happens to consist of two rooms over a ukelele repair shop. That degree's not worth the surfboard that it's printed on, my friends." He winked roguishly.

"And you — you've known that all along," said Jeffrey Bung, just stating a fact. "But because Professor Mowbray was doing a half-decent job, you sort of *saved* the information. . . ."

"For a rainy day," said Holt. "Very good, Jeff. You never spend your capital when you don't have to, right? But now" — he rubbed his hands together, briskly — "*now* we slip our darling president a little unsigned note, suggesting *he* check out . . . you know. And Port-coo-coo will have to do it; he couldn't dare *not* to. He uncovers the deception and he acts: Mowbray goes out on his ass, and it's his own stupid fault. Needless to say," Holt added, "he wasn't hired by *me*."

He locked his hands behind his head and stretched his legs way out in front of him. "But as soon as Mowbray's gone, the martyr-makers in A-CHOIR start to do their stuff," he said. "All it'd take'd be some letters, no more than five or six, just to start things up. They'd go to the *Riddle News*, maybe to a couple of professional journals, and even to *Barron's College Guide* itself. Each suggesting that Professor Mowbray was fired not for the little 'typographical error' on his *curriculum vitae*, but because he was TOO HONEST FOR HIS OWN

GOOD. The administration, you'd go on to say, had felt it *had to* eliminate Mowbray as the only way to keep him from continuing to tell his students about the comparative worth of a degree in a business or technical area and a degree in any of the so-called humanities. The man had refused to be muzzled and he'd paid the price, poor guy: a victim of shortsighted leadership that was trying to turn back the clock to the nineteen-sixties style of education!"

Holt leaned forward in his chair. "Can you imagine the brouhaha that'll set off on campus? Can you imagine what *Barron's* might do with that — what sort of rating they'll give Riddle next time around? I'll tell you what *I* think: *I* think in less than six months' time — if you add this to the other stuff we do — Portcullis and his gang will be huddled together on Martha's Vineyard or wherever the hell they have their summer 'cottages,' wondering why their friends at *The New York Times* and CBS and Harvard hadn't lifted a finger to save them. And the trustees will have appointed a committee charged with the general reorganization of the university.

"And it isn't hard to guess in which direction those fine gentlemen will look." Holt smoothed his right lapel. "Who, after all, is pretty much the opposite of Grebe, Portcullis, and that bunch? Who stands for growth, a sound economy, and values?" He bowed his head just slightly.

"Wow," said Jeffrey Bung. "That's just magnificent, professor."

"It *is* exciting," Holt agreed. "Years ago, the incoming president of the University of Oklahoma was meant to have said that he planned to create a university there that their football team could be proud of. Well, we six, right here in this room, are on the way to creating one that all *America* can be proud of!"

"Halle*lu*jah!" shouted Clovis St. James, in an accent much more similar to Uncle Tom's than to Thomas Babington Macaulay's, say.

But no one even noticed *that*, of course.

21

Like a Stranger

By the time it was Tuesday, and Simon was due for his first official, all-business, and presumably Kate-less meeting with his freshman adviser, he'd started to wonder what on earth they'd talk about.

He'd chosen his courses already, with the advice and consent of his parents; that'd been a little scary, but fun. And, in the last two days, he'd gone to the first meeting of each one of them. His professors underplayed their roles like mad, but still managed to imply the wit and wisdom of the ages, but packaged for the market of today. On his own, he'd roamed around the campus with his map from the freshman handbook, and had quickly memorized the names of all the buildings and what (officially) went on in each of them. Ranging even more widely, he'd then explored the *town* of Riddle — making condescending fun of it, of course — with a couple of his classmates from Bliss Hall. He'd also done some laundry in the basement of said hall and gotten on the list for intramural soccer. In various settings, he'd carried on a lot of fairly hyper conversations (and avoided others) and he was pleased to find out that his views on Barry Manilow, Vermont, the length of the reading assignments in Comparative Political Analysis, and Woody Allen weren't all that different from a lot of other kids'. That is to say: "incredible," "far out," "unbelievable," and "too much," respectively.

On the face of it, then, he didn't have a single thing to ask his father's one-time roommate, his adviser, except unsayable absurdities like, "Have you gotten any details on the plot to overthrow you?" or "Listen, what's the story with your daughter?"

He didn't even have anything to complain about. The one item he kept hassling himself with was something that neither the president of the college nor anyone else could do anything about: the problem of his own inexperience. Not just his inexperience with women, but in general: the 800 or so fewer days he'd lived than other people had. The only thing he could do about this situation was exactly what he *was* doing, just as fast as he could: Live more days. But because he couldn't do that any faster than anyone else, he kept on feeling awkward, like a stranger. Not always, just from time to time.

That (he thought, as he walked along in the direction of the Portcullises) would make a good title for a rock 'n' roll song. "Like a Stranger." Music and lyrics by Simon Storm.

"Like a stranger, comin' from a manger,/Headin' into danger. . . ."

Simon snapped his fingers and actually sang a little made-up melody under his breath. Was Bob Dylan still doing that kind of material? He wasn't really sure.

The previous Thursday, at registration, was one of the times he'd felt a trifle strange, uncertain of himself. He'd watched a guy flip out; he was pretty sure that's what you'd call it.

This person, whom Si had never seen before, had been standing in the L through P line, the one next to Si's own, and all of a sudden he'd started moaning, just staring at the schedule card he had in his hand, like everybody else. And moaning real, real loud. At first, Simon had thought he was kidding around, but then the guy had dropped the hand holding the card to his side, and raised his head toward the ceiling, and started hollering. There wasn't anything to holler at on the gym ceiling, of course — other than maybe the sign that they'd forgotten to take down after the previous year's wrestling season: IF YOU CAN READ THIS, BUDDY, YOU HAVE HAD IT. But anyway, it seemed this guy was yelling at his parents.

"I know it's all my fault," the guy had shouted. "I know that I'm the reason that you drive a Plymouth Fury. I realize you only ate out three times last month, and one of those was local, franchised Chinese. I accept the fact that I'm responsible for keeping you from moving to Rumson, like the Westermans. But you can't make me do this anymore. I *hate* it!" He'd dropped to his knees at that point.

"Why can't I sing on steps like Uncle Walter used to do, and talk with lifelong friends about happiness and the meaning of life? Why can't I have a girl who knits me argyle socks and tells me we can live on love? Why don't I ever read a book that wouldn't even be *suggested* reading in a course?" His voice rose to a wail. "Why do I have to worry about everything that might go wrong before, or even *if*, I make a big success?"

He'd broken off, sobbing, and then reached into his pocket. A moment later, with several hundred people watching, right there in the gym, he'd proceeded to set his schedule card on fire.

Simon had told Amanda Dollop about this incident the next day, when she'd dropped into his room. She'd done that almost daily since he'd gotten there — on Sunday, she'd come by twice — and Si had been trying to figure out if these visits were what his mother called "duty calls," or what. Of course he didn't know that Amanda was worrying the same bone. She realized she got a kick out of Simon's fresh, uncalculating enthusiasm, his lack of affectation, his quick perceptions, the comparative neatness of his room. He wasn't anything like most of the medical students, or the rest of the guys in the dorm. She would have said that she looked on him "like a little brother," which in fact she *did* say to her roommate, Clee Clymer, whose eyebrows didn't seem to buy it, and whose single word response, *"Bizarro,"* she wasn't all that wild about.

On his part, Simon told himself that whether Amanda came by out of a sense of duty or not, she almost certainly looked at him as nothing more than a younger brother, which meant that some of his feelings about her, if known to her, would seem like borderline incestuous. But he couldn't help having them. He was definitely not used to seeing girls who looked something like Jennifer Beals walk into his (or any other) room and throw themselves onto his

130

bed in such a way that he could learn the color of their underpants, beneath their skimpy nylon running shorts.

"I think a lot of the guys here are under even more pressure than the women are," she said, propping her head on one hand and rolling onto her side, which relieved *him* of the pressure of having to look up her shorts if he was going to look at her at all. "I mean, like with expectations. A lot of girls I know are like Clee. I mean, I dearly love her, and I can't stand the idea of her graduating and leaving me with three more years to go. But *you* know. She's Daddy's girl. Whatever she does is super-K okay with him. Last year she flunked Romantic Poetry and he gave her a new Fiero so she wouldn't feel too bad about it."

Si'd nodded. He'd seen the golden one behind the wheel of the shiny little black car. Her front license plate was one of those special kinds you can buy, not from the state, but from an auto supply place or a novelty store. Sometimes they read FLORIDA, THE SUNSHINE STATE, or KING OF THE ROAD, but Clee's just said SPOILED ROTTEN.

"Well, this poor guy was really in trouble," Simon said. "I think. After his schedule card was completely burned, he sat on the floor with his knees up and tried to set his jeans on fire. That was when some other guys started pouring cans of soda on him, and the emergency people got right over and talked to him and finally led him away." He didn't mention to Amanda that he'd been surprised these white-shirted paramedics with RIDDLE RESCUE SQUAD in golden capitals across their backs (and *Stefan*, *Kirk*, and *Eric* in cursive, red-thread script upon

131

their breasts) were in the gym at all.

"The very beginning of a term and the last two weeks are the worst," Amanda told him. "From midterm on, you'll see a lot of ads and notices for stress-reduction seminars, and they start keeping people from the squad on duty in the library, and at The Pub. Personally, I'm pretty secure, but I like to . . . I don't know, *underline* my belief in myself about once a term, usually sometime just before finals. I just want to more or less remind myself that *I'm* the ultimate reality, that I can get any grade I choose in my courses — or anything else I want, when you come right down to it."

"Really?" Simon had said. Again — how many times had this happened? — he wasn't sure if she was kidding or not. Eight hundred days from then, he would have known, he'd bet.

"You're really all that evolved?" he'd added, keeping it light.

She'd rolled onto her back and sat up, folding her legs tailor-fashion and smiling at him.

"Hey," she'd said, "everybody is. It's the one thing a lot of people's parents have right. They tell their kids they can do anything they want, but the kids don't believe it. But they should. The guy you were just talking about, the one at registration? That was *his* problem, probably. What he probably needs at this point is . . . well, some kind of proof. Then he'd be fine."

"Proof?" said Simon. He'd stood up and walked over to his desk, pretending to straighten up some books and papers. Actually, he was trying to avoid looking at the insides of Amanda's smooth, tan thighs anymore. "What kind of proof? A million bucks in earnings? But that'd take some time, wouldn't it?"

Amanda'd gotten up, too, and now was waving a dismissive backhand in his direction.

"No, no," she'd said. "There's a lot of quicker fixes. He could go and learn to levitate, for instance, or walk barefoot on hot coals. Don't laugh. This is the therapy of the future. After he'd done something like that, he'd *know* he didn't have to worry about his courses or anything. It's neat. There's a help group called Research Associates in Unlimited Success. They can absolutely change your life by showing you how to do stuff like that. They set up a lot of workshops here. All you have to do to get your shit completely together is *really* believe you can.

"That was the great thing about Jesus, they realize now. He was so tuned in, so focused, he was able to construct a reality in which he could do all this different stuff that seemed miraculous to everybody else." She was almost out the door by then.

"Anyway," she'd said, "I gotta run. Don't worry about that guy, Si. They'll take care of him; he'll be okay."

Simon kept his face in neutral. He didn't know what gear to put his mouth in, so he chose reverse. Or sideways. Maybe high.

"Boy," he'd said, "that Jesus would have made a terrific doctor, I'll bet."

"Oh, absolutely," Amanda had said. "Actually, one of the apostles *was* a doctor. Matthew . . . or *Augustine*, I think it was. Really makes sense, when you think about it."

And she had left his room.

*　*　*

Although Simon was pretty sure Betsy Portcullis would have liked him to walk right in, and then call up the stairs, he didn't want to risk it. And knocking on the door, and *then* walking in and yelling, "Anybody home?" seemed dangerously presuming, too. So he ended up ringing the doorbell and then, when nothing happened in the next minute or so, ringing it again, but this time for a little longer.

After he'd done that, he almost wished he'd chosen either of his other options. For, coming from a distance, he heard footsteps on a staircase, and a voice — the voice of Kate Portcullis, hoarse and unmistakable.

"All right, all right, all right, all right, all *right*," it said. And then the door had opened; there they were. Face-to-face, again.

"Oh, it's you," she said. And, "Sorry," not because she was (he knew) but just to lip-serve etiquette. Or maybe she was sorry he was there, and saying so.

"I'm meant to have a meeting with your father," Simon said. "He told me to come over now."

"I know," she said. She was barefoot and had on short white tennis shorts today, and Si was pretty much surprised to see her legs had proper muscle shapes in them, were not the least bit scrawny. "He called a little while ago and said he'd been held up. Some stupid committee or something. He said to wait if you could."

Simon started in and she made way for him.

"Or *not*, if you don't want to," Kate continued. "Mom's just played golf, she's almost in the tub. My father said I should 'entertain' you." She stuck out her tongue, but not pointing it at him, just letting it loll over her lower lip.

Simon wasn't sure if it was the prospect of "entertaining" him that was making her sick. Maybe it was her father's language, his use of just that word, a word with many meanings, one quite heavily suggestive (so he thought).

"Huh," he said, without inflection. He looked around and wondered whether he should start upstairs. Perhaps not. He wouldn't want to surprise Mrs. Portcullis, after all, in transit to her bath.

"So, how about a beer?" said Kate, then snapped her fingers, added, "Whoops. I guess I shouldn't say that. Or what I mean is, I shouldn't give you one, should I? You aren't even allowed in the college pub, are you?"

"Sure I am," said Simon. "In fact, I'm meeting a guy down there tomorrow night. Phil Hedd. Maybe you've heard of him." That sounded a little . . . Hollywood-ish, *stupid*, so he shrugged. "I've been told he's meant to be some kind of a big shot on the campus. I wouldn't know, of course."

Simon had been totally taken aback at Hedd's suggestion — he *did* know that. And also a little surprised to discover that Hedd, himself, was a campus salesman. His products were pretty upscale, in terms of both sophistication and expense, but still. Si had just assumed that guys like Phil Hedd and that Grant Kahn would never go from door to door themselves. What he figured was: They'd hire other guys, subordinates who'd just take orders for stuff that Hedd and Kahn already *knew*, from cagey market surveys probably, everyone would just go ape about. Phil was offering two software packages, one called *The Academic Angle*, the other by the name of *Power Dating*. Three hundred and fifty bucks apiece, but still a steal. Each consisted of a user's guide, output and program diskettes, a manual containing more than forty case histories, and a workbook in which to chart your scores and progress, your successes. Basically, both programs worked the same. The computer would first ask you, the user, a series of questions about yourself, and you'd punch in answers that described your looks and character, your likes and dislikes, your whole style. A real, dimensional, personal profile, in other words. *Then* it asked you questions about the professor or instructor, in the first case, or the girl or guy (in the second) that you wanted to get something from, impress, *control*. In seconds after you'd finished doing that, your computer would start preparing a detailed analysis, which'd take the form of a strategy for you to follow with that particular person. A strategy that (as the literature said) "will pay off BIG in *Real Results*." No matter how aloof or cynical the professor, or how unapproachable and worldly-wise the campus beauty, you — that's anyone — will "get them" (it maintained). "You can use their very *strengths* against them," Hedd explained. And of course, he said, the thing was infinitely reusable. Term after term after term.

Si had pleaded poverty, in lieu of ordering, but diplomatically agreed that Hedd "had something there, all right." He'd even wondered, laughing, what would happen if two *Power Dating* owners punched each other into their machines and then went out together, both of them armed to the psychological teeth, as it were.

"There'd probably be a melt-down on Date One," Simon had gone on to say, answering his own question and amazing himself with his easy, collegiate wit. Shortly after he said that, Phil Hedd had suggested they have a beer together, Wednesday night, down at the college pub.

"I've never heard of him," Kate said. "To me, they're all a bunch of assholes anyway." She paused. "Present company excepted, of course." She said that last part in a real sarcastic, stagy tone of voice, it seemed to Simon.

And then she added, "We can go outside, if you want to."

But she didn't wait for an answer. Instead, she started across the large, formal room to the left of the entrance hall, obviously heading for the French doors that opened onto the lawn behind the house.

Simon followed. Above the shorts, Kate had on an oversized faded blue workshirt, on top of some kind of T-shirt. Her legs looked as good from the back as from the front, he had to admit — maybe a little better — and her rear end wasn't scrawny, either. He thought it looked as solid as third base, but better shaped — like, nowhere near as flat.

"You don't have your beeper on," Si said. He'd noticed, so the words popped out of him. He hoped she wouldn't think he'd been giving her body some kind of an ocular pat-down. But on the other hand, why shouldn't he? His motives were perfectly . . . normal.

"I left it in my room when I went to answer the door," she said. "It's a pain in the ass to wear, sometimes. And anyway, with you here I'll know if it goes off. I assume you're a good little normal adolescent, with all your equipment primed and ready for action."

She'd turned her head around at first, to answer him, but by the middle of that last sentence she was opening the French doors and stepping outside, so Simon couldn't see her face. He wasn't sure, of course, but it sounded very much as if she could be smiling wickedly.

"Well, if I'm taking their money," Simon said, "it seems as if I ought — "

"What *I* am is sick of that stupid checkoff thing, already," Kate proclaimed. She'd headed straight for a little fieldstone patio with outdoor furniture scattered around the edges of it, and surrounded by a low brick wall with more flat fieldstones on the top of it. She jumped up on top of the wall and then sat down on it, with her feet outside, on the lawn.

"Trying to decide which of *his* labels you want to put on *you*," she went on. "I decided I'd rather write the little paragraph and just *say* what I'm doing, and how it feels, and stuff."

Simon had to agree with her.

"I'm doing the same thing," he said. He sat down on a white metal chair with a striped canvas cushion on it. "It's a lot easier."

Kate craned her neck around. "But it *could* be embarrassing, don't you think?" she said, looking him squarely in the eye, with a little crooked smile on her face. "I mean, writing down *exactly* what you're doing? Especially — from what I've read — for a *guy*, even a *college* guy. . . ."

It was just chance, of course — he wasn't the least bit flustered — that Simon chose that moment to look away from her and do a little check on his surroundings. There was a badminton court, with clothesline lines, and a small inground pool with a poolhouse, and another homemade-looking little structure tucked back into the shrubbery, way past the pool.

While doing this, he shrugged. "I went and saw Professor Grebe," he said. "He seemed like a pretty cool guy. And as he said in his letter" — he let his head swing slowly back, till he was looking straight at her — "there probably isn't anything kids do that he doesn't know about already." He'd tried to give that "kids" the subtlest bit of emphasis, so that she might possibly *hear* "*you* kids."

Her eyebrows went up and she ducked her head at him. "Oh, yeah?" she said. "Maybe he'll be surprised. I'll bet *you* would be, if you. . . . Never mind." She grinned. "What's the old line? From the Bible, is it? 'Out of the mouths of babes and sucklings'?" She had a field day with those words, and then kept grinning and staring at him until he looked away again.

The next moment she was on her feet, on the lawn.

"You want to play some badminton?" she said, starting toward the court. "Did you know it used to be called 'battledore and shuttlecock'? That sounds like something out of the *Kama Sutra*, to me. I can see why they changed it to badminton."

It seemed to Simon that maybe a game of something would be a good idea, about then; maybe it'd shut her up a little. Besides, he liked racquet games, and was pretty good at them.

So was Kate, it turned out. She whipped off her workshirt before they started, and in her shorts and

139

baggy purple T, and barefoot, she was much better-dressed for a game of lawn badminton than Simon, who had on painters' pants and running shoes, plus a few scraps of a college guy's dignity. In addition, she had a good, deep serve, a deadly drop shot, and a remarkable overhead smash for such a shortie. And she was absolutely the best retriever Si had ever played against.

What's more, she *did* shut up and just play hard, winning the first game 15–9, before Simon took the second, 15–13.

"Let's stop," she said, when that one was over. "Nice game. You're good. I thought I'd murder you." She was standing at the net, and she stuck a hand under it, at him.

He reached and took it. Her hand was small and strong and warm, and slightly moist. There were droplets of sweat on her forehead, just at the hairline. And, where her baggy T-shirt hit her chest (he noticed), it didn't simply lie there, altogether flat. This discovery — the fact that Kate had small, but salient, nippled breasts — gave Simon one quick rush of tenderness, *protectiveness*, toward her, a feeling he'd not had, specifically, about a girl before.

Then he realized he'd been holding her hand a little longer than the situation called for, and he dropped it quickly, looked across the lawn again.

"What's that?" he said, as soon as his eyes hit a potential topic of conversation, the little hutlike thing on the far side of the lawn. It was sort of igloo-shaped, circular, like a yurt, maybe, or a Navaho hogan, except it was only about four feet high, and maybe six across.

140

"That?" she said. "That's my sweat lodge. Want to see it?"

He had to admit he did, sweat lodges being, at that point in time, another inexperience of his. He'd heard of them, of course, and knew they were sort of American Indian (was it?) sauna equivalents, except that a sweat lodge (he thought) got you even more involved with other kinds of purification — beyond the cleansing of the pores and getting all the body poisons out. It was hard to imagine Kate Portcullis setting out to purify her mind — but all too easy (he reluctantly admitted to himself) to think about the way she'd (maybe) look, all glisteny with sweat, in the dimness of a special little hut.

When they got close, Simon could see the lodge was not too badly put together. It was actually a geodesic dome, made out of two-by-fours covered with scraps of carpeting, and one piece of black plastic over the very top, to provide a bit of rain-proofing. A flap of carpet covered a crawl-in door, and inside there was a small pit dug in the ground, surrounded by a wooden platform.

"How does it work?" Si asked. "Exactly."

"Well," she said. "I have to use an old woodstove to heat the rocks. It's out back of the garage. Then — obviously — I put the heated rocks in the pit there and sprinkle them with scented water. Beforehand, I do some other junk to get ready, but basically that's it. I close the flap once I'm inside, of course, for privacy."

"Privacy?" he said. "You mean you always do it by yourself?"

She narrowed her eyes. "Yes," she said. "Always.

And I *do* take all my clothes off, if you *really* want to know. Which of course you do."

"Whoa," said Simon. "But how about the beeper? You take the beeper in there with you, don't you? And your notebook? Maybe *that'd* be a first for Grebe: what happens when a normal naked adolescent girl goes into a nice, hot sweat lodge."

"You're disgusting," she said. "You know that? You really are disgusting. I don't think either you *or* Grebe could understand something like this. And you know why? Because you're both men and you're both intellectuals. Or think you are. Male scientists like Grebe and little smarty-pants guys like you are only interested in stuff that you either *a.* get off on, or *b.* put on a graph and feed to your little Apples. You're so far gone on your gland and head trips you don't even *notice* how fucked-up most people are at that crummy little college of yours."

"Hey, wait," said Simon. "I was just kidding around. The same as you've been, right? Come on. I didn't mean to make fun of your sweat lodge. Really." He felt misunderstood, unfairly charged, a little angry, and a little bit like crying.

"Listen," he went on, "I was talking to someone just the other day — a medical student, actually — and *she*" — he stressed the syllable, but just a little bit — "was telling me about some of the things people are doing to try to be a little more mellow. . . ." Looking at her, he felt he hadn't hit on exactly the right word. ". . . or less, *you* know, stressed and hostile, and all. A little more *spiritual*, you might say." That seemed good. Kate's face looked — definitely — less stressed and hostile than it had.

"It was really interesting," he said. "And it *is* a

big problem at the college, just like you said." It didn't seem necessary to go on to say that Amanda Dollop's approach to stress reduction had seemed to be based entirely on such spectacularly *un*spiritual tendencies as human greed and selfishness.

"Damn well-told," Kate said, grudgingly. "If some of those people are going to be the leaders of the next generation — "

She broke off and looked intently at the ground; she tried to pick up a small rock with her toes, but dropped it. Simon watched, appearing much more fascinated than he really felt. He was sure that in 800 days he'd know *exactly* what to say — or maybe she would.

A familiar hearty voice boomed out, from near the house.

"Yo!" it said. "Yo, Kate! Yo, Simon! Guess who's finally been paroled for good behavior?" Gates Portcullis was back from the office.

Kate looked at Simon; Simon looked at her. And both of them broke out in major grins, then turned and waved and started back across the lawn in his direction.

22

Feedback

With Simon and her father now sequestered in his study, and her mother gliding back and forth between the kitchen and the sitting room muttering what sounded mostly like a desperate prayer to (could this be?) the muse of chicken-cooking, Kate decided what *she* needed was . . . a little privacy. As usual. She tiptoed to her room, there closed and locked the door, and sank face forward on the birthday present of a lifetime, her enormous water bed — the Sea of Serendipity, she'd named it.

She was in an excellent mood. Taken as a whole, the time with Simon had been good. Because he'd turned out to be an athlete, she didn't even have to feel guilty about the badminton — which, of course, she'd gotten dressed for as soon as her father called to say he'd be delayed. She wasn't exactly *glad* he'd beaten her the second game, but she wasn't sorry, either. This way, they had the rubber game to play, still. Maybe next time they could take a swim, too; she had that sort of racing suit, cut really, really high, she hadn't dared to wear in public, yet. He had a nice build. Typically, she let the fantasy go on another step, to the outrageously implausible:

the two of them in the sweat lodge, both bare naked. How would she sit, in a situation like that? Would she actually dare to look at him?

Suddenly, *infuriatingly*, her beeper went off. It was over on her desk, so she had to get up to shut the darn thing off. Grebe seemed to be a *genius* at picking inconvenient times! She grudgingly picked up her notebook and a pen and returned to the bed.

And got a *great* idea!

So Simon thought, and Grebe thought, too, that Grebe had heard it, seen it all, did they? Everything that kids might do, alone or with each other? But how about in a sweat lodge? (Her mind raced.) With an older man? Who was also a psychology professor, with experience?

She flipped open her notebook, grinned enormously, and hurriedly scribbled her name and the time on the top of the first blank page. This would be a hoot, an absolute *hoot*. She'd give a lot to see his face when he read this one.

> *Darling . . .* (she began) *it seems a little silly to be writing this particular report, I must say. After all, you're right here in the sweat lodge with me, and what I was doing had so much to do with all the things that you were doing — to me, with me, for me — that it's hard to separate one from the other. . . .*
>
> *What would I call it? Socializing? Well, you might say. But I'd rather begin with: the most intense, enormous, soaring, all-encompassing, body-bending, mind-blowing series of sensations that any girl. . . .*

145

23

Brewskis at The Pub

When Phil Hedd was a sophomore in high school, the teacher of his honors class in plane geometry had told them it was "impossible" to trisect an angle, using only a compass and a straight edge. So of course a lot of Phil's most snotty and aggressive classmates spent a lot of pissed-off, secret hours, foolishly attempting to do just exactly that.

But not the fruit of Mrs. Hedd's attractive loins, oh, no; he had other scallops to sauté. Proving teachers wrong was "ego-tripping on a tricycle," he said — and anyway, too easy. Besides, in this case old MacMillan might be right.

The boy already knew there were a bunch of other problems — fundamental, global ones — that were totally impossible to solve. In fact, that knowledge shaped his whole philosophy of life. Instead of wasting time worrying about nuclear proliferation, overpopulation, or pollution (or sillier yet, making efforts to prevent them), Phil Hedd, at fifteen-plus, decided the most moral thing for anyone to do was to get the absolute max out of whatever talents he'd been given. That is, to use his wit, and all sharp body parts, to get directly to the top.

In his view, as it evolved over the next few years, the job of institutions — the federal government, let's say, or on a smaller scale, a college — was to create, like, an environment, which would encourage and facilitate, indeed *accelerate*, his progress.

The Reagan administration, which came to power just when Phil was thinking these deep thoughts, was simply great in this respect. From 1980 on, the message that the country got from Washington was clear, and it was: "Go for it!" To grow, accumulate, achieve was in, it told the world. Feeling good was very much the style again, and many folks discovered that there was, in fact, "free lunch" (and also dinner and the theater) for those who knew just how to order it.

Riddle had been much less clear in stating its priorities, Phil Hedd believed, and so he'd been delighted when A-CHOIR called on him: first, to be a member of the group, and then to help it bring the college more in line with . . . well, the country as a whole, the times. The fact was (he further thought) that too much study of, and talk about, such gloomy topics as "re-ordering priorities," "depletion of resources," "a sustainable society," "equal opportunity," "social justice," and "the dangers of deficit financing and nuclear overkill" could turn a respectable university into a *wimpstitution*. And that was just what had been happening at Riddle. Don't get him wrong (he insisted). Guys like himself were very much into learning, into certain kinds of useful research. But hey, at 12 to 15,000 bucks a pop, a college year was an *investment*, man — a major one. And no way would a knowledge of the soil erosion facts in Central Africa produce a dollar's worth of

147

dividend. Sure, they had a messy situation over there; he felt real sorry for the people and had done what he was able to. He'd bought the hunger record, hadn't he? And even got another for his little sister's birthday present. But college . . . hell, you had to let college be college. A place that taught you stuff that you could *use*.

His offering to check out Simon Storm as a potential member of A-CHOIR was typical of him as a person, Phil Hedd decided, as he sipped a Molson's in the college pub that Wednesday night, the cocktail stirrer at a jaunty angle in his mouth (he'd just picked up another free supply from Eddie, at the bar). He *was* a caring sort of guy: He cared about himself and his society (A-CHOIR), his college and his country. It was very, very possible he'd care about young Simon Storm. The kid was carbon steel, no doubt about it; he could take an edge. That little thought he'd had about what'd happen if two people used the Power Dating program, both at once? Sharp. The breakthroughs often come from "what-if" guys; Holt had told them that. This kid was one of those. Hedd gave his mind a little slack, imagining that Power Dating scene: one guy, one gal, both of them aware of everything they had to know to make, like, perfect moves at one another, turning one another on like —

"Uh. Uh, Phil?" Simon Storm was standing, holding onto the chair back, right across the table.

"Hey — Simon!" Hedd jumped up, stuck out a hand, shaking off his reverie.

"Eddie-babes," he yelled toward the bar, "a brace of brand-new brewskis over here, okay?"

* * *

Simon had had an easy, pleasant time with Gates Portcullis, talking excitedly and happily about many, but by no means all, of the different situations he'd encountered in his first eight days at Riddle. He didn't go into his feelings of youthfulness and uncertainty, however. There wasn't any point in doing so, and besides, he didn't want to sound alarms that might be heard, eventually, in Peacemeal. He'd already decided that he definitely wanted to stay at Riddle — that he liked his profs and courses, and a lot of the kids he'd met. And because it was obvious that his father's old roomie loved to hear nice things about the college, and took a healthy pride in programs that he'd fought for, teachers he'd recruited, and student attitudes he thought that he'd encouraged or observed, they'd talked about the positives a lot. They'd also both laughed heartily when Simon's beeper had gone off, and he'd had to take time out to "do his thing for primary research." Simon didn't think it necessary, wise — you name it — to bring up Asmussen or Mr. POP, and what they had for sale, or to mention all the stuff that Grebe had talked about: the government-supported (?) plot (??) to overthrow the president (???) and, in general, retool the university (????).

And of course he didn't mention Kate at all. As far as Simon knew, a person didn't go around talking about girls with their fathers. It was difficult enough for him to say something to *himself* about Kate that wasn't followed immediately (in his mind) by some huge "but." For instance: She was sort of like the type of girl he'd never gotten along with at home, the kind that smoked cigarettes and thought he was a jerk, BUT. . . . And she certainly seemed intelligent enough, and not the least bit babyish, for a kid her age, BUT. . . . Or, you couldn't say she really seemed to like him all that much, BUT. . . .

Yes (he thought), he wasn't sure of anything about her; there always was that huge "but." He'd smiled: But *she* didn't have a huge butt, no way; "well-proportioned" was more like it. Simon had to admit (to himself) he liked her "overall" looks quite a bit; the admission made him lick his lips, unconsciously. Of course, she talked like some kind of a sex maniac, just about, but (there it was again) that was probably just talk. And what had he, just then, been thinking of? Her prowess as a carpenter? Whether she could make a prune whip? Or what his father often called, when speaking of a woman's chest, her "ninny-pies"? He'd already overheard guys in his dorm refer to their "off-campus" girl friends. Wouldn't it be amazing if *he* came to have one? And she was the daughter of his father's old roommate? That sounded like something out of a sitcom, or a Shakespeare play. He told himself to — please — be cool.

When he'd left the Portcullises', there'd been no sign of Kate, but Gates *had* told him, in this fantastically offhand tone of voice, that "Betsy and Kate and I" all wanted him to think of their house as a place where he was *always* welcome, where he could just show up for a meal, or could bring books over to, if he needed a quiet place to study . . . anything. Really. Simon thanked him, said he'd take them up on that. He thought he meant it, too.

With all that on his mind, he actually forgot about

his "date" with Phil Hedd until sometime Wednesday afternoon.

Of course he was nervous, standing there, his first time (ever) in The Pub. He'd thought about the whole deal coming over, and no wonder.

First off, this felt more like an *appointment* than a meeting with a friend. He'd only talked to Hedd that one time, in his room; the guy was an upperclassman, and Si couldn't see at all why he would possibly *want* to "have a beer" with him. In the natural course of events, Simon had already gotten pretty friendly with three or four freshman guys in Bliss, and knew a bunch of others to say hi to. And Amanda was certainly *acting* like a friend, and there were some other girls who knew his name and he knew theirs, and one of them *had* come by his room to check on an assignment. But Phil Hedd was from another world. He probably had never even *talked* to any of the people Simon knew, except for Amanda. Maybe she, for reasons of her own, had asked Phil Hedd to . . . give him some advice, or something.

It was also a fact that Simon had never before been asked to have, specifically, a "beer," like at a *bar*, with anyone. Within the past week — and a bunch of other times back home — kids had offered him beers that they happened to have, and he'd taken some of them, and even drunk them, just to be . . . well, *normal*. In fact, he was a little wary of alcohol — his father drank a lot of the stuff, probably *too* much, he thought — and he'd more or less decided not to get involved with it, at college. It didn't seem to taste that good to him — even beer —

and he figured that a drunken fifteen-year-old might be a pretty ridiculous sight, even to the average college person.

But when he sat down at that pub table, with a large mug of "brewski" in front of him (ordered and paid for by Phil Hedd), he knew he didn't have a choice; he had to drink it and, if possible, enjoy it.

"Prosit," said Phil, and raised his glass to Si, who smiled and did the same right back. He sipped. The beer was cold and bitter, but okay.

His first impression of Phil Hedd, in this quite different setting, was better than okay. The guy seemed really nice: relaxed but knowledgeable, funny. Si couldn't believe he kept that plastic dingus in his mouth all the time, even when he was drinking something; Phil said he'd started doing it two years before, right when he'd given up cigars. He had some great stories about his struggle with "the demon nicotine," and how he'd finally won it. Phil made himself sound helpless, lucky, just a piece of flotsam on the sea of life, but Si could see through that; the guy was simply modest and laid-back.

Almost before Simon knew it, more than an hour had gone by, and he was chatting away like a magpie himself, and making Phil laugh with stories about the dumb flatlanders who'd moved into Peacemeal, and how Solzhenitsyn had told him that Vermont's climate reminded him of home: "eleffen munts uff vinter and vun munt of mediocre shledding." Phil thought he'd passed through Peacemeal once, going up to Stowe.

When Simon had finished his first beer, a full mug had appeared almost magically, in place of the

empty one. He sipped again and found it was —
or seemed — a lot less bitter than the first one. And
he, peculiarly enough, was thirstier. The beer certainly didn't seem very *strong*. He figured maybe
beer in bars, that just came by the glass like that,
instead of out of cans or bottles, wasn't quite the
same, that it was weaker. Two things occurred to
him: One, if he started to feel the least bit drunk,
he'd stop right away; and, two, he could probably
trust an older guy like Phil not to give him more
than he could handle. So he just nodded, feeling
excellent, and soon beer number three showed up
and was attended to. Phil was such a nice *guy*: He
seemed so interested in hearing all about Si's prior
education, calling it "a-may-zing" and "exotic."

About ten-thirty or eleven a couple of Phil's friends
showed up and asked if they could join them. That
Brad Hammond guy was one of them (but his lips
didn't move when he wasn't talking, Simon noticed)
and Grant Kahn was the other — the one Amanda'd said was so important. Si thought it was neat
that he was actually sitting around bullshitting with
the great Grant Kahn. The amazing thing to Si was
how interested Grant *and* Brad, as well as Phil,
appeared to be in *him*, and the things he knew
about. He realized he might be showing off just a
little, like when he explained the mechanics of the
major human joints when Brad bemoaned his "tennis elbow" — but they really did ask for it, and egg
him on. They even seemed anxious to find out his
reactions to all aspects of the life at Riddle: the
people that he'd met so far, his courses, the whole
ambiance of the place, you might say.

All of them — by that time two other guys, Jeff

Bung and Clovis St. James (Si scooped up these new names, real fast) had pulled up chairs to their table, making it about the most popular one in the room — all of them knew and *really liked* Amanda, it turned out, so they were all delighted to learn that she was already a good friend of his. It was kind of a bond between them all, it seemed to Si, having the lovely Amanda D. in common. And they thought it was the greatest that his dad and President Portcullis had been roommates once, and that he had a "home away from home," right on the edge of campus. He didn't mention Kate, of course; *kids* were not on the agenda.

Everyone thought he'd been really, really smart to take one business course, though Phil Hedd joked around a bit about his schedule, with all its varied and "peculiar" courses. Phil claimed it sounded "sort of undecided, like an egghead salad."

"What's that twenty-dollar word?" he asked. "Epleptic? Something like that."

"Eclectic," Simon almost shouted, with a smile, taking another swig of beer right after that, as the other people laughed and laughed at Phil and sent, he thought, respectful looks in his direction. And ordered up another bunch of brews.

"As a matter of fact" — so Simon, soaring, said — "I heard a rumor just the other day. About how maybe there could be some changes coming in the . . . *you* know, in the setup here. Schedule like mine might go the way of dodo birds. End up obs'lete."

After he'd said that, Simon shrewdly noticed that a couple of the guys seemed to take a kind of quickie little glance at one another. It could be he'd been talking louder than before, too loud. He *was* feeling very slightly different, he had to admit. Maybe it was time, he thought, to try a little mind over matter. Sometimes it was good to be smart; you could do things with your mind. He bet if he really concentrated, he could make the "slightly different" feeling go away.

Meanwhile, he realized Grant Kahn was speaking to him.

". . . doubt that very much." Was that a mildly patronizing tone? "I mean," he said, "they might get somewhat stricter about the number of electives anyone can take, over the four-year span, but still I'd guess that the basic structure . . . I mean, every year the freshmen seem to start the wildest rumors. . . ." Kahn had this little, sort of supercilious, smile on his . . . sort of swarthy face.

"No. This came from a professor," Simon interrupted. He consciously lowered his voice. "He told me there was, like, this real gross possibility that Riddle might become . . . *you* know, like Wharton, only better. Total business school. An' the federal government — you know? — was pushing the idea, like maybe even planning it."

That semi-gathered their attention, once again, at least. Some of them, however, still looked skeptical. Or maybe even bored. Grant Kahn was still smiling, as he looked at his watch.

"It's about that time, for me," he said. Then, looking back at Simon, he added, "You've got to take what a lot of the profs around here say with about a carload of salt. The iodized. Now if Vincent Mowbray told you that, I ought to tell you something about *him*. He's just about the biggest bullshi— "

"No, no, not Mowbray, Grebe," said Simon quickly, interrupting before Kahn could stand up and get away. He wasn't so smart.

Si turned to Phil Hedd, who was still looking at him in an easygoing, friendly, and respectful sort of way. "He's a really funny kind of guy, of course," he said. "You probably know him, right? All the robots and all that? Crazy. He didn't have . . . *you* know, a lot of facts. Or any, really. Maybe he was kidding. Yeah, I bet he was," he decided to say. This story seemed to be losing it. "He seemed like a real big kidder."

He was starting to feel . . . tum-da-dum-dum, distinctly odd. Di*stinkly*. He wished he hadn't mentioned Grebe, and he wished he hadn't drunk just that last mug of beer. And he wished he wasn't sweating funny and he wished his head didn't seem so loose on his neck, and he wished that he was sure if he got up he'd move like regular.

"Amanda!" he heard someone say, and he turned his head to see Amanda Dollop walking toward their table, smiling. And then, when she saw *him*, stop smiling, start to frown.

"Hello, Amanda," Simon said, and tried to look completely . . . *average*. And unconcerned.

"Hey, guys," she said to all the rest. "Hey, Simon." Now she was smiling again, at him. "Looks like I'm a little late for the party." She grabbed an empty chair and slid it over next to him, and sat down.

Simon didn't enter into the conversation that followed. It seemed to be about what night it was — Wednesday — and Amanda's schedule, and something about what lab she'd just been at, and how she still had skatey-eight hours worth of studying still to do, when she got back to the hall. And how compared to her the rest of them were, like, on holiday. Si couldn't think of anything to say about all that. At times he felt pretty good, but then there'd be other moments when the deal got all slip-slidey kind of feeling. Dum-de-dum-dum, mighty like a stranger, headin' into danger. . . . How'd that go?

Then Amanda turned to him, and she said, "Simon? You going back to the dorm? These guys are looking settled in, to me."

No one contradicted her, though Simon wanted to say he thought Grant Kahn was leaving, too. But Grant didn't get up after all, so he was glad he didn't — say anything, that is. And besides, he didn't particularly want to walk back to the hall with Grant Kahn.

Simon stood up. It felt as if the soles of his running shoes had become convex — was it? Grown rockers? He couldn't remember, but he managed to balance on them anyway. Then he made a little half salute, to Phil and to the table in general, and headed toward the door. Amanda followed right behind him, her hands upon his shoulders, slightly steering.

24

Shooting Up the Road of Life

"Boy," Amanda Dollop said, "you're really *waffled*, Simon." She undid the lace on his left Nike and pulled it off his foot. "You big beer-drinker, you. You and your barroom buddies. I didn't even know you'd *met* those people." She picked up his other foot.

"Phil's'n awful nice guy," said Simon, smiling broadly. He was lying on his back on his bed, a little messily, all angles and extensions. This was the position into which he'd semi-stumbled, semi-thrown himself a bit before, after Amanda'd steered him safely to his room. Now he was watching her as she attempted the pretty hilarious task of trying to untie the knot in the lace of his right running shoe.

"We're having a couple beers. Jus' me'n' Phil," he added. " 'N'a'restof 'em came along." He shook his head. "Hoo-ee! 'Fraid I mighta got myself a li'l . . . spifflicated, right?"

"Just a little," said Amanda, nodding. She gave up on the lace and pulled the shoe off Simon's foot, dropping it on the floor beside the other one. Then she straightened up and looked at the whole patient.

It seemed as if the smartest thing to do, right then, would be to get his jeans and long-sleeved shirt off and put him into bed and hope he'd fall asleep and stay that way awhile. She'd also move the wastebasket closer to the head of the bed, just in case he woke up booting.

"But why — how come?" she said. "How come you'n' Phil were having *any* beers together? What have you got to do with Phil Hedd? Was he trying to get your views on maple syrup futures, or something?"

She realized this fine irony was being wasted on Simon, but she wanted to keep him answering questions — although chances were the guy wouldn't know, or even remember, exactly what'd been going on at The Pub. *She* was sure it had to be more than coincidence that all the members of A-CHOIR, other than herself, were sitting at a table there with Simon Storm, *her* candidate for membership. None of the other four *ever* hung out with Clovis St. James, except on society business; that was the tip-off. But had they come to bury Caesar or to praise him, so to speak (Amanda'd read a Shakespeare play, her sophomore year of high school). On the face of it, it seemed as if maybe they'd taken her nomination seriously. If so, that was pretty neat. Maybe she was having more of an influence on A-CHOIR than she'd realized.

"Mablesirrup *what?*" said Simon. "Don' know whatcha mean. Jus' having a beer. Phil asked me to. 'S'n'awful nice guy." He smiled some more, then, "Hey! Wudja doin', Amanda?"

It was really pretty clear what she was doing, although he hadn't had the trick performed on him in years. She'd grabbed hold of the end of his belt, and its buckle, and with a couple of expert yanks and flicks had got the thing undone. Another quick, no-nonsense move and the metal button at the waistband of his jeans had also been undone; a final rapid pull and he was neatly zippered-down.

"Taking off your pants, you load," she said. "You don't want to sleep in blue jeans, do you?"

And even as she spoke, she lifted up his legs and bent them, sort of rolled him backward, like the first part of a somersault, far enough so she could get his trousers partway down. After that, she grabbed them by the cuffs and slowly drew them over both his feet, and off.

"There," she said, and looked at him with what, it seemed to him, was satisfaction.

Below the waist he was wearing only sweat socks and his bright red briefs, a really skimpy nylon pair he'd bought that very summer after reading they were what you'd find most members of the Red Sox wearing. The fact that Amanda was a medical student worked against his having any feeling of embarrassment; she'd seen a lot of guys' . . . equipment as a part of her *education*, he felt sure. Plus, this was *college*, anyway. *All* girls saw guys in underwear, or less, at college (he believed).

"Now, all we need to do is get that shirt off . . ." she began. She lifted his upper body off the bed and, in order to keep him in that position while she tried to get his left arm out of its shirt sleeve, she draped his right one around her neck. Simon suddenly became aware of the fact that what his right hand was hanging down almost against was her right breast, and that her cheek was only inches from his nose.

It wouldn't be the truth to say that Simon didn't think *at all* about what happened next, ahead of time. But, to be fair, the thinking that he did was not too balanced, moderate, mature. No, put it down as "crypto-crafty," "Dutch-courageous," "go-for-it-ish." Put his thoughts in *words* and they were more or less the following:

Well, here's my chance; it hadda happen sometime.

And so he very gently touched Amanda Dollop's rounded bosom, felt the side of this forbidden woman-part, and found it . . . wonderful! Though it was covered by a tank top and a cotton camp shirt both, it was still a woman's breast that he was touching — in a sensitive and subtle, rather grown-up way, he hoped. Amazing! It was — this thing that he was doing ("feeling up" a girl, he'd always heard it called) — the greatest thrill he'd ever had, by far. He could almost feel himself go shooting up the road of life, at least 200 days' worth.

Then Amanda turned her head in his direction, and so he kissed her, too, hitting her by (mostly) luck (he'd closed his eyes by now) quite squarely on the lips.

In thinking of this moment later on, Amanda (squarely) faced the truth: that for a moment, there, she'd kissed him back, and that, indeed, her lips had started opening (she *could* say, but she didn't, "in surprise").

But then she'd jerked her head away, tossed him like a rag doll back onto the bed (his shirt not even

161

off one arm), and blurted out some semi-outraged sound, like, "Hey!"

Simon's eyes had opened as his head went crashing back upon the pillow. Now they flat-out stared, in horror, as he realized what he'd done. And more than that, to whom. This wasn't any tube-topped teenie who'd used to let the boys cop feels for quarters out behind the Peacemeal Volunteer F.D. when Simon was eleven (and indeed he *hadn't*, thank you very much!). This was Jennif . . . uh, *Amanda Dollop*, college woman, M.D. up the line, resident assistant, buddy. He was a *beast* (Si told himself) — in attitude, presumptuousness, not all that different from a rapist. Horrified, he realized he . . . *yes*. He grabbed his blue jeans, slid them over on his lap.

"Amanda, gee . . ." he — somewhat sobered — said. "I didn't mean. . . . I'm sorry . . . gosh." He felt his cheeks just burning, burning, burning; too typically, his eyes began to fill.

She'd folded up her arms in front of her and she was looking stern, he thought.

"Shut up," she said, and, "Look. That isn't the worst thing that's ever happened in my life, so far." She even gave him half a smile, with that. "Or anywhere near the best, either, so don't get any bright ideas. What I suggest is: You just get some sleep. And maybe from now on be a little more . . . *mature*." He winced. "As far as drinking goes, I mean. It isn't a *requirement* here, you know. And maybe you'd be smart to. . . ." She waved a palm at him. "Forget it. I'll bring that up some other time. Okay?"

Simon nodded rapidly. "Right, right, sure. And thanks, Amanda. I mean, for taking me home and all. And I *am* going to go easy on the drinking, no

kidding. And I'm really so terribly, terribly sorry
I — "

She waved the hand again. "It happens — don't
worry about it. I'll see you in the morning."

And then she bent, put both hands on his shoulders, and kissed him lightly on the forehead.

Simon would have sworn he felt the imprint of
her lips until he whirled off into sleep, some forty
seconds later.

25

Two Separate Problems

As Simon, with Amanda as his rudder more or less, weaved his way between the tables in The Pub, and eventually out the door, the manly members of A-CHOIR sat and looked at one another. None of them really saw St. James, of course (although they knew that he was there), but the expressions on the faces that they *did* see ranged from outrage (Hammond), to grim resolution (Bung), with stops for petulant annoyance (Kahn), and amused exasperation (Hedd) along the way.

"Grebe!" Brad Hammond said the word with utter loathing. "Why, isn't he that gross, disgusting swine that Dr. Holt said might be playing hide-the-weenie with the local teens? The psychology queer? The one he said we maybe ought to sic Amanda onto?"

Jeff Bung nodded his agreement. "Onto, under — doesn't make a hell of a lot of difference, I suppose. Just so long as she gets into his drawers." Bung chuckled. "His *file* drawers, that is."

"It just frosts my buns," Grant Kahn contributed, ignoring what he thought was Brad's and Jeffrey's rather childish dirty-talk, "that just as we have a great scheme coming into place, we find we have a leak to take care of. Already. How could this Grebe have gotten access to the master plan? That's what I'd like to know. It must have been from someone near the source. In Washington, I mean. Up here, at this end, the only ones who know are us and Greg, and none of *us* would ever — " Once again, he got his eyeballs moving; a lap around the table yielded Brad and Phil and Jeffrey and himself: impossible. Every one of them, in spite of certain other . . . weaknesses, was tight-lipped — leak-proof, he would say. He was sure of it.

"Wait! How about those kids of Holt's?" Brad Hammond asked. "What's-her-face — or Freddy? *Jessica*, that's it. In eighty-four, my freshman year, I swear I saw her with a Mondale-Ferraro button on her little overalls."

"On the front or on the back?" Jeff Bung demanded, quickly. "If it was on the back, it could have been a plant. Some English professor's kid in nursery school, with a perverted sense of humor. What *is* Jessica — six, now? She couldn't even *read* in eighty-four then, and on TV it was all Reagan. I can't imagine any four-year-old not going for Reagan. Really. Can you?"

Phil Hedd moved his cocktail stirrer — a clear plastic one — slowly, with unhurried calm, from the lefthand corner of his mouth to the extreme right.

"Guys," he said. "It doesn't much matter who, or how, or even when. Not for the time being, anyway. What's done is done, and what we have to do is make damn sure it doesn't do us in before we're done with what we have to do. You understand what I'm saying?"

Everybody nodded, but only Clovis St. James smiled.

"We're looking at two separate problems," Hedd continued, "both of which are going to need attention. On the one hand, we've got Hansen Grebe, the classic odd duck, who's somehow gotten his beak — at *least* his beak — where it doesn't belong. But there's also someone else who knows too much, young Simon Storm. Who knows how much too much? It could be plenty, and we know — we just found out — that he's a blabbermouth, at least when he's knocked back a beer or two. Remember, this kid's a buddy of Portcullis's — at least his father is — and he's tight with our Amanda, too."

"You're saying Simon Storm . . ." Grant Kahn began.

". . . *and* Hansen Grebe . . ." Jeff Bung chimed in.

". . . must *both* be neutralized," Phil Hedd concluded.

"*Neutralized?* But wait a minute, Phil," Brad Hammond said. "Isn't it *Professor Mowbray* who gets neutralized? Didn't Dr. Holt say, quite specifically, that he was going to — "

"No, no, Brad, no." Hedd patted Hammond's hand to shut him up, give him something else to think about. "Professor Mowbray, *he* gets *martyred*; neutralized is different. Neutralized means 'rendered neutral' — like in a car? *You* know neutral in a car, right?" He made a little waggling motion with his hand. "Where you can't move at all,

166

either way, either forward *or* back? Well, that's what neutralizing someone involves. It makes them, like, incapable of motion, movement, action. Out of it. Defunct."

"Oh," said Hammond. "Right." He nodded, getting the idea in place, inside his head. Pretty soon his lips began to move. A hearing-impaired special ed major on the other side of The Pub just chanced to run his eyes across them — Hammond's lips — a moment later, and he read, "Brad Hammond," and repeat.

"I'd like to suggest," Grant Kahn suggested, "that we ourselves, and not Amanda, do the job on Grebe. At Grebe's. The B, E, and L, to put it bluntly."

Brad Hammond looked at Kahn. His lips stopped moving, pressed together. He couldn't remember any talk concerning Grebe and sandwiches before. B, E, and L. Bacon, egg, and lettuce that'd be, right?

"Breaking, Entering, and Larceny," said Clovis St. James, very clearly. "Well. Imagine that." He smiled again, then lay back in his chair and closed his eyes.

"I'd rather think of it as research of a sort," said Jeffrey Bung. "Or a form of *caretaking*, in a way. On behalf of that ever-increasing segment of the student body interested in improving the moral climate here on campus. I mean, if there're stories going around about some professor taking advantage of minors *on university property*, I think it's high time someone looked into it."

He leered, and Grant Kahn thought, again, that it was only under a free enterprise system that he would be found in a room with Bung for more than five minutes. Under any other arrangement, he would

167

have long since had the guy exterminated by government troops under his personal command, at no cost whatsoever.

"I think you're right, Grant," Phil Hedd said. "We have to act real fast, in the case of brother Grebe. There really isn't time to . . . well, *convince* Amanda. Plus, if we do the job ourselves, we can make a thorough check on everything that's in his files. Maybe Greg'll have some thoughts — suggestions — about what other kinds of things we might go looking for. I mean, just in case the adolescent study thing's a dud."

"But what about the little twerp?" said Kahn. "Your drinking buddy. What can we dig up on him? Or have we got another way . . . to hang him from the yardarm?" Grant's weekends on the sound had left some salt stains on his way of speaking.

"I don't know." Phil chewed a hangnail on his thumb, which necessitated his taking the swizzle stick out of his mouth momentarily. But he slipped it back in before he spoke again. "And until we *do* know, I suggest we all stay friendly with the kid. Act like we like him and et cetera. Amanda's right about one thing for sure: The kid's *extremely* sharp. You should have heard some of the stuff he came up with earlier. I'm talking Harvard MBA type sharp, that kind of total-picture vision. We don't want him putting any two and two's together, if you understand what I'm saying, and coming up with — "

"Maybe we could take turns bringing him in here for drinks, like every night," Brad Hammond said. "That'd seem like a friendly thing to do. Plus, he might blab some other stuff to us, and it's even possible he might become an alcoholic, which'd probably solve our whole problem. And even if he didn't, I read somewhere — the *Digest*, I think it was — that booze kills off a person's brain cells. Did you guys know that? Like several hundred, or maybe it's in the thousands, every time you have a mixed drink. But it's less for wine and beer; I remember that. If he stuck to beer, like tonight, it might take quite a while to get him down to normal intelligence, like an average BS or BA might have. But I imagine we could trick him into trying stronger drinks, don't you? I've got a whole lot of different ones written down, back in the room, that my father told me about. Recipes for real strong drinks that just *taste* weak? He used to use them on girls when he was in college — I guess they were different, then — and they'd think they were drinking something mild and harmless, like grapefruit juice, and then suddenly, before they knew it, *kazango*! Well, the girls'd be, like, just about helpless, if you know what I mean, and — "

"And in the meantime" — this time Grant Kahn did stand up, and stretch — "we can all be thinking up some slightly more *certain* way of dealing with the lad. I'm sure we'll hit on something. Maybe I'll ask Dads to run a check on the father. I mean, why would *anyone* who didn't have a thing to hide go plant himself in — what's-it-called? — Vermont? 'Pee-smell,' is it, Phil?"

The rest of them were also on their feet by then, and all four started for the door, leaving Clovis stretched out in his chair, appearing (to the other patrons of The Pub) quite fast asleep.

26

Aftereffects

When Simon woke up the next morning, he was still wearing the blue-and-white-checked long-sleeved shirt from the front of the L.L. Bean catalogue, the black Richard and Linda Thompson T-shirt from the back of *Rolling Stone*, and the red nylon super-briefs from the store in Boston with Wade Boggs's picture in the window. But, to this ensemble, he'd added (1) a headache: heavy, dull, starting in skull-center and then pounding down the back of it, into his neck; (2) an unfamiliar, putrefactive flavor in his mouth; and (3) a gloomy sense of having made an ugly mark in what had been, till then, and in that setting, a fairly unstained self.

Well, the good part is, he thought, I'm not at home. My parents, they need never know what a drunken, philandering lout their son and whilom pride and joy's turned out to be.

"Whilom," he thought next. Hey, good one.

He made himself sit up; he groaned. He stretched a hand out straight, about chest height, like boozers in the movies; at least it wasn't shaking. Yet. Nor was he seeing elephants or cows or snakes in unexpected colors, sizes, places. What he didn't expect to see, for the foreseeable future, was any kind of genuinely respectful expression on Amanda Dollop's face — not while *he* was in her field of vision, anyway. She'd probably be enough of a professional R.A. to keep the sneers and snarls to a miminum, as she'd done the night before. Conceivably, she'd even *seem* no different than she used to be, and act as if being sexually assaulted was all part of the R.A.'s job, no more remarkable than breaking up a food fight in the corridor and being nicked by, say, a flying meatball. But he'd know what she was *really* feeling. He wondered if she'd feel it part of her responsibility to make sure that other girls — in Bliss, for openers, but maybe everywhere on campus — were properly forewarned about him. He really couldn't blame her if she did.

Simon got to his feet, let out another groan — more as the proper thing to do than because of any new discomfort — and walked over to the desk where he, or possibly Amanda, had put his watch the night before. But neither of the two of them had wound it; it had stopped. Now he *really* groaned; he *hated* that. From the time when he'd first learned to tell the stuff (that's time) and gotten his first watch (age of four, at 7:42 A.M., his birthday), he'd been a time fanatic. Watches weren't just to help him be *on* time, like always; they also told him how long something took: the crossword puzzle, showering and dressing, reading fifty pages, and a lot of other things too trivial or personal to mention. A watch invited him to . . . well, set *records*, and it made double sure he knew that everything began and ended, had a midpoint.

He looked out the window and guessed it was

close to eight o'clock right then; he seldom over-slept. But he didn't relax completely until he arrived at breakfast and was able to find out for sure what time it was and set his watch again. He got the Eastern Daylight facts from Phillips Hedd, in fact.

Phil was sitting near the door of the dining room and sipping a cup of coffee, and he greeted Simon with a friendly smile on his face and a bright black stirrer *in* it. The smile gave Simon quite a feeling of relief. Apparently he hadn't made a complete fool of himself in The Pub, at least. Phil had a Rolex on, with a wide gold band, a beauty, and he admitted, on the dot of 8:19, that he, too, was an hour/minute freak, totally undressed without his watch on.

Long after Simon left the dining room, Phil Hedd just kept on sitting there, looking into space and tapping his front teeth with a piece of coal-black, pointed, shiny plastic, sharp enough to stab a mara-schino cherry with, stab it to the heart.

For the next few days, Simon managed to avoid Amanda completely. One hundred percent. The thought of seeing her was just too sickeningly em-barrassing. It wasn't hard, this avoiding business — just, at times, a little inconvenient.

During the day, he wasn't apt to see her, anyway. As a rule, she got up about an hour earlier than he did, and all of her courses, except one, met at the medical school, which was off on a distant corner of the campus. The one exception was Rational Portfolio Selection, the business course that she and Simon had in common with about three hundred other young capitalists (and a handful of *aspiring*

172

capitalists) including Phil Hedd and Jeffrey Bung, as a matter of fact. But because there was assigned seating in alphabetical order in the enormous lecture hall where the course met, they were many, many rows apart from one another.

Evenings posed some problems, however. Although he knew that if he went in to eat as soon as the dining room opened, he could be out of there before she got back from her lab, or her rounds, or whatever, he had to remember to take his books and notebooks with him to the meal, so that as soon as he was finished, he could blow right out of Bliss and hole up someplace else to study.

He tried the Forsythe Library just once; by 7:30 the sounds that go with soda cans, potato chips, boredom, and seduction had penetrated even *his* fantastic concentration, and he had to leave. His next stop was a storage room in the Pribble Activities Building, where he stayed until almost midnight, when a watchman noticed the light under the door and told him to vamoose. After that, he used the Widgin Nursing Library, common rooms in two other halls, and the lobby of the Rayforth-Basefield Student Theater. But on the sixth night he got outmaneuvered. Amanda went and found a place she knew she'd spot him from, eventually: the soft, old, dusty easychair from Peacemeal, right beside the bed in 211 Bliss.

"Oh . . . hi," he said to her, when he'd lurched in the door, his head still freighted with the heavyweight reading he'd been doing for Comparative Political Analysis. Could he have left the door unlocked, he asked himself, or did she, maybe, have a pass key?

"Well, greetings," she replied. "I was wondering if you'd dropped out of school. Moved to Zanzibar, wherever that is — do you *know* where it is? — or possibly the highlands of Sumatra."

"Oh, no," he said. "It's off the coast of east Africa, part of Tanzania, actually." He was making quite a production of putting his books away: three standing in a row against the wall, another flat on top of them, his notebook in the middle drawer of his desk, where he also put his pens. "I've had to use the library a lot — reserve books, different things I had to . . . like, you know, look up." He knitted his smooth brow, trying to come on serious and scholarly. Amanda thought he looked adorable, such a perfect little colt.

Out of things to put away, or say, he headed for the bed and once again flopped down on it, his hands behind his head, and looking at the ceiling.

"So . . . Amanda. How're you doing?" he said. "Got the ol' biochemistry under control?"

"*Si*-mon," Amanda said. "I haven't camped out here all night so's I could talk to you about my course work. I think you've been avoiding me, and I want you to stop."

"Avoiding you?" he said. He tried to laugh. It sounded like a minor cry of pain, or the beginnings of a bray. "I haven't been *avoiding* you. I've just been . . . really, really busy." He searched his mind for something cooler, more collegiate. "Bookin' up a storm."

"Sure," she said. "At totally different times and in entirely different places than usual, right? I haven't even *seen* you, except the top of your head in lecture. I couldn't tell if you were taking notes or sleep-ing."

"The former," Simon said. "Emphatically the former. Diddleman stuffs a lot of juicy information into his lectures — don't you think? — and I just about have trouble keeping up with all the — "

"Look, Simon." She stood up, took two steps forward, and sat down on his bed, the edge of it. He had to look squarely at her for the first time, really, since he'd come into the room. She looked almost unbearably attractive, in a pinkish silky shirt, and her dark curls soft and shiny. And her tan, and she was smiling.

"I don't want you to think we've stopped being friends, on account of the other night," she said. "Because we haven't — or *I* haven't, anyway. I've really missed you, missed seeing you around. As far as I'm concerned, what happened's ancient history: forgotten, obsolete, the pterodactyl. So what do you say? Can't we get back to normal?"

"Oh, yeah . . . *sure*," he said. But he couldn't *look* at her normally. He'd told himself to look only at her eyes when they were talking, and not at any other . . . parts. But after a while *his* eyes would have to blink, and then he'd look away, at some-place neutral, like the ceiling. It was very hard to look at *just* a person's eyes.

"Well, then, shake on it," she said, and stuck a hand out, over his chest. He shook, but when he was ready to let go, she kept her grip on him.

"And just so's I know you mean it, I want you to do me a favor," she continued.

"Sure," he said. "Why, absolutely. Anything."

That seemed the best, the *only* way to satisfy her. By which, of course, he meant: to end this present and discomforting discussion. His eyes were now bouncing wildly from the ceiling to the window to the wall to *her* eyes, and back again.

"Good," she said. "The favor is: I want to do a practice physical exam on you sometime. We're learning that now, and it's hard to get guys who aren't medical students and who don't . . . well, tell me how *they'd* do it — better, of course — all the time. I can get all the females I want, but guys tend to be a real problem; it takes a real friend. Plus, it'd be interesting to do someone . . . well, your age." She smiled. "This doesn't have to be real soon, by the way. We can work out a time that suits you. The whole thing takes about an hour, and you *would* be doing me the *most* fantastic favor."

Simon checked her face; he had to. She was smiling, but she also looked . . . well, *serious*, not joking. Clearly, she really wanted him to let her . . . *palpate* him, and stuff. Great. *Grotesque*. But there was, it seemed to him, only one possible, *mature* response for him to make — if he could speak at all, in the sort of major panic he was in.

"Sure," he said, offhandedly. Or at least he didn't gulp. "Be happy to oblige. . . ." What age did she think he was, for gosh sake? *How* interesting would she expect to find him? Not to mention why and where, to what extent, et cetera.

During the next few weeks — while pretty much avoiding the whole social scene but not, specifically, Amanda anymore — Si really did hit the books with great, and also pleasurable, effect. Studying helped him *not* to think about the past, or the practice physical in his future. And also he plain enjoyed the various learning experiences. For the most part, anyway. There were some peculiar moments, too.

One of those occurred when Phil Hedd came by his room to help him with the course they had in common: Rat-Port, a.k.a. (and aforementioned) Rational Portfolio Selection. Phil was a finance major, in the department of business administration, so the course was bread and butter to the guy. And because he'd taken other courses with Professor Diddleman, he'd not only had a lot of experience with the kind of tests he gave, but also thought he knew how to deal with them. That's what he'd come to talk to Simon about: the weekly fact-quizzes that Diddleman was famous for (Si had taken three of them already), and especially the many tricky questions ("Goddam near unfair") that could be found in them: the so-called "Diddleman Destroyers."

"What I try to do," Phil whispered (*why?*), sitting on the edge of Simon's bed and tapping the face of his Rolex, "what I *always* do, is budget out my time. But never like it says in the instructions, see? That's one of the ways that Diddleman destroys a guy. By putting 'twenty minutes' next to PART I he makes you think you ought to go real slow and careful on that part, which is always the fill-in-the-blanks, right? And then you come to PART II, the multiple choices, and it says 'ten minutes,' so you're picking up speed and maybe even jumping at the first choice that seems to make sense, and pretty soon you're at the true-falses with only 'five minutes' left. But you're relaxed because that's how long it says they ought to take. And then and there he's got you zapped. All of a sudden you're looking at questions like, let's see, oh, yeah: 'It doesn't make investment sense to not buy gold in years you may not need a tax loss.' True or false. Say — *what?* Maybe thirty of those little buggers. You're going to do one of *them* every ten seconds? No way in the world. So here's what I suggest, my Time Adjustment System — the way I use the time, myself. Fill-in-the-blanks: not twenty minutes there, but eight-point-five. They're all straightforward facts; you know 'em or you don't. So what *that* means is, then, you can. . . ."

Simon nodded. He wasn't going to say this, naturally, but so far he'd taken no more than twenty minutes *total* on any of Diddleman's quizzes; when he finished the first one, he was actually afraid that he'd left out a page, or something. What the course was teaching was a set of rules, and Simon learned rules fast and easily. But still . . . he still could nod at Phil, and at Phil's strategy, and mean it. He, too, always checked his watch as he moved through a test, any test. It was good to *know*, have proof of what you thought the situation was, how far ahead (you hoped) you were.

So, in addition to nodding, he said, "Thanks a lot," to Phil. And, "I'll use that method next time."

"Good man," said Phil. "On the midterm it'll make all the difference. There'll be a lot more questions on that sucker, plus an essay, which I personally always hate, I don't know about you. But if you use my system, you'll see your grades go shooting up." He smiled. "I can almost guarantee it."

Simon smiled right back. They stood, exchanged

high-fives as Phil went out the door. Si didn't have the heart to tell the guy he hadn't missed a question yet.

His other peculiar moment was of a very different sort. It came in his Expository Writing class, which was much more of a challenge to Simon because he actually had to *do* stuff there, as well as learn a bunch of rules. He hadn't written weekly "papers" back in prep school, someplace, or in the AP English class at New Trier, Stuyvesant, or Beverly Hills High, so in terms of practice he was pretty far behind the other kids. Which was part of the reason he was mucho impressed by some of the *A* papers Mr. Waxman, his class instructor, read out loud to them from time to time, to highlight certain kinds of excellence.

But in the seventh week of the term, the "im-" in front of "-pressed" became a "de-." What happened was: He learned what he was up against, in terms of competition. You might say.

Waxman, beaming, had produced a fast 500 words entitled "Winning the Battle for Household Hegemony: How To Turn the Dog Against Your Parents." It was, he told them, from the pen of one Carruthers, first name Sydney, a guy from Bliss whom Simon knew and who had never struck him as a wit, before.

Well, Waxman wasn't halfway into paragraph two before the girl on Simon's left began to make peculiar sputter sounds. He turned and looked at her, thinking this was just the way they laughed in Oregon, or somewhere, and saw her eyes were even wider than her mouth — in horror, or at least sur-

179

prise, he thought. He raised a sympathetic, and in-
quiring eyebrow.

"The title's different, but *I* wrote that paper,"
Tracy Stoddard told him, speaking in a whisper
from behind her hand, "my junior year at Exeter,
in 1984. I got a ninety-three on it. What he's reading
is my paper, word for ever-lovin' word."

"My gosh," said Simon, "that'd be a violation of
the honor code, then. You'll have to turn Carruthers
in." With a sinking heart, he realized that "Mr.
POP" was not, as he had dared to hope, an upperclassman playing silly games with freshmen. The
guy must have made a sale to this Carruthers, right
in Bliss. That was really rotten — rotten of "Mr.
POP" and rotten of Carruthers. If stuff like that
went on, unchecked, it could, like, totally destr —

"I can't, though," Tracy Stoddard was going on,
to his left. "You see, the thing is, I kind of adapted
it, myself. From one my roommate's *brother* did,
when he was at St. Marks." She giggled. "His was
only worth an eighty-five down there, and Exeter's
tons harder."

It didn't take Kate Portcullis very long to notice
that Simon didn't "just show up, any time" for a
meal at her parents' house, nor was he using it as
a quiet place to study — both of which, her father
had mentioned to her, he had told Simon he was
more than welcome to do. She'd asked her father —
extremely casually, she thought — what Si's reaction had been to this display of *mi casa es su casa*
hospitality, and had been told that it seemed pos-
itive. So what was going on? If their roles had been

reversed, she told herself, she would have damn well found a reason to show up at *his* folks' house, at a time when everyone but him was out (if possible), and, *with* a reason or without, started in seducing him.

Sure you would, she told herself right after that. Don't try to kid a kidder, feebroid. Constant candidate for Virgin of the Month. And worse: not anxious, in her heart of hearts, for any major change of status.

What she actually suspected, almost assumed, was that Simon was "seeing" some girl on campus, an older woman, an *experienced* woman, who was probably using him in heaven-knows-what unsavory way.

Oh, yum, she thought, and shivered, imagining one.

It seemed totally unfair, though, that this girl — these girls — just because they were *slightly* older than she, should be able to live, and probably even shower, cheek-by-jowl, with literally hundreds of cute (albeit *disgusting*) boys their own age. And should *also* have dibbies on Simon.

But on the other hand, and to be truthful, Kate didn't expect either fairness or favors from the gods of dating. She was prepared to make her own breaks and take, like, all the single steps that journeys have to start with. Even enjoy them, in a way.

To that end, she made a phone call to Bliss, and then another. If she could believe the voices at the other end — both girls', both sounding (in terms of poise and general attractiveness) like younger Jennifer Bealses, she thought — Simon wasn't there and really didn't seem to be spending much time in the hall "these days." But would she like to leave a message?

Kate thought not. She imagined Simon returning to his room after sharing (not a pizza but) a fifteen-hour sexual smorgasbord with . . . Daryl Hannah, say. And picking up, from underneath his door, a note that told him "Kate called." She could almost *see* her message, balled and crumpled, arcing toward the nearest trash container.

But still, she thought, a few days after that, there could be other explanations for his absence from her house. Maybe he spent all his time hacking away at the computer center. Or possibly he was locking his room door and never answering a knock, for fear that everyone would learn that he was red-eyed homesick, and ashamed of it. In need of comforting, poor baby.

She decided she would write the guy a letter, and straight-out *ask* him over. All he could say was no — as her mother had been known to say. Maybe he was (simply) shy.

Dear Simon (she wrote),

How about coming over for the rubber game of our badminton series? If you win, though, it's best out of five — and so on. After, we could take a swim and have something to eat.

Appearances to the contrary, I'm a pretty good cook, and if you can make it Thursday, when my parents are in Cleveland (no kidding), you'll discover if I'm also a pretty good liar, or not. If Thursday isn't any good for you, next Tuesday's another possibility. Then, you'd get my mother's cooking and her chaperonage, too, at no extra charge. Not that you're in any real danger Thursday.

Regards,

Kate

P.S. That game you beat me was the only b'minton game I lost this summer, so I'm feeling outstandingly vengeful.

P.P.S. I'm curious. What did you say you were doing when the beeper went off while you were talking to my dad, last time?
1. "Chatting with the college president"? — sounds pretentious.
2. "Socializing"? — borderline inaccurate.
3. "Being advised by my adviser?" — childish and unlikely.
4. "Rapping with the sire of the incandescent Kate Portcullis"? — AHHH!

Of course she crossed her fingers when she mailed it.

27

Anonymous Letter

Dear President Portcullis,

A fact has come to our attention which, after a great deal of (painful) soul-searching, we have decided to pass along to you. Here it is, unvarnished, unadorned, almost unspeakable:

Vincent Mowbray, Professor of Marketing and Trends Analysis, is at Riddle under false pretenses. He no more has an earned PhD than "Doctors" Seuss or K.

Nothing against Vinnie personally, but rules are rules and credentials are credentials, "as the saying goes." Western Hawaii A&T — the supposed source of his degree — has a staff of one, a 400-square-foot campus, and, as its main physical asset, a printing press. Mowbray has some nice tweed jackets and a reasonable overspin forehand, but he is otherwise unqualified to be a full professor at Riddle. We feel sure that in the light (aroma) of that fact, you will do your (painful) duty for the sake of the academic integrity of the university, thus making it entirely unnecessary for us to dispatch a carbon of the body of this letter to the *Riddle News*, in a week or two with other (painful) questions attached.

I think you will understand, given the extreme delicacy of the situation, why we choose to sign ourselves,

Sincerely and sadly,

Dr. A. and Dr. B.

P.S. In case it's slipped your mind, there are, we notice, a couple of *highly* qualified *associate* professors of Marketing and Trends Analysis, both of whom are worthy by any standards — and perhaps even *overdue* — for promotion to full professor (with resulting raises in salary, of course).

Professor Greg Holt smiled a final time at the letter before he slipped it into an envelope. He was sure Portcullis would never suspect it was his work. And that the president's secretary, Miss Plangent, would guess, and broadcast all over campus, that those two young snots, Sparhawk and O'Grady (each of whom had made no secret of his ambition to be chairman of the econ department), were the Judases who'd blown the whistle on their likable colleague. Holt had never gotten less than an A in Business English, either in school *or* college. One of his teachers, a real magician with words in his own right, had even put it to him straight:

"You could of been a writer," this guy had said.

28

Break-in

Most of the male members of A-CHOIR were pretty darned excited — and would have been even without the fatigue inhibitors they'd dutifully chosen to ingest — as they tiptoed down the second floor corridor of Frabbit Hall. Phil Hedd checked his Rolex; it was 2:19 A.M. They were on their way to break and enter into Hansen Grebe's domain — larceny to follow, hopefully. Amanda Dollop was asleep and unaware, in Bliss, exactly as they wanted her to be; B, E, and L was no job for a lady. Seduction and entrapment were a very different matter. There was still one vacancy in the society; the candidates were being "compu-analyzed" — in other words, the stall was staying on.

Grant Kahn and Jeffrey Bung had flown over to Hedd and Hammond's suite, Bliss 108, about midnight, and there the four of them had further prepared for the mission by applying camouflage paint to each other's faces and, over his protests, to Kahn's white tennies. After that, they got in costume for the "raid."

As it turned out, they'd all picked out pretty similar outfits: running (or tennis) shoes, a black or

186

dark blue turtleneck, green or dark blue sweat pants, and, in the case of Brad Hammond, a navy blue woolen watch cap and a large commando knife complete with khaki sheath and canvas belt. Bung had thought to pick up four pairs of rubber gloves, which they put on at the last minute and joked about, but which also made them feel not just slightly criminal, but very near *professional* as well.

Clovis St. James had gotten their attention when he volunteered to be the "inside" man on the job — in other words, to secrete himself somewhere in the building before it got locked up for the night, so that he could then let the others in through an agreed-upon back door at 2:15 sharp. The secreting part turned out to be a cinch, just as he'd known it would be. Instead of hiding anywhere, he'd put on work clothes and his Walkman, carried in a mop, and started "doing" halls, as closing time approached. No one even noticed him, of course. Pretty soon, he had the building to himself (except for Dr. Prettyfield, of Rat Experiments) and could go to the faculty lounge and view some video cassettes in big-screen color. Psychology profs were *very* big on movies, using them to illustrate such major human frailties as "mob behavior," which apparently they felt was hard to understand without spending a few hours watching (and then rapping about) *The Ox-Bow Incident*, a classic.

Based on the cassettes St. James discovered in their library, they were also taking a pretty long look at the phenomenon of "male arousal" and, as a matter of fact, Clovis's own involvement in that study made him a couple of minutes late for his 2:15 rendezvous with his fellow male A-CHOIRers.

When he finally did show up and let them in, he thought that they seemed pretty well aroused, themselves: bathed in nervous perspiration.

Now, the only challenge that remained for them was dealing with the office door — its spring lock, or whatever. Naturally, they'd come prepared. Grant Kahn clutched his MasterCard in his rubber-gloved right hand, while Phil Hedd fingered a Visa and Brad Hammond as always (away from home) had his American Express, in addition to the big knife. Instead of flexible plastic, Jeffrey Bung had brought along a combination nail cleaner and cuticle pusher from the traveling manicure kit his aunt had given him the Christmas before, which he planned to use as a pick-lock. But when they got to the door, St. James, who'd been leading the way (and whistling), just turned the knob and the door swung open. Amazingly, they'd done it: They were in.

Hammond went first, sliding into the room the way that Tubbs or Crockett would, offering the absolute minimum in the way of a silhouette. He was still in his crouch, well out of any possible line of fire, pointing his knife in front of him and wishing he'd remembered a flashlight, when Clovis flipped the switch that turned on the office overheads.

"We shan't have to worry about the outside watchmen," he said. "The profs who work in here are always coming in odd hours. And the chap who checks around inside's not due again till half after four." He dropped into the palm of one of the hand chairs and gestured 'round the room, as if to introduce it to his colleagues.

The place is yours, old beans, he might have said.

Brad Hammond, straightening, said, "Wow!" as

his eyes took in the unexpected clutter. He could hardly believe that this was a *professor's* office. Business and econ profs were more into flow charts and conference tables, with chrome and leather accents, seascapes on the walls. He went and picked up Grebe's Batman mask and put it on. If he could just wear *that* to interviews.

The other three bit back on any similar desires. Though none of them had said this to another, Bung, Hedd, and Kahn had all rationalized their presence in the office in the same way: They were — though unofficial, "free-lance" you might say — actually *government agents*, there to plug a dangerous leak. Secret information had dripped, at least, or maybe poured, out of some office in the executive branch of the federal government, and Hansen Grebe had got a bucket under it, somehow; he couldn't just have *guessed* the stuff he'd said to Simon Storm. They, as proper patriots, were sort of doing the investigative equivalent of making a citizen's arrest which, as everyone knew, was a person's civic duty. Even if they found and . . . *liberated* something, it wouldn't be stealing, exactly. They were sure their parents would understand that, if it ever came up.

So it was as one (responsible, red-blooded, hypertense) man that Hedd, Kahn, and Bung marched toward the green metal filing cabinets at the back of the office, with Hammond (in disguise) not far behind. And because he took the nearest one, which started with the letter A, it was Phil Hedd who struck . . . well, *pay dirt*: the section headed ADOLESCENT STUDY.

His lips tightened, but at first he didn't speak. He pulled out a folder and opened it. Inside, there was

189

a thick sheaf of what looked like mimeographed answer sheets of some sort, interspersed with pieces (and some scraps) of other kinds of paper, these with paragraphs, short essays written on them, almost all of them by (rather ill-formed) hand. Hedd squinted, wrinkled up his brow. There were names on the tops of all the sheets of paper, some of them familiar and others not. His lips moved as he read them; his cocktail stirrer also moved and also made no noise. Mark Trail, Madonna, 646, Gorodish, Itchy, CeCe Ryder, Lady Jane, Sting, The Pace, Cretina, Coo Blahcon, Pete Rose, and Sleaze (he read).

He stopped and shook his head, decided he should maybe read what they had written. He tried one paragraph and then another one. They both were strange, for sure, like borderline nonsensical:

> *I was picking fleas off of my mother's Airdale, Jordy, and putting them in this juice glass with water and some Ivory Liquid. She gives me a dollar for every one I find. She goes: You can do yourself and the dog a favor, both at once. I was feeling poor but ~~virtious virtuos~~ like I was doing a good thing.*

and,

> *I was staring at the celing rite above my bed. The cracks and fly-do remind me of the vaper trails I make in space vanilla where Im gonna find my homesweethome someday. There, or California, one. I'm feeling pretty ripped I guess you could say.*

Phil riffled through more page tops, seeing most of the names come by again a time or two. And then . . . and then, a different one whizzed past. A newie. Not altogether unfamiliar, though. He had to stop, go back. Eureka, he was right! Lined sheet, ripped out of spiral notebook. The name on top, writ bold and unmistakable:

Kate Portcullis

and underneath it, this:

> *Darling — it seems a little silly to be writing this particular report, I must say. After all, you're right here in the sweat lodge with me, and what I was doing had so much to do with all the things that you were doing — to me, with me, for me — that it's hard. . . .*

"Oh, *boys*," sang Philips Hedd. "I *dooo* believe I've found a leedle somet'ing. . . ."

The others crowded around him, except for, or possibly including, Clovis St. James.

"Oh, my," they said. "Oh, my." With knowing grins and active eyeballs. *Kate Portcullis* doing stuff with Hansen Grebe! This was better than Amanda — yes, by far! This was the mother of all mother lodes.

It didn't really matter that their search of all Grebe's *other* files proved fruitless, juiceless, even. Oh, sure — it would have been a treat to find some stuff on how Hansen Grebe had learned about the federal government's interest and involvement in the plot to take over the university. But what they had was

191

basic, down-to-earth — real smut. And super, super useful.

After washing off their camouflage and stripping off the rubber gloves, they carried it, that page, across the campus to the twenty-four-hour Xerox machine in the library lobby and ran off two Quik-Copies; luckily, St. James wore pants with pockets and had change. Then they headed back to Bliss to talk a little strategy.

As Phil Hedd put it, backhanding one of the copies of Kate Portcullis's steamy, sweat lodge prose: "It's two big baddies with a single bullet, guys. Port-coo-coo and Handsome Hansen Grebe have caught the deadly double. They'd both drop trou in Macy's 'dow before they'd let a thing like this go public."

And so it seemed to all of them in 108 Bliss Hall, the Hedd and Hammond suite. What father, after all, would want the world to know his fourteen-year-old daughter opened up (at least) her pores with fortyish profesors of psychology, under Native American circumstances? And what professor of psychology would ever find professing-work again, if he were known to hit on nymphet pupils, drip-pingly, in humid heat?

"Professor Holt is absolutely going to *flip*," said Jeffrey Bung. "I vote we trundle over to his place right now, five A.M. or not. He's told us that" — he made adjustments on his wristwatch — "his 'latch-string's always out.' Or that's the way I have it here, anyway. Means we can come over if we have to, anytime, I'm pretty sure. I want to see his face when he first gets a load of this. And hear just how he says we ought to handle it." Jeff gave a wicked snicker, just anticipating. Holt always made . . . well, *everything* okay.

Brad Hammond nodded and started tightening the muscles in his legs and back that people have to use in order to stand up. But then he saw his roommate hadn't moved, and neither had Grant Kahn. They *were* exchanging glances, though — glances Hammond thought meant something, maybe lots.

"Belay there, Jeffrey," Grant Kahn said. "Put a reef in it. When the cap'n knows the harbor . . . well, he don't pay pilot's fees." Slowly and majestically, he rose. Bung hadn't understood a word of what he'd said, except it wasn't, "Yes, let's go." He hated Kahn anew.

"Men," G.K. was saying now. He seemed to be addressing not just them, the male members of A-CHOIR, but many, many others — generations, either way, or a national TV audience. "I think it can be said that one of the purposes of a Riddle education is to enable a man to stand on his own two feet. Stand tall." He glanced at Bung, about five-seven, tops. "To reach for the brass ring. To grab the ball and run with it. All over America, hundreds of small to midsize companies are doing that." Kahn dropped his head and gave a little self-approving chuckle. Now, even without his father, he saw safe ports ahead for him.

"I believe it's fair to say Professor Holt *himself*" — he tossed another look at Bung — "admires independent action and initiative. And has urged such attributes on us. In fact, at times, I've sensed — and Dad feels the same way — that he — "

"What Grant's suggesting," Hedd cut in, a silver

swizzle flashing in his mouth, "is we end-run old Greg on this one — do it on our own. Like so. . . ."

In less time than it takes to tell the story (or it took for Kahn to sit down), Hedd spelled out a plan. They'd collectively compose two letters — "a pair of little masterpieces" — one to President Portcullis, the other to Professor Grebe. Each letter would demand the resignation of the person it addressed, said resignation to be mailed, by such-and-such a date, to a post office box they would rent in town. The letters would both be accompanied by a Xerox copy of what Phil called "The Sweat Lodge Princess Piece." He realized it'd take them a while to compose the letters — none of them being "what you'd call too great of a letter writer" — so that they might not even go out until after midterms, but it'd be worth the delay, in the long run.

"This way, we do the whole damn thing ourselves," Hedd said to Jeffrey Bung. "We neutralize those two, and then young Simon Storm, because he knows too much. At about the same time, actually; I've got a little something planned for him already. And *then* we've got the makings of the atmosphere we're looking for — the stuff to put the campus in a ferment or whatever you call it. You want to see Holt glow with pride? Just watch. He'll give each one of us the kind of letter that makes major corporations start a bidding war. For us. You'll see."

"Before the fall, pride gloweth, what?" said Clovis St. James, quite suddenly and loudly. "And all that rot." He laughed, agreeably.

Everyone else joined in on that — the laughter, that is. It was *already* autumn, so St. James's timetable was a little off, but that didn't matter. The guy had made a cute little rhyme there, sort of like a calypso or something. What an easygoing, lucky dude, they thought — that Clovis. Didn't have a care in the world.

29

Presidential Burdens

Henry ("Gates") Portcullis was astounded when the information in the letter he'd received from Doctors A. and B. checked out. Astounded, then disgusted, then enraged.

Like most large, open-faced, athletic men of action, he didn't like anonymous letters worth a damn, and his first temptation was to crumple up the rotten little thing and throw it in the wastebasket. The reason that he hadn't done just that, in fact, was that the letter had been opened first, and had its contents scanned, by Angela Plangent, his secretary. That was standard office practice so that he, as president, could deal with "first things first." Miss Plangent kept a constantly updated list of the 500 wealthiest Riddle graduates under her blotter, which insured she didn't miss a (first) thing, ever.

So though this letter, obviously, was not the *most* important item in the morning mail, Miss Plangent thought it worth some special mention.

"You have a letter here from Doctors Sparhawk and O'Grady, sir," she said, her heavy, liquid voice pounding at his usual good humor. "Although they didn't sign their names, I'm almost certain it's their work. And even if the charges that they make are true, it seems *despicable* to me that those two back-sta — "

Henry'd waved her off, but when he read the letter, minutes later, he agreed with her indignant tone and didn't question her conclusion. Plangent knew department politics: If she said A. and B. were Sparhawk and O'Grady, you could wear that on a sandwich board while standing in the middle of an open field partway through a major August thunderstorm.

And so Portcullis made a call. A classmate of his and Jared Storm's had made a small, surprising fortune from a chain of herb farms he'd started in the sixties and had retired at the age of thirty-two to the island of Maui. He agreed to buy a ukelele, hurt it, and then take it to a certain fix-it shop. Using that as a pretext, he could then check out the "university," upstairs. The next day he called back and told ol' Gater that his worst suspicions were the truth. Western Hawaii A&T was, basically, an overweight Chinese named Langdon Ho. A PhD was now $200, printed on nice heavy paper stock, or $325 on Australian sheepskin, plus $8.75 postage and handling.

Portcullis rocked back in his chair, then thanked the man and hung up. He felt a little sick. It wasn't that he was particularly fond of Vincent Mowbray. As a matter of fact, the guy had always seemed a little . . . *plastic* to him, a little too slick, too ready with that are-you-with-it smile. But still.

Damn! He dropped a heavy fist down on the letter. Damn Mowbray, anyway. He hadn't had to do this. The man was plenty bright enough to earn a PhD — from lots of places. Or an EdD, anyway. All it took was time and money; you didn't have to be *smart* (God knew).

There wasn't any doubt in his mind about what he had to do. He had to fire Mowbray. Even if Miss Plangent hadn't seen the letter, he would've had to. Cheating was one of the Unacceptables at a university, whether it was done by a student *or* a professor. It was one of the Unacceptables in Gates Portcullis's *life*. Honesty and consistency had helped to give him a happy marriage and success in his present job, and (even) a kid who liked and loved him, both. Messy and unpleasant as the thing would be to do, he had to fire Mowbray, and at once. There doubtless would be flak, but he could take it. That was part of what they paid him for. Doing what was right for Riddle, never mind the short-term consequences. Doing what was (just plain) *right*.

30

Return Engagement

When Simon opened his box in the Bliss Hall basement mail room and saw the letter there with "K. Portcullis" in the upper lefthand corner of the envelope, he felt an unexpected, nonelectric jolt go through his body.

"Whoa," he said out loud, looking at it, smiling cautiously, as if it were an unfamiliar dog and he was trying to judge its personality and style and, more important, its intentions. He felt pretty sure the letter would be special, one way or the other: that it'd either lick his face or take his hand off near the elbow.

He turned it over, got a thumbnail underneath the flap to open it, began to, and thought: No, he had to be alone, unseen, uninterrupted. He slipped it in his pocket and snuck up to his room, where he closed and locked the door behind him, as if he were preparing to perform some foul, forbidden ritual.

"You *are* peculiar, you know that?" he muttered to himself. He sat down on the bed, filled his lungs to near capacity, and finished opening the envelope.

He read the letter once, real fast, and then let out the breath and took another big one, let *it* out, and rolled his eyes around the room. And smiled.

"Ta-da!" he sang, fortissimo, a mini-fanfare. He read it through again, but very slowly, savoring not only what the letter said but what it *was*: the first he'd ever gotten from a girl.

She really did seem to want him to come over; no way you could read it otherwise — as irony, let's say. He decided he would go on Thursday, what the heck. But *not* in order to take advantage of either her or the situation, he hastily assured himself (and any gods of love or luck who might be looking for a little hubris to strike down, an overweening, evil overconfidence). No — hanging out at her house with both her parents gone would be . . . well, different and relaxing, both. *Good* for him. For once, he wouldn't have to talk to and keep up with a single person who was older than himself. Or be subject to the high-pitched, oscillating vibes of other people *wanting it* (so badly *he* could almost taste its rich, full flavor), or worrying that "it" might be beyond their charms and talents.

He had to smile again, this time at himself. He'd walked, talked, read, had a hydroponic garden, seen an amniocentesis done, and gotten into college earlier than other kids. Perhaps he'd have to "take a little break" or need "a change of pace" before most people did.

"Pressure getting to you, kid?" he asked himself, and made a face. He got up and walked over to his desk. He'd decided to write a formal reply:

Mr. Simon Storm, Esq., accepts with pleasure
the kind invitation of Miss Kate Portcullis
for Thursday, 3 P.M.

with an informal addendum:

P.S. What I wrote was: "Conferring with the
parent of a pigeon, court-sport-speaking."
Be prepared to grin and bear it, Vera
Vengeful.

"Slammer" Storm

He thought she'd like that answer; it sounded (to
him) a little like *her* — that is to say, like a kid. As
a matter of fact, for maybe a second and a half he'd
considered writing "bare" it, but in the end had
decided it'd probably be a little *too* childish. Or,
even worse, that she might take it seriously and
either be furious or . . . (gulp) prepared to.

In terms of dress — athletic attire — Simon was
determined not to give Kate even the tiniest advantage this time; if anything, the opposite. And so, on
Thursday, he arrived in the closest he could come
to tennis whites: rugby shorts, a Peacemeal Regional T-shirt, athletic socks, and all-court Pro-sters
(overall effect, not bad, considering his darker eyebrows and his tan). In a little zipper bag he had a
towel, two different swimsuits, clean socks and underwear, maroon warm-up pants with gold piping
on the sides, and this cream-colored sweater that
his mother, drinking cocktails, had declared he looked

"delicious" in, one time. He also put the beeper in the bag.

Kate answered the door in cut-offs, the same bare feet, and a black sweat shirt that said *GIGI* on the front of it, in huge pink cursive script. And a purple headband. Pretty radical cut-offs. She'd spent a few moments in front of a full-length mirror, groping for the word that best described her look. When it came to her, it was: jizzmatic.

Now she said, "*Hey*, Slammer," in that husky voice of hers and stuck a hand out at the guy, and smiled.

He matched the smile, extremely glad to see her, slightly nervous, pleased to see that she was smiling. Hostility — even fake hostility — might have been a little harder to deal with, now that it was just the two of them.

"I'm ready for action," he said, spreading out his arms a little.

"So I see," she said, giving him what had to be a once-over (he thought). "Well, come on in. Action is the special of the week in this saloon. All that you can handle, absolutely free." She smiled again. "Big boy," she had to add.

She told him he could take his bag upstairs and leave it in the living room, that she had just one final bit of dinner-prep to do before they started playing.

"Food-processing the *flapadouce* — that's French for 'bat' — for gravy," she explained. "And don't worry, you can't hardly taste it, in the final product. Not unless you know what you're looking for."

She also told him that it was still nice and weirdly warm for this time of year — wasn't it? — and her parents had called from Cleveland and claimed to be having a good time and her mother had wanted him to know that a half teaspoon of baking soda in about four ounces of water would settle his stomach nicely after dinner — just kidding — and was he getting so sick of that damn beeper, the way she was, that it almost didn't seem worth it, except she certainly would miss the money, every week. And she hoped he liked beef stew, sort of. A sort-of beef stew.

All that was packed into the trip from the front door to the top of the staircase, and there was more coming down and getting to the court. Simon wasn't sure, of course, but he *thought* he could recognize nervous babbling when he heard it. He was a little surprised to be hearing it then, and from that source. But when they started to wallop the birdie back and forth, just warming up, she put a lid on it, and Simon heard a new voice, rap-rap-rapping, ninety M.P.H. Sounded strangely like his own.

"Hey, nice. . . . Look out! Up there — it's a hawk, a redtail. Last week I thought I saw a buzzard flying over where the women's soccer team was practicing, no kidding. . . . Come on, no drop shots, Gabriela; this is just a warm-up, y'know. They've got a real good team, from what I understand, better than the men's. . . . Anyway, it was really huge, whatever it was. I *thought* it was a buzzard. . . . You ready yet? You want to start? Okay, I'd like to try some serves, myself. . . . We've got them where I live, up home — buzzards, that is — so it isn't like I'd never seen the things before. . . . That's out. No, wait, it hit the line, I think. We'd better wait for the instant replay. . . . D'you watch the Giants-Dallas game last Sun-

203

day? I don't blame you, really. I think the players have actually gotten too strong and too fast for. . . ."

Once, when he paused to catch a breath, he asked himself what this was all about. More nervousness? Or something else? Was he, maybe, trying to be "the guy"? (He chipped a backhand down the line and watched the bird fall — barely — in.) Mister Big, male-player-pig? Keeping his cool with a wallow in the word puddle? He must have made a face: Kate raised her eyebrows. So he touched his shoulder, rolled that arm around a little.

They began to play for real, real games. Kate said she'd rather play a bunch of shorter games this time, in which instead of fifteen points to win you only needed seven. They could start a new series. Simon said okay with him. If she'd suggested games of three, or fifty-eight, he knew he would have said, "That's great." He really liked to please her, see her smile.

At first he kept on talking as they played, commentating almost. Kate just played, making only little grunts of effort or of "nice," laughing at a netcord point of hers, and at him when he dove for one and his racket went flying. Simon took an early lead in the first game and held it to the end, but the second game was even, seesawed: 5–4, 5–all, 5–6, 6–all. He stopped the chatter, concentrated hard. She got him with a drop shot: 7–6. Had to win by two, though. Her next serve was high and deep; it pinned him to the baseline. He returned long and, fearing that she'd dink it artfully again, he started toward the net. Instead, she gunned an overhead, wide to his backhand side. He lunged, but only ticked it. Second game to Kate: 8–6.

She grinned. "I'm off the schneid, at least," she said. "No bagels for the Slammerootie." She'd gotten off the sweat shirt, too, in the course of that game. Her top — and bottom layer of clothing, very clearly so — was a silky violet camisole. She looked a little flushed, and happy, and excited. It was his serve.

After a while they stopped keeping track of who'd won how many games; that had ceased to be the point. Long before they stopped, they weren't strangers anymore.

He put on his swimsuit in her bathroom, hurriedly, excitedly. He saw she used the same kind of toothpaste he did, and the same kind of dental floss, and he would have liked to brush his teeth, right then, using her toothbrush, except he was afraid she'd notice it was wet and think he was disgusting or perverted. He looked at her shampoo and her deodorant, getting a funny little charge from all this snooping. He bet she'd smell great, like fields up home in summertime, with wildflowers. The suit he put on was his racing one, his Speedo, instead of the baggy Hawaiian job. Then he walked downstairs with his towel.

She was already in the pool, bobbing froggily around, with her head up and her wet curls shaken out. The sun had gotten lower, but she told him it was nice and warm, the water was, to come on in. She kept her eyes right on him, smiling, didn't look away. He had the same sense of being checked out that he'd had at Lake Dunmore the previous summer, but this time he didn't mind, or wish he was

. . . more this or that. It wasn't just the lack of cigarette smoke, either. He dove, but didn't make a big production out of it; the water wasn't bad at all.

Kate had worn the suit she hadn't dared to wear before, in public. She liked the way it made her legs look — long — and it really didn't show anything it shouldn't, except maybe a little of the sides of her fanny, she guessed, so what was the big deal? The suit didn't *do* much for her chest, but then she didn't ask it to. She had her faults, but lying wasn't one of them. When she got out of the pool to jump up on the diving board and do her forward somersault in lay-out — showing off (a bit) *was* one of them — she peeked but didn't pull her suit down and saw that he was watching. Good; so here I am, she thought. She absolutely liked his looking. She wanted everything to be, like, open: on the up-and-up, between them. She giggled, underwater, thinking that.

Simon used her shower before he got dressed and walked down the hall to the kitchen. She smiled when he came in and told him to help himself from the refrigerator. She said there was white wine open, also beer, both light and regular. And also orange juice and ginger ale — and maybe seltzer, she thought. She said dinner'd be ready in about fifteen or twenty minutes; she was washing lettuce in the sink, wearing black sweats with an enormous pink top and big red beads around her neck. She'd turned away from him because she thought he was so good-looking in that creamy-colored sweater she wanted to scream.

Simon guessed where the glasses would be, got one,

and poured himself some juice. He asked her if she wanted anything, and she said maybe a little wine, so he got out a stemmed glass — showing he wasn't a *total* nerd — and poured, and handed it to her. She held the glass up so as to touch his with it.

"Here's looking at *you, champero,*" she said.

And after that she sipped and said, "I don't much like the taste of this, so I hope you're impressed." And she gave that husky laugh and put the glass down by the sink, where it just stayed.

She set the table in the dining room, where he'd eaten before, but this time they took the seats her parents had had.

She held up matches, pointed at the candles. "Would you mind?" she said. "I know it's corn, but. . . ." He even took the matches, did it for her.

The food was very good, Simon thought: this really rich casserole of tender beef and white beans and carrots, with French bread and salad. That talk of bats in the gravy, that had been a joke. The stew was very nicely seasoned; it was typical of her to say that there were bats in it, typical of the way she joked around. In the candlelight you couldn't tell what you were eating anyway.

"Boy," he said, "you weren't exaggerating about your cooking. This is *delicious.*" That sounded funny to him, him saying that — his *father* said "delicious." But she didn't seem to notice.

"I wasn't kidding," she said. "I *do* like to cook. It's sort of soothing. Maybe I'm a *re-*tard. Phyllis Schlaflyette. Seriously."

"I always liked playing house," he said. "Seriously."

"Yeah, but with you — with guys — it's not a

real option," she said. "You couldn't just play house full-time if you wanted to. Admit it. There's a difference."

"Well, I guess," he said. "But I still like it."

"You know something?" she said. "I want *everything* I do to feel like playing — something like playing. You know what I mean?"

"Yeah," he said. "I think so, maybe. Like doing something hard but having it be fun. Like our badminton game."

She nodded. "That's right," she said. "Or figuring something out. Don't kill me for this, but some of the stuff they ask me to do in school is fun like that, almost like playing around with . . . I don't know, an idea. Or making something come out. If I wasn't so cheap, I'd send some of my Grebe money to Greenpeace. You know what that is, right?" He nodded. "*They* have fun, I bet. It's a lot of risks and they work hard, but I bet they have fun." She shook her head and dropped her eyes. "Except when people start blowing up their boat and killing them. I'd forgotten for a minute."

He picked up another piece of bread and broke it in half.

"One thing that's surprised me here," he said. "At college, you know? Is how most people aren't into that. I don't mean the fun part. I'm talking about stuff like what Greenpeace is doing, that kind of stuff: pollution, nuclear arms control, you name it. Even on an intellectual level, they don't seem to be."

He'd been looking at the nearest candle, but now he looked at her. He didn't know whether this was a good idea or not. It seemed a little heavy for a *date*, if that's what you could call this — and it seemed like you could, in a way. But she'd started it, after all.

"I mean, here we are, like Einstein said" — well, why shouldn't he quote someone? Everybody quoted people, trying to make a point — " 'drifting toward unparalleled catastrophe' and hardly anybody seems to want to *talk* about it, much less change the way they think."

Without thinking, himself, he smushed the bread he was holding down into the gravy on his plate and wiped it all the way around before sticking half of it directly in his mouth.

"It really pisses me off, sometimes," he said.

She was looking at him steadily, with her lower lip between her teeth.

"Before," she said, "the last time you were over here, you said you were still trying to figure out who you were, or something. Words to that effect. Well, didn't you just say, sort of?"

Simon scratched his head over one ear, then put his elbow on the table and leaned against the same hand, and looked at her. She thought he suddenly looked a lot older, with his gray eyes solemn like that, and very slightly narrowed, staring. He looked *smart* to her, too; that was how he looked to her, real smart. It made her sort of tingle, something did.

"Well, maybe, in a way." He sighed. "But I'm such a long way from *doing* anything. *You* must know what I mean. You wonder whether. . . . I don't know." He shook his head.

"Well, I *do* know there's dessert," she said. She bounced to her feet. Things could get *too* heavy. She didn't want him getting off on smartness. "*A* dessert, anyway. So-called. It's an experiment, so don't blame me if it's inedible. Too chocolatey, or something." And she laughed.

He got right up, too, wondering if he'd been boring her.

"*That* I'd have to see," he said. He reached for the casserole; be *fun*, he told himself. "Could I have a doggie bag for this?"

They headed for the kitchen, he, too, apparently content (she thought) to leave the future of the planet in the dining room.

The dessert wasn't too chocolatey. They ate it at the kitchen table and Simon said he wasn't sure after his first piece of it — a kind of cakey pie with home-whipped cream on top — and he tried another piece that just about made up his mind. But then he had to have a third, so as to cinch it, absolutely, not a shadow of a doubt. Afterward, Kate made some coffee, which she served in her mother's formal demitasse cups, just to see what that felt like. He asked if he could have a second little cupful, and she got up and poured it for him, which gave her a peculiar feeling that she wasn't certain if she liked or not. During dessert, they'd talked about less . . . PBS-type stuff, Kate thought: music, movies, even sports and videos. *Mystery!* was going to be on a little later, and they both said they wanted to watch it.

Simon did the dishes. Kate let him insist for a while and then just let him, partly because she wanted to see if he'd have to make a joke of it and partly because she wanted to see if he knew how. Well, he did, all right. He did them thoroughly, intelligently, athletically even — no jokes or bumbling. And didn't even seem to mind.

"Where'd you learn to do dishes?" she asked him.

"Oh, around," he said vaguely, circling a hand above his head. "Actually, my parents let me do them sometimes, as a treat. But mostly I have to sneak a plate here, a cup there, at other kids' houses. Some parents just don't care. They let their kids do all they want, even on a school night."

When they went into the den, where the TV was, it was just the natural thing (Si told himself) for him to drop onto the other half of the little couch, next to Kate. The couch faced the TV straight on, and the chairs that flanked it were both at an angle. He was just going to watch *Mystery!* and leave; he had a lot of work still to do; he hadn't so much as touched her and he didn't plan to.

As the last credits were being flashed on the screen, she said, "Simon?"

And he said, "Huh?"

And she said, "There's something I've been wanting to ask you. Seriously." She leaned forward and turned the TV off. "What's it really like being in college at . . . well, the age you are? I mean, just day-to-day — the regular routine and everything. I wanted to ask you last time. Seriously. But I was too busy being a jerk."

"No, you weren't," he said. "It was just . . . the situation. But, you mean, like. . . ." He waited. He didn't know exactly what she wanted, or how much he felt like saying, either. He thought he'd made a pretty good impression, so far.

"Oh, I don't know," she said. "But, like, with me: I'm a little younger than you, and a girl, so maybe it's different. But I've had almost zilch experience with alcohol and drugs." She paused. "*And* sex — face it, I'm a virgin, as you've probably guessed already. Everybody does, I don't know how. I think I must have a see-through. . . . Never mind." She waved a hand. Si thought he could be blushing and was thankful for the dimness of the room. "See? I don't even know how to talk right. In college, I wouldn't know what to say in class, or at parties, for God's sake, or . . . *any*where. I don't think I'd know when people were serious and when they were putting me on — like, when guys say different things, you know? I guess I'd be afraid of feeling like your basic wimp a lot — over and over and over."

"Oh, well," said Simon.

What he felt like saying to her was that he *liked* the way she talked and was *glad* she was a virgin, same as him, and that as smart as she was, it'd be a cinch for her to get along in class *and* understand the other kids, who weren't all that subtle or mysterious. What he did say was, "It isn't really *that* bad."

With which he started talking. At first he stuck with war stories, you could say: things he knew she'd like to hear because they were funny, or gross, or sensational. Then he switched to bedtime stories, more or less: how interesting and not-too-hard the course work, mostly, was; how friendly and intelligent some students were, "just regular, not assholes in the least." When he'd finished doing that, she didn't say a word, just kept on sitting there, and waiting.

So then he told her how many times he'd wished he was 800 days older and how freaked he'd been when he'd seen the guy flip out at registration, *and* when Asmussen had tried to sell him on The Last Resort (in the event of a nearby nuclear attack), *and* when Mr. POP had come around, and later when he'd realized how much cheating was actually going on. And finally he told her about getting drunk for-the-first-and-last-time-in-his-life and making an idiotic pass at a woman who was old enough to be his . . . baby-sitter.

When he'd finished telling her that, he realized that not only had he told her ten times more about college than he'd told his parents even, but that he'd also mentioned everything that really had impressed him *except* what Hansen Grebe had said about her father and the college.

Mostly, she'd just nodded while he talked — and smiled a little at the part about him and Amanda, making the childhood naughty-naughty gesture with her pointer fingers. When he had finished — shrugging, wondering if he'd maybe gone too far, his own embarrassed smile just jerking at one corner of his mouth — she started saying, "Wow, it really seems you — "

He'd looked down at his watch and jumped straight up. He felt a little panicked by how late it was, but also honestly relieved. Graceful exits sometimes were a problem; now, he had to "run."

But before he opened the front door — she'd walked him down the stairs, of course — he stopped and looked at her and said, "Boy, thanks. I had the absolutely *best* — " And suddenly shut up and reached and grabbed her by the shoulders, pulled her right up next to him, she not resisting. There was a pause, perhaps to give her time to ask a

213

question, plead a previous engagement. She didn't, so he bent and kissed her, and when she opened up her mouth it wasn't (he was pretty sure) to speak.

Good Lord (thought Simon, slithering delightedly on unfamiliar ground, and typically, a real fast learner), the girl, this girl — *my* girl? — is *hot*.

Probably he was surprised; he didn't think about it. In Peacemeal, "hot" did not equate with "virgin," just as it did not equate with "mother" (yours or *anyone's*, in fact). But if he was surprised, he didn't act it, or like anything at all, except a person with a case of terminal delight. She'd wrapped her arms around his back and was plastered up against his front and was making little mm-mmm mouth sounds. He responded in a lot of different ways, all of them unplanned, some of them unprecedented. He was smelling, tasting, feeling more than Kate — like dreams, imaginings, *impossibles*. It occurred to Simon, fleetingly, that he was having the best time of his entire life.

And then, like that, she'd pushed herself away, but not too far, and was holding both his elbows, looking up at him and smiling. Her lips were glistening; her eyes were also shiny, wide.

He had "I love you" in his heart, to say, but his mouth could barely croak, "I think I'd better go," not because he wanted to at all, but just because . . . because he had to say *something*, didn't he?

She raised her eyebrows, but she didn't tell him that he absolutely had to stay.

"I'll be in touch," he added. *That* was cool.

To which she said, "You'd better be," and turned away, still smiling.

31

From the Riddle News

**MARKETING PROFESSOR OUSTED;
PHONY DOC MUST GO, PREZ SEZ**

*Bizzy School in Tizzy;
Mowbray Charges: "Smokescreen"*

President Henry Portcullis announced today the firing of long-time Professor of Marketing and Trends Analysis Vincent Mowbray for "gross academic dishonesty." According to Portcullis. . . .

And later in this article:

When contacted by the *News*, Professor Mowbray said, "This is nothing but a smokescreen and a cover-up. The real reason for my extermination has nothing to do with me or with my competence. I'm being crucified for telling it not only like it is, but also like it will be in the future. You can't cream potatoes with the milk of human kindness, friend — *or* expect to land a decent job with a BA in any of the so-called humanities, and especially including that most useless of all majors in the universe, Women's (ha-ha) Studies. . . ."

32

Rat-Port Midterm

The morning of the Rat-Port midterm test began
almost exactly the way every other weekday morning at Riddle began, for Simon Storm. He woke up
more or less at seven, took whatever time he needed
to collect himself, his towel, hairbrush, Oral B, and
toothpaste, and went out the door of his room and
walked the twelve steps down the corridor that would
get him to the bathroom. When he was through
with his business there — which included the con-
clusion/fact that once again he did not need a shave,
as well as the familiar fantasy in which Clee Clymer
entered, doffed her robe, and asked him if he'd
please, please crowd into a shower stall with her
and put the loofah to her back — he returned to
his room to dress.

The fact that he would soon be taking the midterm test in Rational Portfolio Selection did not
affect his heartbeat or his appetite at all. He knew
perfectly well he would do well (for sure), or even
perfectly (conceivably). Professor Diddleman was a
proven academic terrorist, but *he* was very, very
good at spotting and disarming verbal booby traps.

All he had to do was budget his time, more or less as Phil Hedd had suggested, and there would be no problem.

When he'd finished dressing, he reached for his wristwatch and didn't find it in its usual place on his desk. He didn't exactly panic, but he did spend some time looking for it. First, he looked in all the possible places in the room where it might have fallen, or where he might have, accidentally, put it down. After that, he tried the bathroom and the common room — but not real hopefully. And then he even knocked on the door of Barry Seraphim, the hall adviser and, as such, the person in whose office items lost were often found. Barry shook his shiny head regretfully.

"Sorry, Si," he said. "At the moment, I got neither tick nor tock, pocket nor wrist, Seiko nor Sanyo, quartz nor jewel — why *seventeen* jewels? I've always wondered — solar nor batt — " Simon left him; Barry babbled on. By the time Si got to breakfast, he was (he estimated — accurately) some fifteen-twenty minutes later than he would have liked to be.

He wasn't the only one, though. Thirty seconds after he sat down, Phil Hedd dropped into the chair beside him. Up since four A.M., Phil said, just cramming, cramming, cramming.

Naturally, Si told him all about his problem — his timelessness — and Phil was not just sympathetic, he had something to suggest.

"Borrow one from Amanda or Clee," he said. "They've got a gross of watches, I'll bet. Clee has one to go with every outfit in her closet, swear to

God. And med students — cripes — they need a lot for taking pulses, all that crap, see if people are alive, or what."

Simon brightened, thanked Phil for his inspiration, and quickly finished off his sogged-out flakes and coffee. When he knocked at the door of Amanda's suite, he got no answer so he tried the knob. You'd think she came from Peacemeal, too; it was unlocked. He charged directly in, grinning; it was definitely his lucky day.

"Amanda? Clee?" he called. The place *felt* empty. He crossed the room to touch Clee's four-thousand-dollar electric tanning bed, the BGG Solarium; they hadn't been gone long, it was still warm.

And right there, on Amanda's desk, there *was* a watch, one of those fancy digital jobs with four different buttons and probably the ability to resist water, shocks, temptation, and the three most common venereal diseases.

He was sure she wouldn't mind if he borrowed it. He scooped the little beauty up and buckled it onto his wrist; it cheerfully informed him there were seven minutes, still, to test time. Chances were, he told himself, that he'd have handed in his paper and brought the watch back where he'd gotten it from, before Amanda'd even finished checking over.

In a really popular course like Rat-Port it wasn't possible to make people sit in alternate seats for a test; there wasn't a lecture hall in the college big enough for that. Some people avoided the crowding by taking the test to the library, or back to their rooms (as the honor system let them do), but Simon wasn't about to go that route. If he happened to get a hundred on the test, he didn't want to also get, like, *looks* from anyone. He took a seat a little off to one side, and pretty soon that guy Jeffrey Bung, whom he'd met at The Pub that much-too-memorable night when he'd assaulted Amanda, came in and took a seat almost directly behind him.

Some graduate student assistants of Diddleman's handed out the blue books and then, when that was done, the tests themselves. Simon gave his a quick once-over as soon as he got it, and before he started in. It was exactly as expected: a bunch of fill-in-the-blankses, followed by multiple-choices and true-and-falses, followed by an essay. He went back to page one and started filling blanks.

He hadn't done more than four — all cinchy — when he remembered to check his watch and make a time plan. The instructions suggested fifteen minutes for this part of the test; he'd give it ten. He wondered if the watch had a stopwatch feature; it ought to, from the looks of it. He pressed the top right button, hopefully.

Well, the actual time of day disappeared all right, but instead of reading seconds (01, 02, 03, et cetera) he got (to his complete amazement) words, familiar words, withdrawals from the data bank inside this programmed timepiece-plus. Staring at his wrist, he read:

REMEMBER:
GINNIE MAES
ENERGY P'SHIPS
TAX-FREE MUNIS
NO-LOAD CONV. FUNDS

And the list went on.

Instantly, Si knew what he was looking at: crib notes for the test. And on Amanda's watch. She must have *planned* to cheat, but then, by force of habit (or forgetfully) put on another watch, perhaps the white-faced, doctor-looking one with the sweep second hand that he'd noticed her wearing, before.

Good Lord (he thought). *Amanda*, of all people, had planned a flagrant violation of the honor system. Of everything that Riddle through the years (or formerly) had stood for. And she, a resident assistant, like part of the officialdom; to a (fairly) young Vermonter this was simply unbelievable. His mind careened; she must (he thought) be under awesome pressure (the watch continued spewing information and advice: IGNORE P/E'S IN PHARMACEUTS, have bank loans in the tens of thousands, mounting up. But still, she didn't have to stoop to —

He felt a tap-tap-tapping on his shoulder, turned, and there was Jeffrey Bung, looking at him very solemnly, first squarely in his eyes, then at his . . . *wrist.*

Simon blushed; he felt it happen, couldn't help it. Clearly Bung, this guy, thought that *he. . . .*

"Please see me after the test," Bung whispered (viciously, thought Simon), then bent his head and went back to the exam in front of him.

Simon finished the test with parts of his mind in a total whirl. Not the parts taking the test, though. He got a ninety-eight on it; Diddleman would take off two on the essay part because Simon had written "IBM," instead of the full name of the company.

Diddleman also didn't like the fact that Simon's essay included relevant and cogent arguments he hadn't ever thought of — not to mention being wittier than he had ever been.

The whirling parts of Simon's mind had two things going 'round and 'round in them.

First, was: He had to keep Amanda out of this, take all the medicine himself. Even if she'd put that program in the watch's memory, she hadn't *used* it. Maybe she had never meant to, maybe she had changed her mind — or maybe, as he'd thought at first, she'd absentmindedly put on some other watch. Her plans and motives didn't matter in the slightest, though. The fact was that *she hadn't used the watch.* She'd left this watch behind, never thinking for a moment that anyone would come along and *steal* the thing — as he (let's face it) had. No, he had to keep Amanda out of it.

And second, was . . . just utter gloom and doom. He was going to be accused of cheating. Accused and probably convicted — tossed out of the university. How could he ever face his parents — even with the truth?

We believe you, Simon, they would say, when he had finished with the whole foul story (changing — just — Amanda's name in case she might be wholly innocent). We believe you, they would say, and look away, and he would never know for sure if they were telling him the truth — any more than they would know if *he* was, to begin with.

It was just about the worst thing he could imagine, facing his parents. And *then* there'd be the rest of his life. No other decent college would consider him, for sure. He'd be a second-rater, all the way.

And (oh, my God, he thought) this would absolutely finish him with Kate. She'd think he was no better than the rest of them: just another piece of college scum.

How could this possibly have happened? Why was it happening to *him*?

Bung was all business when the two of them met in the corridor. He told Simon that the correct procedure under the honor code was for each of them to write out a "report," detailing the "facts" — what had happened in the "case." On a separate sheet Simon could also write out, explain, any "militating circumstances," Bung said. "Like, your excuse." Simon would hand his report in to Bung, who would hand them both to the honor committee, which'd decide Si's fate.

"I'm sorry," Jeffrey Bung said, in conclusion, sounding just exactly like the hypocrite Grant Kahn had always known the little swine to be.

33

Resigned

Henry ("Gates") Portcullis, sitting in his study in the Thomas P. Riddle House (a.k.a. his home), was a deeply troubled college president. His experience at Santa Cruz had not prepared him for this. Even growing up in Bronxville, New York, was no defense against a bombshell of this magnitude.

Beside him, on the floor, was the extremely badly written letter, the "demand" that he resign . . . "or else." On top of it was . . . well, that other thing, in Kate's own hand. Her love letter to Hansen Grebe or (to be a great deal more descriptive, also accurate) her *victimized*, *unbalanced*, *tragic howl*. Far, far better-written than the other one, but that hardly mattered now. The substance canceled out the style; there was nothing "good" about the letter.

Also beside him, on a table though, was a bottle of Remy Martin cognac, its contents lessened by a third since earlier that evening. Gates Portcullis wasn't what you'd call a drinking man. A little glass of Dubonnet, a bottle, maybe two, of ale and that was it, for him. But in this crisis he had thought he "needed" something, and "a good stiff brandy" came to mind. That's what you gave to people who'd just had an awful shock; literature was full of good stiff brandies being handed to, and downed by, people in those circumstances. *He'd* had not one, but four such brandies; this was life, not literature.

Now it was pretty clear to Gates he didn't have a choice. He *would* resign; he *wanted to*. If what poor Kate had written there *ever* were made public, she'd . . . just die. (He could really hear her saying that.) Things like this could mark a girl, and follow her all her life. ("Kate Portcullis? Hey, I read about you once! In *Midnight*, wasn't it?") Kate must be (also) taken out of this depraved environment. He should have realized long ago (he told himself) that her constant pseudo-good-humored harping on the *students'* sexual remarks/advances had been nothing more than a . . . a muted cry for help. An indirect appeal for his and Betsy's support and guidance on, their understanding of, a far more gruesome problem. Why hadn't they been wise enough, *tuned-in* enough, to hear what Kate was *really* trying to say?

He didn't think that he could face the women of the household yet. Neither Kate nor Bets. Of course he *would*, in time — because he *chose* to, not because he had to. Being truthful with the two of them meant everything to Gates Portcullis; that was the way they loved each other, in utter truthfulness. But just for now he didn't want them — either one — to see how sad the thought of leaving Riddle made him. He was glad to do it (for the sake of Kate). He knew that, deep inside himself. But still it would be hard to leave this place he (also) loved so much — leave it in the hands of evil men who couldn't even write a decent prose.

He didn't know where Grebe fit in. Was he a part

of this — a member of the group that wanted him removed? He really had to doubt that. Up to now he'd thought of Hansen as a friend, and Betsy'd told him once that Grebe had said to her he thought her husband was "a dream come true — the perfect college president." Plus, it seemed unlikely that Grebe (wasn't he a Princeton PhD?) would conspire with people like the ones who'd done that letter.

But on the other hand, Grebe had obviously taken foul advantage of Kate. There was no getting around that. The man was as rotten as they came. He would have to find some way, sometime, to deal with Mr. Grebe. The Gater's large, strong fingers flexed each time he thought of him. He didn't know, just then, precisely what he meant by "deal with." Picking up the professor by the ankles and whirling him around and around his head before casting him over the side of a whaling vessel directly into the foaming midst of a pack of great white sharks who were engaged in what is called a "feeding frenzy" was one distinct, attractive possibility. Meanwhile, he would just make damn well sure (if that was possible) that Kate stayed far away from him.

Sighing, he got up and walked, with only one small stumble, to his desk, and typed his resignation in two short but well-constructed sentences. He dropped it in a mailbox the next morning, wishing he could send his headache to the same address.

34

Physical

Between the ecstatic moment when they kissed on her parents' doorstep and the heart-sunk one when Bung believed he'd caught himself a cheater, Simon and Kate had time for only one more "date" (as guess-who liked to call it, in his mind). They'd gone to see a movie, and then had an ice-cream cone, and finally came back and sat in her parents' Saab in its garage and took their chances on freezing. That was what they'd wanted to do from the time he'd arrived at her front door — not freeze but have a little privacy. To minimize the risk of frostbite, as a matter of fact, they climbed at once into the backseat of the car, where they could both be downright prodigal with body heat.

What followed was the best of times — that was the way they thought about it, then and later. Kate's father hadn't yet received the sweat lodge letter (let alone talked to her about it), the midterms were a week or so away, so neither of them had any heavy-duty stuff to think or talk about. What they did — could do — was curl up close and let out all the light and lovely — funny! — things that they'd been thinking of: their first, identical reactions to the other one's existence ("Gimme a *break*!"); the different moments each of them began to get this little buzz from some interior detector: Beware of possible relationship ahead; and of course this large-screen Technicolor deal they both felt now, together.

"With you, it's just like being — I don't know — with some sort of ideal person," she said.

"A giant," he suggested, nodding.

"Not exactly a giant," she said, "but someone I hadn't even imagined ever knowing. When we're together now, I'm as relaxed as I am by myself, but I'm also so *excited* all the time. I know that doesn't make any sense, but. . . ."

"Sure it does," he said. "I know what you mean. I used to worry — I bet a lot of people do — about how I'd know when it's really *love*, with someone. Well, now I'm sure that's one of the ways, maybe *the* way. When you feel completely peaceful with them, but also like you want to jump up and down."

"On them," she said.

"Exactly." And he laughed. "Listen to Tom Cruise, Junior — right?"

"I trust you, too," said Kate, not unexpectedly.

"Did I say that?" said Simon, smiling this time.

"You didn't have to," Kate replied, and proved it, kissing him. She felt they were right together, not just on the same page, on the same *line*. She laughed.

"What?" he said.

"The breeding-readiness test — you know I'd flunk it still, for sure," she said.

"I know," he said. "Me, too." Message signed for and accepted.

With that out of the way she was able to tell him

that she thought she'd felt more like a woman since she'd met him than any time in her life, before.

Simon nodded. He'd been amazed at how, when they were kissing and stuff, she seemed so much *older*; that was probably the same thing she was talking about. He told her it was funny: He'd started out thinking of himself as a friend of her parents — he was used to thinking of adults, friends of *his* parents, as sort of older equals. But now he thought of himself as *her* friend; he didn't know where her parents fit in. He said he hoped they wouldn't be shocked or feel betrayed, when they realized what was going on.

"Like this?" she asked and gave him another kiss, this one really hot and wet and wiggly. It cracked them up, but there were others later on that both of them took seriously enough. They laughed, delighted, when, opening the door to leave the car, they saw the windows on the inside had been all steamed up.

Simon's "report," the thing he handed over to Jeffrey Bung, admitted that during the Rat-Port exam he'd been wearing a wristwatch that had material "relevant to the content of the course" stored in its data bank, and (also) that said watch had the capacity to "display such material." He also insisted that he'd never used the stuff, that he was guilty of possession, but of nothing more.

Of course he didn't think "they" would believe him. Why would he have it, if he wasn't going to use it (they would ask)? He wouldn't have an answer other than the classic: "Well, a friend asked me to hold it for him." They'd never in a million years buy *that*. He wouldn't, in their place. Let's face it, he was doomed. He could (and did in the "report") request a retest, as a way of proving that he knew not just the content of the lectures and the text but also all the "suggested supplemental reading" — books that no one in the course (but he) had even touched. They'd probably refuse to give him such a test, claiming that what he knew *now* didn't prove a thing about *back then*.

He couldn't tell Kate; he just couldn't. That was driving him crazy. Every fiber of his being, of his history and style and upbringing, said, "Tell her the whole truth" — and still he couldn't. The problem was: Her father was the college *president*. When Simon was convicted of the cheating charge, she'd (almost surely) feel she had to tell her dad the truth, the truth *he'd* told her. She'd (almost surely) feel she had to try to save her boyfriend. But that would bring Amanda into it — and probably destroy her.

(The other possibility, which he refused to think of — much — was that she *wouldn't* tell her father, meaning she did not believe him, either.)

And so, he just did nothing . . . but avoid her. The other midterms that he had to study for would serve as his excuse. This was the best thing he could do for her (he told himself); let her find herself another boyfriend — she wouldn't have much trouble doing that, he guessed. She'd soon forget about her little fling with him. That thought — which he kept running through his mind — was an exquisite agony for Simon. But still he thought of her each night, before he fell asleep; he'd kept her husky voice inside his head, and a picture of her body, wet-flanked on the diving board. He found out what it meant to ache for someone.

He was in his room one early afternoon, avoiding everything but the facts and implications of U.S.-Soviet relations, when there came a peremptory rapping on his door, a most official answer-me-in-there.

"Come in. It's open," Simon hollered, hoping he sounded like someone with nothing to hide.

It was Amanda. The first time they'd been face-to-face since . . . well, since before. . . .

"Hey," said Simon, neutrally, trying to keep all of his various and conflicting feelings out of his voice. Feelings like . . . well, disappointment and contempt, pity and . . . red rage. Was it even *possible* she'd figured out who had her watch — that Phil, perhaps, had mentioned he'd told watchless little Simon S. to go and borrow one from her? He wondered what she'd say if he just whipped it out and dangled it before her eyes. He did still have the thing, hidden in a bureau drawer. (Bung, being the incompetent that he was, had neglected to secure the "evidence.")

Even as he struggled with those other emotions, Simon had to (still) admit she looked fantastic. For a person with extremely suspect moral fiber. That was the thing about that particular kind of fiber, moral: Apparently it didn't show on surfaces — like change the shape and texture of a person, or her general, like, *juiciness*.

"Look, Simon," she said, urgently. And for a moment there he thought that a confession might be coming next. "We have to do our demonstration physicals this week, on Friday. I'm really, really desperate for more practice. I know it's midterms and all, but . . . could I possibly take you up on your offer? It'd just be an hour, I promise. An hour, *max*."

"Well," he said, "it isn't the absolute best time, for sure." Was this the ultimate in gall? he asked himself. Getting a guy kicked out of the university and then asking him for favors?

Then, of course, he realized — reminded himself — she didn't know he'd taken that damn watch, that he was in this total, desperate stew. And he also realized that this might be his one big chance to get her off her guard and talking — about her debts and other pressures she was feeling, mitigating circumstances. About, in other words, some *explanation* for the watch that *maybe* he could use to save *himself*.

"But I said I'd do it," he went on, "and so I will. When were you thinking of? And where?"

"Well, how about tonight?" she said. "Right here. At . . . oh, say ten o'clock?"

That seemed pretty late for a physical exam, to Simon. That was more like the time for a late date, from what he'd heard. People didn't take off their clothes at ten P.M. so other people could . . . *examine* them.

"Okay, sure," he said. "I only hope I pass the thing."

He was weakly nervous-laughing as she waved and headed out the door.

"Thanks a *billion*, Simon. Really. You're a sweetheart," she opined. "If there's *ever* anything that I can do for you, just say the magic word. . . ."

231

Ha (thought Simon)*! Talk about the ultimate in irony!*

At nine o'clock that night Simon was in the shower getting painstakingly prepared to be examined. He'd already chosen what he'd wear and was trying to remember how long he'd probably get to keep it on: fleece-lined slippers, running shorts (in lieu of underwear), his Vassar sweat pants (a present from his mother), and a light jacket that zipped in the front (so he wouldn't muss his hair when he removed it). He used some Aqua Velva out of the bottle someone had left on a bathroom sink, but in a more . . . *general* way than Pete Rose seemed to, in the ads. When he was dressed, he sat very still and tried to keep from sweating.

She was right on time for their appointment, and the clothes she wore were also rather unprofessional. Under her medical student's white jacket (with the stethoscope sticking out of a side pocket), she had on a pair of Clee's lounging pajamas: flowing, silky, clingy things featuring huge red and purple flowers against a black background. Si had seen the Goddess in them once, before, so in a way he was just as glad Amanda had a jacket on. It crossed his mind that her having to borrow her roommate's clothes was evidence of the economic pinch she must be feeling. Poverty explained a lot of desperate acts, even excused (a bunch of) them.

"Okay," she said, all business, setting down her bag beside his bed. "We'll call this our examining table." She patted the edge of the bed. "So you sit there. And I'll" — she turned and seized the desk chair — "put this over here in front of you."

She sat, glanced at, then placed, her clipboard on the floor beside her, gave him one quick flash of smile, and latched onto his wrist with seeming confidence — looking as she did so at the white-faced watch on her left wrist.

"Hmm," she said, after a bit, and changed her grip a little. More seconds passed and she looked up, let go, smiled again, and made a note on the clipboard. She bent and took a blood pressure cuff out of her bag; then she hung the stethoscope around her neck.

"Boy, you sure have got a lot of equipment," Simon marveled. "On top of your books and all. Not to mention the extra tuition. It must cost an absolute fortune to be a med student."

"I guess," she said, pushing his jacket sleeve up and wrapping the cuff around his upper arm. "Actually, I got this loot — my bag, the instruments, and stuff — from different relatives. Of course when I get certified I'll have to treat them all for nothing, I suppose. So, here we go. . . ."

She finished taking his blood pressure, then started her examination of his fingernails, his hands, his arms, giving him some small instructions, saying "fine" and "very good" a lot. Simon could feel some drops of sweat go running down his sides; he bit his lower lip and crinkled up his nose. By then she was examining his head.

As she looked into his ears with whatever that instrument is called, she startled him by asking, "How'd you do on the Rat-Port, d'you think?" He said okay and then, seizing that opening, he added that he guessed it'd be a while before *she* got to use any of Diddleman's great portfolio advice, seeing as she was a med student with (doubtless) zillions of dollars in loans to pay back before she could begin to start any serious investing.

She didn't reply for a couple of minutes, not until she'd gotten to the part where she was more or less looking behind his eyes with her ophthalmoscope. Her answer, given in a calm and even voice, made him wrinkle up his nose again.

"Not necessarily," she said. "My mother's father's helping me. With the tuition. I guess you could say he's putting me through; I'm kind of a pet of his, I suppose." Her white jacket had come open and Simon inhaled a lungful of a scent more rare and delicate, by far, than Aqua Velva. His nose twitched still another time.

After that, she looked up that same nose awhile and surveyed the inside of his mouth and got him to say, "Ah"; then she felt around his neck a bit before she asked him to take off his shirt so she could listen to his lungs.

She used the stethoscope for that, moving it to different places on his front and sides and back, while he took real deep breaths. He was sure she must have noticed his wet sides, but she didn't go, "Oh, gross," or anything. When she started to do this tapping deal on his back — he knew that it was called "percussing" — he was very conscious of her touch, her hands upon his body. They weren't cold, or hard to take in any other way.

"Okay," she said. "Now if you'll just lie down, like so. . . ."

He bit his lips again; they must be getting close to, *almost* to, the worst part.

"So how do you think *you* did on the Rat-Port

234

test?" he asked her, a little too loudly. "I mean" —
modulating — "did Diddleman destroy your grade
at all, or what?"

"Oh, no," she said. "I really doubt it, anyway. I
had a ninety-seven going in. I guess I'm a pretty
good memorizer. That's most of what med school
is, you know, memorizing. And — I don't know —
I probably shouldn't say this, but I think Professor
D.'s a little overrated as a toughie. If you take your
time, his traps are pretty . . . childish, don't you
think?"

Simon twitched his nose some more and said that
yes, he *did* think so. He also thought that unless
she'd been lying through her teeth for the last half
hour or more, there was no reason in the world for
her to have cheated on the Rat-Port exam. If you
don't count sheer depravity, that is.

"Now," she said, "I'm just going to examine your
heart. . . ." And so she did, with her stethoscope,
and then she started another touching and tapping
routine — which gradually slid down from his chest
onto his stomach. He could feel himself tensing up
as she went along. He'd learned nothing whatsoever
he could *use*, and there wasn't that much left of his
body. Especially if you didn't count parts that he
wasn't all that anxious to have evaluated by a depraved woman (even one who looked like you-know-
who).

"Okay," she said. She'd finished with his belly,
straightened up. "Now if you'd please just take off
. . . those." She gestured toward his sweat pants as
she turned and bent to reach into her doctor's bag.

Simon took a deep breath, undid the drawstring
at his waist and, with one mature, smooth, easy

motion, slid the sweat pants and the running shorts, together, off his body. And then the baby closed his eyes.

Amanda turned back to the body on the bed and made a high-pitched sound, a sort of, "Yeeps." And in the next moment she'd whipped off her white jacket and tossed it more or less between Si's navel and his kneecaps.

When Simon opened up his eyes — of course he did so instantly — she was pivoting away from him already, blushing just as much as he was.

"I just want to examine your *legs*, simp-o," she said. "We don't do private body parts with . . . strangers yet. So get some shorts on, will you, pretty please? And gimme my jacket back?"

Simon found himself resenting that. Not the requests or the "simp-o," but the "strangers." They'd been through a lot together, and he'd done as much for her in the last week as any real close friend could ever do. Plus, he'd just had a glimpse of her in the Golden One's sheer pajamas, so he'd certainly seen a good deal more of her than any stranger ever would, he hoped. "*Strangers.*" That was really cruel of her.

But he wasn't going to argue the point. Better "strangers" than having her . . . whatever. He separated his running shorts from the sweat pants and got them on. *And* tossed the jacket at her shoulder. There.

Amanda finished the exam without a lot of extraneous chatter, and with the jacket on and buttoned. She checked out his feet and legs, got him to sit up for a couple of reflex tests, and had him walk across the room and back. When all that was over with, she told him he could get (completely) dressed again. At that point, she picked up her clipboard and wrote for about a minute before asking him if he'd mind just sitting down again. He did as he'd been asked, but he chose the hassock this time.

"You're fine," she said. "Just about a perfect specimen for your age group — physically. As far as I could tell, anyway."

There'd been a definite, deliberate pause after "age group," he thought. And what did that last part mean?

"There's just one little thing," she added. "You seem pretty tense, I notice. Maybe it's the midterms, but you *do* seem . . . well, stressed-out a little. Some minor facial tics, that kind of thing, pulse a few beats quicker than we'd like to see it. What I'm wondering is, if you've thought of doing anything to . . . I don't know, maybe come to grips with your whole *situation* here."

Simon briefly considered bursting into hysterical laughter, but instead he simply raised his eyebrows.

"Obviously," she said, "you're a brilliant individual. But because of your — *you* know — age, you probably *do* feel a little out of it, at times." She smiled at him, perhaps a little meaningfully, he thought. "Nothing to be ashamed of, of course.

"So what I was thinking," she went on, "was maybe if you did something like a firewalk — you know what one is, right? I think I brought it up before. Where you get to walk barefoot over a bed of hot coals, but after you've been prepped for it, of course? Maybe something like that would help you put the whole Riddle experience in proper perspective, you know what I mean? *Prove* to you there's nothing that's beyond you here, on any level. Jack up your confidence, in terms of the nonacademic side of things."

She leaned back in her chair and crossed a leg. The jacket fell open again.

"There's this . . . like, well, counseling technique called neurolinguistic programming." She smiled as if she'd said something outrageous. "Pretty far out, not exactly horse-and-buggy medicine, but, hey — let's not rule it out without a hearing. Me, I'm frankly just a little bit holistic," she admitted with another smile.

"Holistic-er than thou, no doubt," said Simon, mumbling. He found he wasn't in a real great mood, here.

And she said, "What? Well, what it does is teach you to use something called *modeling*. In your case, for instance, all you'd have to do is learn what they call the *belief system*, and sort of the *style* of successful kids a few years older than you. And — bingo! You'd be able to *be* them. Isn't that amazing? What I mean, of course, is you could be exactly *like* them — to the point of having their thoughts and attitudes and, most important, their *effectiveness*." And *whap!* another smile.

"But wait. I must be missing something," Simon said. "The firewalk — "

". . . is just a *metaphor* for all the rest of it!" she said, delightedly. "What it does is show you — *prove* — that modeling does work. That you can *then* do all the other stuff."

"You mean," said Simon, narrowing his eyes, "that once I've modeled on a firewalking teacher and walked on hot coals and proved to myself I can do *that*, I can then do the same thing: study — model on — Phil Hedd or Grant Kahn and do the things that those guys do?"

"Uh-hunh," said Amanda, nodding vigorously. "You actually could."

"Wow," said Simon, imagining himself with a cocktail stirrer always in his mouth and Brad Hammond for a roommate, and with an absolutely incredible tan and girls crawling all over him and a couple of million in a trust fund. And best of all, still in — that's not kicked out of — Riddle U. "Far out. But the trouble is, I don't believe it."

"But that's where the firewalk comes in, silly. Think about it," Amanda said. "Right now, you probably don't even believe you can walk barefoot over hot coals, either, right? But you can. I'm sure of it. I know people who have *seen* this being done. If I were you, I'd think about it, Simon. Seriously. I want you to. And there's going to be a chance to do one here for free, next week, I think. The Research Associates and some foundation's going to sponsor it. It could change a whole lot of things in your life for the better." She gave him what he thought was a totally meaningful look, followed by — he wasn't sure of this but it could have been — a real fast wink. "It could unlock all sorts of . . . potential, and get you what you want *right now*, instead of having . . . well, to wait for it, grow into the experience, or whatever."

Simon shook his head. He was feeling as if he could use a few hundred extra days right then. What was she saying, exactly? She hadn't rebuttoned her jacket. But yet, she surely couldn't mean. . . . It was getting late. He still had studying to do. She'd seen him naked on the bed — that couldn't possibly have triggered all this? Or could it? Impossible — come *on*. And anyway, he had a girl friend. Except he didn't — all because of her. Was he being propositioned? Promised? *Paid back*, even?

"I'm not sure," he said. "I . . . I'll think about it. Now I've really got to — "

"Fine," she said. She stood up; he stood up. "Thanks again for the practice. You really were a groovy patient, Simon." And she laughed.

She bent, picked up her bag, stepped right up to him, and with her free hand on his upper arm, leaned and kissed him on the cheek. Then she silky-whirled around and floated out, trailing scent and, "Have a real good night now, hon."

Simon sank down on his hassock once again. He'd certainly never seriously considered walking on hot coals before — for anyone, himself included. But maybe, now, he should. Face it, he had nothing else to lose and possibly one thing to gain.

He rose and stumbled toward his chair, and the simple world of U.S.-Soviet relations.

35

Snapshot

Brad Hammond had been thrilled when he was chosen by the other (male) members of A-CHOIR to be the one to check the post office box in the Town of Riddle P.O. for the first two weeks. That was the box (number 138, as a matter of fact) that Phil Hedd's fiancée *pro tem*, Ancy Burdock, had rented on their behalf — not knowing why, of course — so that President Portcullis and Professor Grebe would have a place to send their resignations to. If Brad Hammond hadn't known better, he would've said the word *fiancée* meant any reasonably well-stacked, good-humored female Riddle student who, for a period of several months, tidied up the suite he shared with Phil — and often washed their glasses in the shower (with P. Hedd).

As he shambled toward box 138 for the eighth or tenth time, Brad Hammond took no notice whatsoever of the bag lady sitting on the radiator no more than eight feet away from the box. He'd known for years that (so-called) bag ladies had plenty of money for liquor and lived on federally funded handouts that had slipped through the cracks in the safety net that government officials planned to seal up at the same time they closed the window of vulnerability. But Brad Hammond also believed there was a job out there for every bag lady in the country to get off her ass and get — that's if there *were* any bag ladies after all, which he couldn't say for sure, because up to now, he'd never seen one.

Based purely on appearance, it'd be hard to say what job would've been the perfect one for the bag lady on the radiator. She wasn't much of a looker, with that kinky steel wool hair, parted in the middle and barely held down by a Cub Scout neckerchief. The pink feather duster sticking out of the Neiman-Marcus shopping bag suggested an affinity for domestic science, maybe. But the cameras around her neck proclaimed a photographic inclination, too.

She raised one camera and pointed it at Hammond just as he inserted his box key in the appropriate hole. She pressed the button — and a spring snake, cloth-covered, with big red and green spots and painted yellow fangs, flew out of the "camera" and struck box 99. Hammond turned his head a tad to look at it — his key still in his hand and in the lock — and so the lady got a nice three-quarter shot of him, and then two more, this time with her Canon AE-1.

Professor Grebe had long been quite the amateur photographer, and Cheryl Tiegs had steered him to the AE-1. She hadn't said, specifically, that it was great for shooting blackmailers, but Grebe was pretty sure it'd be perfect for the job.

The box (which three short days before had held just what they wanted from the president — Portcullis) was bare of resignations this time. It held, instead, a single postcard that Brad Hammond didn't understand at all, and threw away at once so that he wouldn't have to think about it. On the back, or message, side, it just said: *GOTCHA!*

36

Upstairs at Biccoletto's

Phil Hedd chose the binder this time — or the cover, the folder, whatever you call the thing you put a bunch of papers in to make them look important. The one Phil chose was royal blue, extremely classy, heavy plastic — sure — but with the look, the feel, almost the *smell* of a quality leather. In other words, this cover was a perfect match for, and almost identical to, the white one of *The Handbook for University Reorganization*™, which Professor Holt had shown them weeks before and which had come direct from central casting (so to speak) in Washington.

Before too long, Phil Hedd believed, he'd go and buy a *red* one, too, and put the resignation that they'd soon receive from Grebe in it. So there you'd have the set, complete: red, white, and blue. Everything you'd need to customize a Model T-type education, and make it like a new Mercedes.

Of course at the time they'd originally extended the dinner invitation to Professor Greg Holt, the (male) members of A-CHOIR had expected that the royal blue folder would have all *four* items in it: the Simon Storm confession (soon to be chiseled

244

into the cornerstone of a major, college-wide cheating scandal), the Portcullis and Grebe resignations (which would open up the presidency of the college; neutralize a dangerous, liberal opposition figure; *and* blow the lid off a campus kiddie-porn ring), and the original of Kate Portcullis's sweat lodge piece (the perfect fodder for the ruminants who read enough to know which one's the *New York Post*). But as the day of the dinner drew closer, there were still only the three in it. Should they consider canceling, they asked each other? The decision was to go ahead; they'd already reserved the private room at Biccoletto's, and Grebe would surely come through any day. Holt would have to be delighted with what they'd already accomplished, and besides, he'd soon be starting on those (glowing) letters for their transcripts.

Grant Kahn, for one, looked forward to the role switch, too — where *they* would be the hosts and Holt would be the guest. "He who pays the piper calls the tune," and he (he knew) was "Born To Run" (it all, someday).

The afternoon before the dinner, Kahn had actually gone down to Biccoletto's to check out the room so he would know what tie to choose. When he saw the place — high-ceilinged, dark wood paneling and velvet hangings, shining crystal, bright white napery — he knew his only choice was black. Evening clothes were called for by this room (or "would look real swanky," as his father's father would have said). G.K. thought it'd be "fun" if all of them — that's Phil and Brad and Bung and what's-his-name, as well as himself — wore dinner jackets and "forgot" to tell Holt that they'd be going formal. The professor had once talked to them about "the natural one-downness of the underdressed," and it'd be interesting and instructive (Kahn thought) to see how a seasoned campaigner would deal with such a problem situation.

Of course he never got to find out. Either because "great minds think alike" (as G.K. decided) or because "children must play" (as St. James thought), Professor Holt showed up in a tuxedo, too. *And* with a rosette in his lapel, which certainly looked (again to St. James) like the French Legion of Honor.

"No, I just assumed that we'd be dressing," Holt said to the crestfallen Bung, who was trying to find out if someone chickened out and spilled the beans to curry favor (Bung ate lots of Mexican) — and whose rented outfit drew a lot of smirks, behind his back.

The food and wine were excellent, as far as any of them knew. Kahn had telephoned the highest-rated Italian restaurants in New York and San Francisco and, using his father's name, had solicited suggestions for the menu. The conversation was well-seasoned, too, for much was going on at Riddle that they all were very much concerned about, and even pleased by.

One and all agreed that Professor Vincent Mowbray's firing had been "a masterpiece of management," by Holt. He'd planted information that had blossomed into action and continued to yield fruit weeks later. As soon as the president released the news of the professor's dismissal (on that phony credentials charge), the *Riddle News* was positively swamped by a wave of indignant student letters (none of them well-written, but so what?), which more or less echoed Mowbray's initial reaction to his firing: that he'd been gotten rid of just to shut him up. And that the chances of a Riddle graduate in any of the humanities finding a job that paid more than the minimum wage were, as Mowbray contended, almost nonexistent, absent nepotistic influence, of course.

Some of the letters made for painful reading, descriptions of young people's dreams turned into nightmares:

> . . . so I sit their with my mouth just gaping open while the guy from M.I.C. goes through my transcrips line by line, laughing till he wets himself. When he gets done he looks up at me and goes 'Well Mr. Herringbone, what I'd suggest is maybe you can find a game show to get on' And then he laughs some more. I ask you: This is what my parents sold my little sister for?

After a few days, the letters had been supplemented by the arrival of a group of demonstrators who marched around the main administration building. Unsurprisingly (in the efficient eighties, when students are careful not to jeopardize their grades, or health, or reputations) these were poor people hired by enterprising business majors outside of offices in the city that were formerly occupied by discontinued social programs. Many of them were black and women and they were paid in cash and off the books out of a discretionary fund controlled by the chairman of the department of economics. Some of the signs they carried were hand-lettered by the same Riddle students who'd recruited them, others they had done themselves. It was hard to tell which ones were which, to tell the truth. DO'NT MAKE RIDDLE GRADS TURN INTO US, one read. Another just demanded: REINSTITATE MOWBRY NOW! A third was almost spiritual in tone: LET MY NET WORTH GROW.

Everyone in the second floor dining room at Bic-coletto's agreed that "*l'affaire* Mowbray" was definitely having a campus-wide effect. Bung had actually *seen* an English major hurl his copy of *Sir Gawain and the Green Knight* at a nut-gathering campus squirrel, and everyone had noticed those few members of the philosophy and religion departments who'd organized a fairly feeble counter-demonstration complete with signs detailing the estimated net worth of Norman Vincent Peale, Billy Graham, Bhagwan Shree Rajneesh, and Art Buch-wald, among others. Two women students wrote the *News* to say that inasmuch as they planned to make their money the old-fashioned way, by mar-rying it, they felt that they were smart to put their faith in romance languages instead of, say, statis-tical analysis, "*n'est-ce pas, mon cher docteur man-qué?*"

Because (or in spite of) all of this, the (male) members of A-CHOIR and Professor Holt were unanimous in their opinion that Vincent Mowbray was turning out to be an exceptionally memorable martyr. Brad Hammond even wondered out loud if it might be possible to name, or even rename, a building after him, "*come de ravolution*" (he concluded, with a grin). No one thought that last bit was very funny, except for Clovis, who would laugh at anything.

Phil Hedd purposely kept the blue folder under his chair until the brandy had been poured, and the cigars were drawing well, and the waiters had withdrawn from the room. To everything there is a season and this deserved (at least) a smoke-filled room.

He handed it across the table with a flourish, and his fellow members all shut up, as one.

"What's this? What's this?" asked Holt, in genuine surprise. He hadn't been expecting a gift of any sort, of any magnitude, just then — though, granted, they were coming into recommending season. So what did this appear to be? Some bonds, perhaps? An oil lease, or some other sort of deed to something valuable?

"Just a couple of heads for the old trophy room," was Phil Hedd's unexpected answer. "We wanted to surprise you, sir."

Holt opened up the folder. Nothing gilt-edged or negotiable, but yet. . . . He started reading through its contents.

"Portcullis . . . neutralized," he said. "Delightful. And the makings of a cheating scandal — starting with Amanda's baby brain, I see. Is that strategic?" He read the next page, smiled. "And here? Do I assume that Ms. Portcullis's fellow perspirer is none other than a certain coo-coo prof we talked about before?"

That set them all to talking more or less at once, each trying to make it seem that *he* had *really* been the one who . . . *you* know. But out of the general bedlam Holt extracted information. About Grebe and Kate Portcullis. About Grebe and Simon Storm (who *had* become a legitimate, strategic target once he'd told them, in a semi-drunken state, about Grebe knowing something — and possibly everything — about Washington's interest and involvement in the reorganization of the university).

"Wah," said Holt, and drank some brandy. That was something of a body blow. Somehow, there'd been a breech of security. Either one of the (male) members of A-CHOIR was a double agent, reporting to Grebe on a regular basis, or someone else had gotten into his files. He was virtually certain that Kahn, Hedd, Bung, and Hammond were all too cautious, greedy, and unimaginative to be traitors. His wife Renée and little Jessica (or Freddy) were better possibilities. They all had scores to settle with their lord and master, and both Renée and Jessica were known to be daily readers of the *New York Post* and the columns of the psychologist Dr. Joyce Brothers. There could be a connection there, he mused. But for now Phil Hedd was talking . . . again.

". . . we can't figure out is how come Grebe hasn't come across as yet — saved his reputation's ass by quietly resigning. We've got him absolutely dead to rights, I'd say. Statutory rape, right, sir? Plus child abuse, corrupting the sweat glands of a minor" — Hedd giggled — "maybe desecration of a Native American custom, something like that? I mean, we got exactly what you said you bet we'd maybe get on him, Professor Holt. Well, didn't we?"

Phil's voice had gotten a little strident, there, because Professor Greg Holt was staring once again at Kate's sweat lodge piece and pursing and un-pursing his lips. He didn't even seem to be listening.

Finally, he looked up and said, "You sent Grebe a copy of this? With a demand for his resignation? And you've had nothing back from him?"

They all nodded, except for St. James, who was blowing smoke rings down the center of the table: nothing, nothing, nothing.

"Well, I believe that I can tell you why you haven't," Holt went on, biting off the words. "This Kate Portcullis piece is just a fantasy. Her father may have bought it, but you all know how smart *he* is. Grebe couldn't have been in the sweat lodge when the beeper sounded — you know why? 'Cause he's the guy — and he can prove this, bet your life — who sets those beepers off!"

While the other (male) members of A-CHOIR sat stock still and processed that, Clovis St. James leaped to his feet, draped a napkin over his arm, and sped around the table filling brandy glasses. Then he sat back down and blew another set of smoke rings, dealt them all around the table, you might say.

The next half hour was not a joyful time in the back room on the second floor of Biccoletto's restaurant. Phil Hedd, Grant Kahn, and Jeffrey Bung all felt like stupid *penguins* in their dinner clothes. Perhaps because Holt himself had suggested the possibility of Grebe being "involved" with some adolescent in the study he was doing, they'd just rushed to the conclusion that he *had* been, and in the way this sweat lodge document suggested. They'd never thought to think about *mechanics*, other than. . . . Oh, never mind.

Brad Hammond didn't get it; Clovis St. James couldn't have cared less.

Kahn and his friends would still have to pay the piper, a gentleman by the name of Brancusi ($487.95, plus tip), but Greg Holt now called the next few tunes.

Grebe was more dangerous than ever, he said; he'd been alerted and now knew that someone knew that he knew . . . something. But Grebe would know that *they* knew that, so possibly that meant he would be *less* alert, and would even assume that they'd never dare to try to set him up again, particularly in another sex scandal. Holt's idea was to move quickly to plan A (for Amanda). He'd make a deal with her: trade her Simon Storm's admission to A-CHOIR for Grebe's . . . neck in a noose, let's say. Or if she knew about Simon's being caught cheating, he could even trade her a guaranteed exoneration or a *nolle prosequi*. All she had to do was get some stuff with Grebe on film, or videotape. He had some real California-type activities in mind, he said, things that'd necessitate the use of a second girl, too, namely Amanda's roommate, Clee Clymer. That'd be expensive, Holt told them; it just so happened that he knew Clee had her price, and it was one set by the Bavarian Motor Works, and went on four digits after the two. But it'd be worth it, Holt said, and maybe they could get a good chunk of that back after selling the film or the tape to a studio or a magazine. He would right away get started on Amanda.

When they broke up for the evening, no one was in all that good a humor, as far as anyone could see (who didn't see St. James, and that was everyone). It was just a lucky thing, Greg Holt opined as they went down the stairs, that Portcullis was as dumb as they were, or too chicken to control (or failing that, confront) his fourteen-year-old daughter.

37

One-on-One, Times Three

The sun was shining brightly Wednesday afternoon as Simon dragged along the black-topped walk that connected Bliss and the library. He had one midterm left to take, which didn't bother him at all. His hallmates, classmates, and even strangers on the Riddle walks had never seemed more friendly, nattily attired, or in better shape. He had just done, dried, and folded a large wash, and before that, for lunch, he'd eaten three tacos which, digestively, had left him feeling strong and basic and a man of courage. He didn't owe anybody in the world so much as a postcard, and he believed his downy face-fleece might be turning into *beard*.

Yet he still was feeling close to totally bummed-out, buried in a dark blue slime, lower than the abdomen of *Señor Anaconda*.

His problem was — what else? — that Damoclean cheating mess, still hanging over not just short-term peace of mind but his entire future. Never had he felt so helpless, so lacking in control. His fate was in these other people's hands, he guessed — this honor committee — and they were certainly taking their time. He'd tried to figure out if this was good or bad. Maybe it was *great*. If the case had seemed completely cut-and-dried to them, chances are he would have been long gone; the fact that they had not just glanced at it and then said, Hit the bricks, kid, meant (perhaps) his arguments were working. Maybe he would get his re-test and the chance to prove he'd never have to cheat. But another explanation — the more likely one — was that they'd been busy with their own exams. Once the period was over, *then* they'd take up any (all the) cases that they had, like: bang, bang, bang. Take that — there, Mister Cheater.

There wasn't anything that he could do. Except the firewalk. It was scheduled for Saturday night, down at the Riddle Stadium, and he'd decided he would do it. Not because of anything . . . about Amanda, but for other reasons. What the heck (he'd thought), maybe it'd help him, just in general. Maybe it could give him back some confidence, some sense of his own worth, some hope that he might have a decent future (still). Some idea of what on earth he'd say to Kate, if he ever dared to talk to her again.

"Simon! Hey, Simon!"

He recognized the husky voice before he saw her. She had on coveralls and gloves, a woolen cap pulled down around her ears, and was raking — jabbing at — the leaves beneath the rhododendrons by the library. This was her latest strategy for keeping gross male students off her case, on campus. She dressed like a workman, a member of a group that they were careful not to see.

"I called you at the dorm," she said, "and some-one told me you were playing touch on the college green. You weren't there, so I came over here. I figure everybody's gotta go, sometime." She did a thumb thing at the library.

"Anyway. Come here," she said. "I've *gotta* talk to you." And she pulled him by the front of his jacket around behind the rhododendrons, where she didn't talk, but kissed him. Simon liked the kissing part, which also meant he didn't have to talk. Also, he was glad that they were out of sight. In his present frame of mind he really didn't want to be seen kissing a workman.

They ended up sitting with their legs dangling into the well outside one of the library's basement windows, and Kate sure did have a lot to talk to him about. She simply *had to* tell him (she explained) about the awful thing she'd done: merely wrecked her father's whole career and possibly his mental health as well, while also jeopardizing the future of *their* thing, by forcing her parents to move. Simon goggled at her.

It was just the night before (Kate said) that Gates Portcullis finally showed her "Sweat Lodge Slop" (as Kate referred to it) to Betsy. Who'd merely laughed at it and taken him to Kate. Who'd also laughed — hysterically, almost — and then explained the whys and wherefores of the thing, and asked her father (quite derisively) if he would ever think that she. . . . But then he'd hit them with his heater, with the real bad news. He showed them both a copy of the letter that he'd gotten (with the "Sweat Lodge Slop"), and of the resignation that he'd sent, in consequence. He told them he felt *good* about resigning, that he'd been thinking of retirement for quite a while — at least from Riddle. That he'd been feeling "stale." Kate did not believe him, but he made her *say* she did. The family did not go into, as a group, just how the "Sweat Lodge Slop" had got from Grebe's hands to . . . whoever's. In certain ways, that hardly mattered.

"I stink, you know that, Simon? I just *stink*," she said. "I'm sharper than all the venomous fangs in the snakehouse, I am. What a daughter, what a friend! And Daddy made me promise not to go to Grebe. He said *he'd* do that, later on, sometime."

Simon sat there, stunned. He felt like the twentieth-century small college version of the prophet Job. Talk about unfairness. These were meant to be the happiest years of his and Kate's lives, their carefree childhoods. Could he, by some perversion of the A.P. process, be already in a midlife crisis? He shook his head. And realized Kate was shaking *him*.

". . . all right?" She seemed to have been asking him a question. "You look just awful, Si. I didn't mean to — "

"No, no, no," said Simon. "No, it isn't that. I mean, it *is*. That's the lousiest thing" — except for that one other — "I've ever heard in my entire life. But — I don't know — it isn't your fault, really; you shouldn't blame yourself. You couldn't have foreseen. . . . Poor *you*." He patted her head, and the cap slid sideways off her curls. He groped for something else to say.

"Maybe. . . . Look — you want to do a firewalk with me?" He just blurted that out, without really thinking, but even once he'd thought, it didn't seem like such a bad idea. He and she together. Misery loves company. Maybe they could salvage something from this mess. And anyway, she needed a distraction, too.

"It's free," he said. "On Saturday, at night. Down at the stadium. Some foundation's picking up the tab for everyone who wants to do it."

Of course she had to hear the details, what little bit he knew. When she did, she got excited. It sounded crazy and outrageous. She could learn to be like anyone (she asked)? Like, say, Sean Penn? *This* she'd have to see.

They stayed there for another half an hour, talking (blackmail, parents, what she'd actually written in the sweat lodge thing, how missing someone felt). And they kissed a little, too. Simon felt some pangs of guilt for not telling her *his* world-disrupting news, but he just couldn't, didn't dare. Not yet, not yet. Maybe once the firewalk was over. . . .

Given Simon's kind of mind, it figures that the instant he heard about this scheme to force Portcullis to resign, he flashed back to the stuff that Grebe had told him at the time of their first meeting. Now he needed to know more. He couldn't help *himself* (perhaps), but maybe he could help his girl friend's father. Kate had promised not to go to Grebe, but S. Storm hadn't. So as soon as S. Storm left his own true love, he headed for the second floor of Frabbit Hall.

"In-come," said Grebe's voice — it sounded rather strange — in answer to his knock. Simon opened the door and did as he'd been told. And there was the professor, in the middle of the room, hanging upside down from the ankles in one of those in-

258

version apparatuses that are alleged to do wonders for a person's circulation, lumbar region, and (even) disposition. He had a gray sweat suit on again, with the same black high-topped sneakers, and his thick, kinky hair looked even funnier inverted, falling left and right from its deep center part.

"Oh, excuse me, sir," said Simon, with his manners showing, starting to back out.

But Grebe held up (or, rather, down) a palm and said, "Simon! Yo! Come in, come in, it's good to see you. You look funny, upside down like that. Why don't you put your seat in one of my hands, as the bish — Or did I use that one already? How ya doin', anyway?"

Simon sat on the edge of one of the leather-covered palms and looked down curiously into Grebe's inverted face. It was hard to read someone's expression that way. But he decided to come directly to the point.

"Professor Grebe," he said. "That plot you told me about? The one to change the university into a business school — like, take it over? Well, I've reason to believe" — he found himself sounding like Her Majesty's Secret Service — "it's started. That it's underway." He paused a moment, hoping for a muffled oath, at least a start. When he got neither, he continued.

"Unfortunately, the fact I just received is confidential. But it's bad. Almost the worst. It looks to me as if their plot is working. So what I thought is, maybe we — or I, that is — could try to, well, *fight back*, some way. What I was thinking was: if you could give me, like some stuff that I could *leak* . . . to Woodward and Bernstein, maybe. Or Mike

259

Wallace. Or possibly even Ann Landers, in a pinch; you know how many readers *she* has."

The upside-down professor didn't move or change expression. Simon leaned way forward in his chair.

"Remember what you wrote down on that piece of paper? The first day I came up to see you? That one name? I thought if I could leak some evidence of *his* involvement in the plan, well, that'd be the perfect way to — "

Grebe's head began to move, but it was shaking, back and forth. And rather fiercely, Simon thought.

"It wouldn't work," Grebe said. "What I have is evidence, all right, but he'd just wave it off with some vague explanation and a smile. You know this just as well as I do: No one wants to hear thing-one that's bad about the guy." He sighed. "I know you're right, though. Things are starting up. Some sorry sons-of-bitches even did a number on this office. Looking for I-don't-know-what-but-maybe-I-can-guess." He gave one bark of laughter. "Well, they screwed up completely. Looks to me like they were trained by the same people who trained the guys for Watergate. You know what they got? Two things. One silly scrap of paper — something from our adolescent study — and my Batman mask. My *Batman* mask! How low can you get? We're talking evil people here, my boy."

Simon slumped back in his chair. Fast as you can say, "Computerland," he'd gotten . . . well, if not exactly *It*, a lot of it. A lot of real bad *something*. Here it is, in order.

Item One: He'd told that tableful of people at The Pub what Grebe had said about the college. Which (Item Two): caused them — more than one of them, for sure — to search Grebe's office for some details, and discover (yes!) poor Kate's small sweat lodge joke. Proof (and Item Three): He'd seen Brad Hammond in a Batman mask the day before, swinging from a curtain in the common room in Bliss. Item Four, and proof that there was more than one of them involved: Brad Hammond was incapable of acting on his own, even unsuccessfully.

Add up Items One through Four and you got this: *Simon Storm* had brought about his girl friend's father's resignation, the plotters' first successful ploy, and possibly the end of Riddle U. as (since 1815) the Barron's College Guide had known it. *Simon Storm*, not Kate Portcullis, had done that.

He stared at Grebe again. It was still impossible to tell what he was thinking, upside-down, but Simon — *he* felt worse than ever. He slowly let himself pitch forward, head first, from his chair — then got his hands down, legs up, in a headstand. Now, at last, Professor Grebe looked normal, sympathetic even. Two fat tears squeezed out of Simon's eyes and trickled down his forehead.

"Good Lord," said Hansen Grebe, in horror. "You shouldn't have to cry. A new position ought to be a lot of *fun*. Or so the ingenue informed the man of God, from what I understand."

Simon had to smile at that one, but the tears kept coming, anyway. Floodgates had been opened, and out of him they poured along with words, words, words: Items One to Four, above. You could call it a catharsis, a confession, I suppose. But not a total one. He told Grebe everything *except* about Amanda's watch, and about this new suspicion that he had: that *he* had been — adroitly — framed.

Hammond, Hedd, and Jeffrey Bung had all been in The Pub the night he'd gotten — hey, *been* gotten — drunk; Hedd had told him where to find that watch and little Bung had nabbed him "using" it. What he realized now he'd have to do was. . . .

". . . disgusting," Grebe was saying. "We *must* get Henry's resignation back, and Kate's amusing little fictional adventure, and et cetera. Don't slap yourself around unduly, Simon; the fault is mine as much as yours. I should have put the torch to what Kate wrote the second that I saw she hadn't used her code name. So leave it to me; I think I have a way to deal with this. In fact, it's started up, on line, already. I promise you I'll call you in a day or two, all right?"

In a moment both of them were right-side up again, and shaking hands, their jaws both firm, resolved, their four eyes blazing. In another moment, Si was out the door and speeding back to Bliss. He couldn't believe what a *pigeon* he had been, what a gullible *baby*. But maybe, still, with Grebe's help and Amanda's. . . .

The ashen-faced young man had been talking nonstop for the last fifteen minutes, but now he sat there silently, although his lips still moved.

"You really *do* sing beautifully," Hansen Grebe informed him, with a cheery smile. "Now all you have to do is act. Here's the situation, Brad. Either *you* bring me that white folder, the one that has *The Handbook for University Reorganization*™ in it, and the blue folder containing the rotten fruits of your labor, both of them by Sunday morning, say, or *I'll* take that excellent photograph of you opening post office box 138 — along with the blackmail letter I received — to the police."

"But Professor Grebe," the lad protested. "That's blackmail. Isn't it?"

Grebe smiled again. "No, that is *whitemail*, Brad — whereby a person is persuaded to do something right. Right makes white — you understand me, Brad?"

He nodded. Yes, he understood that. White makes right — same thing. *He* was white. He'd known that all along.

"*If* I have to take the photo and the letter to the cops, *you* will go to jail," Professor Grebe continued. "For three years, easily, or maybe five. That'd be three years wearing esssentially the same outfit, Brad. Three years without your CD player or your speakers; three years without your windsurfer — or eating out, or even *carrying* out. Three years without a Soloflex, a hot tub, or Jacuzzi.

"And then, when you're released from prison, you'll be branded: a convicted felon. The only jobs that you can get will be the ones that *women* have to take. You'll be a laughing stock at your reunions here at Riddle: the most downwardly mobile Appalachian amateur in your entire class."

Brad Hammond wasn't all that intelligent, but he could recognized a threat when he heard one.

"I'll get those folders for you, sir," he said.

38

Amanda's Suite

"That's not my watch," Amanda said. "Who said it was? I hate those — whachacallem — *digitals*, or something? I think a watch should have two hands, and a face, just like a person does." She paused. "A *friend*."

Because Simon had certainly had a relationship with every timepiece in his life, so far, her preference for friendly ones was understandable and something he could buy — *would* buy — with pleasure. As was her flat rejection of the digital machine he'd dangled right before her nose, shortly after entering her suite. His made-up story was: He'd found it in the common room, thought he'd seen it on her wrist before.

At the time (9:05 P.M.) Amanda was reclining on the down-cushioned chaise longue, a piece of furniture — almost a prop — that Clee had brought from home. It was covered in some silky striped material and she by a white terry cloth bathrobe. Simon still hadn't gotten used to seeing girls walking in the halls, or hanging out, in just a bathrobe — no pajama legs below. In his mind, still, there was this real division between what a person might properly do at home and what she or he could do at college. He kept thinking girls in (only) robes should go and get some clothes on. But that was his problem, and he was working on it.

"Well," said Simon now, "I guess I'd better take it down to Barry's, then. The lost and found." She shrugged; she clearly didn't care. Unless Amanda was the greatest actress in the history of the world, that watch was a matter of total indifference to her.

But Simon didn't head for Barry's. Instead, he kept on standing there.

"Look," he said. "Amanda." She looked up at him, but kept on brushing her hair. "I've got some . . . stuff I've got to talk to you about." She smiled and raised her eyebrows, looking devilish. "I don't mean *stuff*-stuff," he amended. "I mean some confidential . . . things. So I was wondering if we could maybe find a place where" — he jerked his head in Clee's direction — "where just the two of us could, *you* know. . . ."

Across the room Clee Clymer was stretched out on her back on the tanning bed, wearing a very minimal string bikini made of what appeared to be soft leather, tan. She also had on headphones. Her eyes were closed, but the paperback book *Charles and Diana* lay facedown, open, on the bed beside her.

Amanda waved a palm at him.

"*She* can't hear us, silly; she's got some music on," she said. "And besides, she isn't interested. And even if she were, she's got to study for a midterm." Amanda turned and craned her neck, checking out Clee's book. "English history, I guess. Unless she's invited some people over to watch her study, it'll be okay, I promise you. You can say whatever you want. So — shoot."

Simon took a last glance at Clee — he had yet to formulate a policy on girls on tanning beds, and sort of in bikinis — and then went and picked up Amanda's desk chair and brought it over next to the chaise. Amanda had a robe on, and he was going to play the doctor this time. But even with his back to her, he still could feel the Golden One was there, behind him. He'd have to just pretend she was his nurse. Like, *sure*. With Clee back there and Amanda in front of him he decided he felt like part of a Dadaist bread sandwich: a piece of bread between two hamburgers.

"I lied before," he told Amanda. "I didn't find this watch down in the common room; I found it on your desk. And look. . . ." He pressed the upper righthand button on the thing and let her see the tricks that it could do. As he did, he stared at her intently and tried to read her mind — or anyway, her face. Here's what he thought he saw: first interest, then surprise, then shock, then something in the neighborhood of fury, maybe. (Here's what he wondered, looking at the robed Amanda, as a whole: Would Hippocrates, if he had had Amanda as a patient, possibly have come up with a different oath? And maybe lost his license?)

"You're telling me you found that on my desk?" Amanda now was asking him. "You don't believe what I just said? That I've never seen that stupid watch before? You really think that thing is *mine*?" The patient was glaring at the innocent practitioner.

"No, no," he mumbled, looking down. "Not at

all. I'm sure it isn't — now." His head came up. "Before today — earlier today — I didn't know. But what I said *is* true, about finding it on your desk. That's where it was the morning of the test. Someone planted it and — get this — planned that I, *specifically*, would come along and pick it up. Which is exactly what I did. Then at the exam. . . ."

He kept on talking; she just listened. He could see her level of annoyance rising once again. Each breath she took was quicker, more emphatic; she stopped brushing her hair, and the terry cloth robe came open a little, at the top.

Simon didn't even notice — the brush. By then he was dazzling the patient with his erudition: naming all the names, reminding her who-all had been there at The Pub and explaining how, the morning of the test, Phil Hedd, after (presumably) swiping his watch, had aimed him at her room so Jeffrey Bung could pull the trigger of the trap. And at the end he said:

"Why me, though? How come Phil asked *me* to have a beer with him at all? Seniors don't do beers with freshmen *men*. And then his friends just happen to come by?"

Amanda thought she understood that part, of course. She'd guessed as soon as she'd walked into The Pub and seen them all that this was Simon's interview for getting in A-CHOIR. And now what she was thinking was: Her "fellow" members, having found, like, nothing wrong with Simon, had decided to get him kicked out of the university and solve the problem that way. One less candidate to compete with Shep Hewitt and those two other bozos. You want to talk about *overkill*?

But she wasn't about to go into that. She wanted to know something else.

"You said that you just learned *today* about the watch — that the dumb thing isn't mine," she started. "Yet the exam was — what — ten days ago? *You* were caught cheating on a midterm, but *I* haven't heard a thing from the honor committee. So what does that mean? That you didn't tell them anything about where you got the watch? Simon! My God! You haven't been kicked out for this already, have you?"

She leaned forward as she said that, seized his hands. Her robe gapped open wider still.

"No," he said. "At least so far as I know, I haven't." He hoped she wasn't going to switch roles back, and take his pulse again.

But she just kept on squeezing hands, but even tighter. "You were just going to *take* it — whatever punishment they handed you — rather than get *me* involved? Oh, Simon" — tears came coursing down her cheeks — "you are the *sweetest* boy in all the world!"

Simon didn't know if she said that last part so loudly that it got through the music the Goddess was receiving through her headphones, or what. But he heard a sound behind him, and he looked in time to see that Clee'd turned over on her tanning bed and now was lying on her tummy, propped up on her elbows, with the book face up in front of her. And before she started reading it again, she shot a glance across the room, intended for her roommate, which Amanda (rightly) took to mean: "Dumb Dollop, you can go to *jail* for what you're doing there."

Amanda didn't pay attention to the warning,

though. How could she? This boy, right here in front of her, had done the most unselfish, noble thing she'd ever heard about in her entire life. He'd been willing to lay down his education, goals, his whole *career* (whatever it might be) for her. She felt, she *knew*, she'd never meet the likes of him again (at least at Riddle) and her tears of sorrow (for herself and for the difference in their ages) mingled with the ones of gratitude that (to be completely fair to her) came first. For two cents (and if C.C. hadn't been there) she'd have locked the door, shucked off her robe, and — age differential or not — given him a physical the likes of which. . . .

But Simon was talking, had been talking.

". . . plenty relieved that I can, maybe, tell the truth now. That's if you think I should, if I can prove to the honor committee somehow, that *neither* of us — "

"Wait, wait, wait," Amanda said. Her mind jumped back on track, into reality. She had an appointment with Professor Holt on Saturday; surprisingly (to her) he'd called and asked her to come over to his house. "It's a matter of great urgency — of, well, of *national* importance," he had said. "A meeting of A-CHOIR?" she had asked, of course, and he'd said, "No, it's much more major, right around top secret. And just between the two of us." Well, whatever Holt wanted, there was one thing he was going to give her in return: some way to quash this phony cheating accusation. She didn't doubt for a moment he knew *of* it, or maybe even was the cause of it; Shep Hewitt was his type, for sure. So, what Holt had brought together, Holt could darn well tear asunder.

"Let me handle it," she said to Simon. "I *am* your R.A., after all." She'd let go of his hands by then, and had settled back on the chaise, retying the sash that held her robe together.

"I'm seeing someone Saturday," she said, "who I think can probably take care of this. In fact, I'm *sure* he can. So, look — you're going to do the firewalk? I'll meet you there, okay? Just so you know that everything's been taken care of."

"Fantastic," Simon said. "That'd be fantastic, if you'd do that." He hadn't even started the firewalk procedure and he was already starting to feel powerful and confident. "Frankly, Amanda," he said, "I just may not stay at Riddle anyway, after this year, but it'd sure be great if I wasn't . . . well, thrown out."

"Not stay at Riddle?" Amanda asked him. She put on a pout. "Why not? Because of . . . *this*? But I don't *want* you to leave, Simon. I've got three more years, and with Clee graduating and all. . . ." For one crazy moment, she was really tempted to ask him to room with her, a year from then; that'd be pretty neat, having Simon, beautiful Simon, as a suitemate. But then she imagined Dr. Tassetevin from the medical school just happening to come by her room and finding a sixteen-year-old boy there. That'd be cute. She could also imagine herself in three years of compulsory therapy followed by assignment, as a resident, to North Dakota, probably. Or Guam. ". . . I'll be almost friendless around here." She smiled so he would know she wasn't really serious. Actually, she could understand perfectly why he might want to leave the college, after this.

What she still couldn't totally understand was why the guys from A-CHOIR had gone to so much trouble with Simon. And why they used *her* in their scheme — how they'd *dared* use her. They could have kept him out of the society without all that; there was clearly something fishy going on. Professor Greg Holt had better level with her Saturday, at five P.M. She wondered what he'd offer her at that odd hour: a cup of tea with choice of lemon, milk, and sympathy, or a baloney sandwich.

Simon got up to go. He felt a little guilty, not telling Amanda the full story about what all Phil Hedd and his friends were up to, why they'd really wanted him out of the university. But it was probably best if she didn't know too much about — or get mixed up in — things involving folks whose zip code started with a 205. And he certainly was feeling better, now that it appeared his name and reputation would be saved.

For the first time in a while, Simon felt he might survive his education.

39

Phone Calls

"Hello."

"Hi, Kate. It's me," said Simon. He had his forehead pressed against the wall; his lips were almost on the mouthpiece of the phone. That was the position, in the corridors of Bliss. It was also a good way to pick up a disease, some people thought.

"Oh, hi. What's up?" she said.

"It's about the firewalk, day after tomorrow," Simon said. "They have a sign-up sheet on the bulletin board downstairs. The deadline's tonight."

"So what's the matter? Can't you sign me up?" she asked.

"Oh, yes," he said. "I *guess* I can. As a matter of fact, I already signed us both up; I used a made-up name, for you. From what the notice said, there's a limit on the number of people that can do the workshop — or whatever it is — so every hall just gets so many spaces, first come first served."

"Well, what's the *problem*?" she said. "Did someone object because whatever name you put down for me doesn't live in Bliss? That sounds like some of those jerks over there."

"No, no," he said, "there's actually a couple of

272

empty spaces, still. I don't know; I was just wondering." Below his nose, on the wall, someone had written in purple pen: HOW TO CONTRACT HEARING AIDS: BY LISTENING TO ASSHOLES. "I was wondering if you still want to go through with it, or what. According to the notice, the whole thing — getting psyched, I guess, and then actually doing the walk — takes four or five hours. We'd have to be there at five o'clock in the afternoon."

"That'd be okay," she said. "I guess what we ought to do is maybe eat a sandwich before. You could come over here, if you wanted to; we could whip up something good." She paused. "Yeah, I'm still up for it. Why — aren't you?"

"I guess so," Simon said. He tried to change his tone. "Maybe I'm just getting cold feet." The truth of the matter was that his conversations with Professor Grebe and Amanda had reduced his stress and anxiety levels considerably — while totally demolishing the charm of "models" like Phil Hedd, or Kahn. And the firewalk never *had* been a real grabber, intellectually. Simon's mind was much too strong and flexible to *dis*believe in miracles — but could a person by the name of Beasely Dewitt, an Englishman, apparently, be expected to perform what surely *was* a miracle for anyone who had the hundred-dollar fee and wanted/needed one? Granted, the generosity of the Lucretia Hepplewhite Foundation had democratized this particular what-have-you — workshop/session/service — by picking up the tab for one and all, but still. A world where *everyone* could have or be . . . the best? In less time than it takes to knit a sweater? Hey, come *on*.

"Cold feet?" said Kate. "Very funny, S-man. But

I'm not letting you fink out on me. This was your idea, remember. And anyway, it *will* be interesting — you know it will. This is the sort of stuff that can make your reputation as a grandfather, someday."

"I suppose," he said. He certainly was *curious*, no question. "Okay. I'll come over about three. Two-thirty, maybe. How would that be?"

"Fine," she said. "And good luck on your midterm, by the way. It *is* your last one, isn't it?"

"Yeah," he said, and, "thanks. I've got a paper still — to finish and hand in before tomorrow noon, but that won't be a problem. It's mostly typing that I've got to do."

"Good," she said. "So, see you in — let's see — like, forty-seven hours."

"Right," he said. "I'll be the one wearing clogs and an asbestos jockstrap." He hung up on her retching sounds. It was getting so he talked like her, he thought.

What he hadn't bothered to mention — on the grounds it wouldn't mean that much to her — was who their fellow strollers-on-the-coals were going to be. The first three names on the sign-up sheet in Bliss were Hedd and Kahn and (little Jeffrey) Bung.

Saturday, at one P.M.; a voice that echoed in the corridor:

"STORM! TELEPHONE!"

Footsteps. A hand, clean fingernailed, reached out and grabbed the dangling receiver.

"Hello," said Simon.

"Hurricane, it's me." The voice of Hansen Grebe

was unmistakable. "Hope I didn't take you away from anything outrageous."

"No, sir," Simon said. He'd been dressing for his date with Kate, and wondering if he should cut his toenails.

"Just called to say I think that things are going to break our way by nightfall. Unless I miss my guess, before the clock strikes ten, the tide of battle will have turned, our enemies will be confounded, all worries will be over, the college saved, and the names of Grebe and Storm will be as well known — and generally revered — throughout the land as the Unknown Soldier's. Where can I get in touch with you at — oh, say, nine o'clock? Anything as big and good as this should be enjoyed at once, as the actress said to the bishop. Or was it vice versa?"

Simon said he expected to be down at the stadium. "The firewalk," he muttered. "Though I probably won't *do* the thing," he added.

"Ah-*ha*," said Grebe. "You're attending the per-*ember*lation, are you? Well, *chacun à son* goo, said the old lady as she poured the hot fudge sauce onto her mashed potatoes. Tell you what: I'll meet you down there, how would that be? You think they'd mind if I brought marshmallows?"

Simon managed an uneasy laugh, while saying, well, he didn't really *know*, and Grebe said, "See you later, anyway," and then hung up.

Just before he called up Simon, Hansen Grebe had had a call from Brad — Brad Hammond. *He'd* said he'd seen the Holts' new mini-van back out of their garage, and then get loaded up with suitcases; a freezer chest; the Holts' saluki, Muammar; young Jessica; and Freddie. He suspected that the family

275

was going somewhere for the weekend (Hammond did — Brad Hammond did), and so he planned (he told Professor Grebe) to "make the snatch" that very evening, shortly after nightfall. Even if it did mean missing the firewalk (he decided not to add). Grebe thought Brad sounded nervous, but determined: good.

After he called Simon, Professor Grebe went out and bought a big cigar, which he figured he could light and smoke when everything was over and he'd won. It wasn't that he loved it when a plan came together, or that he'd been a lifelong Celtics fan, (although he had been); he just liked to call to mind, from time to time, how much he hated smoking.

40

Warm-ups

Amanda Dollop had never been in Professor Greg Holt's "study," in his house, before.

"It's kind of cozy down here," Holt had said, as he led her down the stairs into this basement sanctum sanctorum of his.

At first glance, Amanda didn't see anything particularly "cozy" about the room — about Holt's desk and filing cabinets, or all his framed mementos and accomplishments: diplomas; an archery award from summer camp; a photo of Holt holding the hand of a surprised-looking Donald Regan; a plaque honoring his past vice-presidency of his college chapter of Young Americans for Freedom; a certificate attesting to membership in the *Who's Who in American Military Schools*; a poem Renée wrote him after their first date; pictures of the children and his Triumph, and his Audi, and his Bentley; a cute sign saying: THE GOLDEN RULE: HE WHO HAS THE MOST GOLD MAKES THE RULES; and a large photo of Jennifer Beals in one of her *Flashdance* outfits on which someone had written: *TO GREGORY THE GREAT, HIS SUPREME HIGHNESS. HUGGIES, EVER, JENNY.*

But when she'd taken in the deep, high-armed, down-cushioned sofa, and the bar in the corner with the lighted Coors sign over it, she thought she maybe saw what he referred to.

As soon as Amanda'd come in the door, she thought she detected a difference in the setup and in Holt's whole *attitude*, you could say. Where in the past she'd always felt peripheral, a very minor player on a very crowded stage, she now felt singular — indeed, *alone*. She didn't hear the children, or Holt's wife; there weren't any kitchen noises, food smells. And just as Holt had said when he'd invited her, there weren't any other members of A-CHOIR in the house. It was just the two of them, and Holt had said, "Suppose we have a little glass of something in my study," and had led her down the stairs. Like that.

Amanda was delighted. Holt wanted something badly (badly, *badly*), specifically from her; there was no way he could know she was equally determined to extract her pound of . . . shall we say, *exoneration*? She looked forward to a little thrust and parry session. She'd been real good at this before she ever met the Golden One, but after years of talking strategies, techniques with Clee, she now was world-class quality.

She asked Holt if he liked, as she did, an occasional martini.

Only an hour before Simon and Kate arrived at Riddle Stadium (at 4:58 P.M.), 7,487 people had been watching the closing seconds of the football game between the Riddle Sphinxes and the Walden College Pond Scum, which ended in a 6–6 tie and caused 312 alumni wits (all male) to tell their stone-bored spouses that watching a tie game was like kissing your sister. As these women could have told the wits, Riddle-Walden was actually more like watching a high school physics class doing, oh, perhaps their fourth experiment, in lab; the players seemed to try, but really didn't have the hang of it.

Now, however, there were just 150 or so student and faculty power-seekers there, including Kate and Simon, three quarters of them male. And they were (mostly) ready. These folks were giving up their *Saturday nights*. Instead of getting drunk, or getting laid, or getting in a fight, they were there to walk on fire and get (only) everything they wanted (from then on).

Roadies from the Dewitt International Growth Institute (DIG-IN) had made some changes on the floor of the stadium. A huge royal purple tarp now covered one entire end zone and continued up to the ten-yard line. In the center of the tarp there was a painting of a huge five-pointed, shining silver star, and scattered elsewhere on the thing were other paintings: multicolored bull's-eyes, fireworks exploding, and a speeding F-14 jet fighter plane. Also, here and there were printed words. College-educated Simon noticed Evian, Vuarnet, and Benetton; Kate saw Miller, L.L. Bean, and Pennzoil.

Behind the goalpost, at this same end of the stadium, there were the makings of a considerable bonfire, heaped up in the broad-jump pit. Chainlink fences had been erected on either side of the pit, about a yard away from it; beyond the *ends* of the pit, the fences angled away, producing (Simon thought) a sort of funnel effect. He got a momentary mental flash to certain stockyard photographs he'd seen.

And finally, on the field edge of the tarp, up on the ten-yard line, there was an elevated stage, about the size of one you'd find in a small nightclub. It had a black backdrop, three standing microphones front and center, and two huge banks of heavy-wattage speakers on each side.

All at once, at five o'clock on the dot, the speakers spoke; a steady drumroll, getting ever louder, hushed the crowd. Two spotlights, hidden behind the backdrop, came on and cast their beams of light to the very top row of the stadium, one on the left side and one on the right. They found, and rested on, two human forms up there. These were both young women, similar in size (just right) and (perfect) shape, with manes of bright red hair and wearing skintight, jet-black, silken bodysuits. And in their right hands, high above their heads, they both held lighted torches.

The watching crowd let out an exclamation: "WO!" (those suits looked positively see-through from down there), and the girls began to trot on down the long, long flights of steps, heading toward the broad-jump pit, from either end.

They reached it, stopped. The drumroll also stopped. Then, together, they both tossed their torches on the woodpile, which instantly exploded into flame. The audience, which had crowded toward the pit, let out another noise, this one of affirmation (Simon thought). People laughed and clapped. A voice from the darkness started up a rhythmic chant, and in a moment everyone had memorized it, joined their voices in staccato sound.

"Yes! Yes! Yes! Yes! Yes! Yes! Yes!" this makings-of-a-mob exclaimed, their faces glowing in the firelight.

The chant continued for a good two minutes, and wasn't dying down at all, when suddenly some joyful, cadenced music started blasting from the speakers: familiar, inspirational and *now*, it was the theme from *Chariots of Fire*.

The stage was flooded with a brilliant light. Everybody turned toward it and right there, right behind the microphone, jogging easily in place and wearing a silver warm-up suit with bright white running shoes, was Beasely ("Bease") Dewitt, himself!

"What ho! Good evening, Riddle!" he exclaimed, his vintage Oxford accent unmistakable. "I'm Bease Dewitt, y'know!"

"Hey, hey, good *evening*, Bease!" most everyone replied. And the congregation moved back on the tarp, approached the stage, heads tilted upward, toward The Source.

"Good friends," said Bease Dewitt, "in fellowship and common purpose, let's all join our hands together. I sense we're going to make a *mahster*piece tonight."

People seized each other's hands — *loving* that idea — which had the effect of putting them in rows, which Bease *then* caused to sit down on the tarp, like happy children at a summer camp. Everyone was asked to introduce himself to everyone in easy reach, and tell that person how afraid of walking on hot coals he was "on a scale of one to ten, ten being *petrified*." There was a lot of nervous laughter in the buzz of happy talk that followed.

When that had been accomplished, finished with,

Beasely introduced his "helpers," who'd appeared up on the stage, and whose hands *he* now had taken. "Rob" had on a white silk shirt and tight black pants; his hair and mustache both were shiny black, and his front teeth were very white. "Niki" wore a black silk shirt and tight white pants; her wavy hair and perfect teeth were every bit as bright as Rob's. It appeared that neither Rob nor Niki had remembered to button up their shirts, but the good-natured crowd made light of their forgetfulness with whistles and remarks intended (almost certainly) as flattery. No question that the "helpers" were a hunk and a hunkette, respectively.

Then, with Rob and Niki seated on the stage on either side of him, Bease began his longest rap about "the work" — how he'd come to more or less discover it, how it had changed his life, and *would* change all of theirs, if they just let it.

He told them, first of all, about the total mess he'd been, just three short years before. Although it seemed to other chaps that he was "quite the swell," he said, with friends, "sufficient worldly goods," and Oxford education, "prospects," and what have you, such was not the case at all. Below the surface, everything was different.

"Eckshally," said Bease, "I thought I was a cipher, the sort of chap you Yanks'd call a puhfect *nuhd*." In his heart of hearts, he said, he doubted his ability to make it. (And Simon, much to his amazement, heard — like, all around — the nearly noiseless sound that heads make, nodding.)

One day, apparently, as Bease was sitting in his gloomy little flat, worrying about his future prospects, or the lack of same, an old fantasy just pip-

pip-popped into his mind, one he'd had from time to time, for years. In this daydream (he now told the crowd) he — Beasely Dewitt, a nobody, unknown — became the greatest runner in the world. But secretly. He'd just go off and work out by himself — eighteen, twenty hours every day, far more than anyone had ever done before — until he was the best. And then — this was the juicy part — he'd enter in some marathon with scads of famous runners in it and just beat their socks off! He would *win!*

That dream, it seemed to him the grandest thing imaginable. And furthermore, just possible. Anyone *could* run; you didn't have to have connections, a fantastic personality. All you had to do was move your legs fast, pump your arms, breathe deeply through your nose, and exhale through your mouth (was it?).

Well, this time, when he had the daydream, he decided he would give the thing a try. Why not, after all? He *knew* he couldn't make it in a business or a bank — not on the scale his family expected, or as his rotten friends most likely would. As a cover-up, he'd simply tell the world that he was going off to "write." Most people thought creative artists were a bunch of wimps and fags, but some of them *had* made a ton of money, lately.

So, using a small inheritance from a dotty aunt, he leased a cottage in the north of England and started in to "train." But on the very first day, after he'd run his hardest for perhaps 300 yards, and then stopped and didn't *feel* much like running anymore, ever again, he realized he needed . . . a *coach*, someone to motivate him, maybe, tell him what to do and when, organize his training. Behind every great runner from Phidippides ("the running newsboy") on, there'd always been a coach; he felt quite sure of that.

The first person he thought of as coach for himself was (naturally enough) the world-class marathoner Freddie Phypphs; they'd been chums at Oxford, after all, and Freddie played the ponies, always was in need of funds. What he could do, so's not to alert the world of running to his plan, was use the "writing" bit again: tell old Freddie that he'd hoped to do a book on him, on one of England's leading sporting heroes. And on that pretext he could find out Freddie's training schedule, and do the same himself. He phoned, and with a hundred pounds as bait, got Freddie's quick acceptance of his weekend invitation.

But before Freddie'd even gotten there, Beasely did some further thinking and concluding. He needed *more* than two days' coaching, *more* than Freddie's training regimen. What he had to do was something more extreme, something *scientific*. What he needed was to make himself *be* Freddie (as a runner), in effect to *clone* him. That definitely appealed to Brease; it sounded very 1986, right there on the *cutting* edge, in fact. And besides, it might not be that hard; they were similar in size and shape, in background, education. He figured that the more like Freddie Phypphs he got — attitudinally, psychologically, physiologically, and spiritually — the faster he would run.

So that's what he did. In the course of one long weekend, he found out — *and made himself believe* — everything that Freddie felt about the act of running marathons: why he did it, basically, his motivation, and the shape and depth of his commitment. Then he learned about the race itelf, its stages, how to cope with uphills, downhills, potholes, and the other runners, when to make a surge and when to lag. And finally, he learned to mimic Freddie's form — exactly — so that if the two of them ran by a crowd, with brown bags on their heads, no one could have said, for sure, which one was which. He'd never worked and concentrated half so hard — especially on a weekend — in his entire life; Freddie left exhausted, Sunday night.

"But then, on Monday morning," Beasely Dewitt told the seated congregation at the stadium, "I got into my little Morris Minor and drove twenty-six and a quarter miles into the country, parked the car by the side of the road, and ran straight back to the cottage. Lacking competition, and in spite of stopping twice to take a drink of water from some bally brook beside the road, I did the course in two hours and eleven minutes flat. World-record time, just then, was two-oh-seven and a fraction, done on a course with hardly any hills at all, compared to mine. I had become, in two days' time, a Freddie Phypphs with better motivation, even: an absolutely *smashing* distance runner."

Well, you'd better believe that story got some crowd reaction. Lots of people jogged at Riddle. They had aunts and uncles who'd done marathons. Two-eleven *meant* (a lot of) something. *No one* ran a two-eleven who didn't train a hundred miles a week for (simply) *years*. Everybody there knew that.

Bease talked on through the buzz. He told them once he'd made the run, he realized he didn't have to race; he'd won already, it was clear to him; there was nothing that he couldn't do, in any field, not anymore. He'd unlocked, so to speak, "the Bank of Excellence — in anything."

The buzz down in the crowd got louder, and took on a certain tone. *Dubiety* is one word to describe that tone; *bullshit* is the word that Simon heard, repeated here and there.

But Beasely wasn't finished — no, indeed. They mustn't simply take his word for this, he told them; of course he planned to offer proof. He — now — would run for them, right there, that very night, a world-class marathon over a course laid out the day before under the supervision of Mr. Reynolds and Mr. Lieberman of Price, Waterhouse (a spotlight picked out two men with briefcases and wearing business suits, standing on the edge of the tarp, who smiled and nodded and saluted jauntily). And while he was gone, Rob and Niki would give his Riddle friends some "warm-ups" for the firewalk.

With which the music from *Chariots of Fire* started up again, and Bease Dewitt (most gracefully) stripped off his sweats and did a little stretch and warm-up of his own, right up there on the stage.

Physically, he was an altogether different type than Rob: fine-featured, with long, dark blond hair that, if it got messed up (by taking off a sweater, say), would float back perfectly in place at a single jerk of his head. Standing on the stage in just his running singlet and a pair of wide-legged silky running shorts, he was almost like an alabaster statue, clean-limbed, fair, with perfect English legs. If Rob was hairy Magnum-macho, here we had a Botticelli angel, grown to be a man: the pure and graceful Earl of Elegance, himself.

As he bounded down the stage steps and off into the dark, a large digital clock lighted up at the back of the stage and started counting off the seconds of his run.

Greg Holt knew better than to drink martinis. He'd known better for years — known that, for whatever chromosomal or hematological reasons, a drink combining gin and ice and dry vermouth (stirred *or* shaken, either way) knocked him off his slender, elegant size nines like no equivalent amount of Scotch or bourbon, rum or vodka, brandy or Kahlua ever could. Not even close. But still he kind of liked a dry, occasional martini — about the same as Pooh bears "kind of like" the taste of honey.

So when Amanda Dollop as good as begged him, right straight out, to join her in a "white one," he agreed. And just two minutes later they were seated on the couch, raising stemmed and frosty glasses to each other, saying, "Cheers."

In order not to spook the girl at all, Holt kept his distance, even pulled a knee up on the couch between them, as he turned and talked to her. He liked that little touch; it almost told her, "Keep *your* distance, wench." And for the next five minutes as they sipped their drinks, Holt put Amanda even *further* at her ease (he felt) by chatting back and forth with her about how *nice* his study was, how *perfect* the martinis were, how *good* an archer he still was — things of common interest, you might say.

Then, quite suddenly, he jumped up on his feet and went behind the desk, where he flicked a lever on a little box that looked much like an intercom. At once, it started making sound: a strange and slightly eerie electronic wail, not pleasant or unpleasant, more or less a background noise, like sirens in the distance. Amanda raised an eyebrow; Holt came back and took the same position on the couch.

"Black Noise," he said to her. "It makes this room completely bug-proof. What it does is set up interference in any sort of listening device that makes it *totally* impossible to hear what's being said in here. Not that I've any reason to believe we're under close surveillance. I just wanted to be sure — take no chances whatsoever. That'll give you an idea of the importance of this thing I want to talk to you about, and of the mission — should you choose to accept it — that I plan to offer you."

Amanda looked impressed, Holt thought. Like, *real* impressed. She should have been. Black Noise had cost him $89.95 plus $4.75 postage and handling; he'd found the ad for it in one of his magazines, *Modern Minute Men*. ("Modern My-*newt* Men?" Renée had annoyingly inquired once, handing him his copy. It was the one with a small Latin-American freedom-fighter on the cover. "Is he a member of some pygmy tribe or other?" she'd gone on.)

So now Holt went right into his sales pitch, after first refilling their glasses, of course. He was feeling very fluent and persuasive; that was nothing but the truth. Amanda'd taken off those cunning little boots that she'd been wearing, and had tucked her feet right under her, all comfy on the couch.

Holt strung it out; he liked to watch her face change as she listened: shock, surprise, disgust, amusement, and appreciation — deep respect. Stripped down, his story was quite simple: Top secret government files had been "compromised"; a Riddle professor was known ("well, *almost* known") to have received highly classified information; the CIA, awash in bad publicity just then, was leery of involvement in a college campus caper — and anyway had total confidence in Holt and any "ops" that he recruited.

With which he moved to some specifics in the case. The stuff — "material" — that she'd be looking for might very well be kept inside a folder, "one that looks like this," Holt said as he got up, established balance, crossed the room again — this time toward his files. As Amanda poured her second martini into one of her cute little boots, Holt opened up the drawer marked: OPERATION METAMORPHOSIS and took out a plastic folder that at that distance looked absolutely just like leather. He held it up so she could see it better, and she nodded: Got it.

Greg Holt nodded, closed the file, and started back toward the couch again. But then he saw Amanda's glass was empty, and the shaker, too. He picked it up, went over to the bar, and mixed another batch by eye. One good thing about a dry martini: You didn't have to be, like, real exact in your proportions. He told Amanda that. He found a jar of peanuts and poured some in a bowl. "A li'l muncheroo for us," he told Amanda. "Gotta watch these babies," and he held the shaker up. He wasn't drunk at all, but he was feeling great. He went back to the couch, filled both their glasses from the shaker, and took a little nibble at this latest miracle he'd made, this mixture of two liquids to make . . . dynamite. Excellent, he thought. He sat down in the middle of the sofa, and he didn't have that leg up anymore.

"Well, now," Amanda was saying, "I guess the next thing that I'd need to know is who the person — the professor — is. And where you think he's got the stuff. And how" — she might have blushed a little — "you think a girl like me could ever help you get it. If that's what you've been leading up to."

That seemed to make Holt think of — like, remember — something. He turned quickly away from Amanda and reached for the lamp that was sitting on the table at his end of the couch. It had a three-way bulb in it, which presently was at its brightest. Why not save a little energy? Holt seemed to ask himself. (Amanda's drink, untouched, went down the other cunning boot leg.)

"Well, yes," said Holt, as he turned back to her. "I'm sure you *can* help lots. We *need* you to, in fact. Notice I say 'we,' Amanda. You won't be doing this for me alone, my dear, though I'm a part of it, of course, and I'll be like your fellow . . . *musketeer*, your *partner*, come to think of it. . . ."

His glance fell on her glass, then on his own.

"Whoops — I've gotten behind again," he said, and slugged his down. If this slip of a (great-looking) girl was still in good shape (yum) — as she sure *seemed* to be — the drinks could not have been that strong. Maybe the maid had watered down his gin,

290

he thought, and poured again. Maybe if he "got behind" again, it would be little friend Amanda's. He tried to think: Had he ever called his pin to her attention?

The clock above the stage had just hit 2:09 and the crowd in front of it had barely finished Rob's and Niki's latest meditation exercise (imagining a large brick wall, say ten feet high, that they walked slowly up to, each alone, and then walked *through* — unflinchingly, relentlessly, unharmed), when a spotlight picked up Beasely's entrance, at the far end of the stadium. He looked superb, striding — even sprinting — down the backstretch of the track, heading for the finish line, where Messrs. Lieberman and Reynolds recently had gone to hold a tape for him to put the chest to. As he did, the clock above the backdrop of the stage stopped counting off the seconds. There, for everyone to see, was *proof* that Bease Dewitt had told the truth about his great discovery, about the power he would help each one of *them* unlock in *his* own self (or even hers). 2:09.34, it said. Incredible! He'd done it. An absolutely world-class marathon *without* those boring, grueling years of training for the thing!

It was almost equally incredible to see how *fresh* he was. No trackside sprawls for Bease Dewitt, no arms around the shoulders of two sturdy friends, no being wrapped in space-age capes or blankets, or lying down on cots. Hell, no. Instead he grabbed a bunch of colorful flags in one hand (all the NATO allies who'd accepted Cruise and Pershing missiles, plus Old Glory, Simon noticed) and in the other one a banner with the words ECCLESIASTES 10:19 on

291

it. That verse, to the best of Simon's recollection, was, "A feast is made for laughter, and wine maketh merry; but money answereth all things." He whispered that to Kate, who whispered back, "That's the same as 'Whoever says money can't buy happiness just doesn't know where to shop,' isn't it?" But, in any case, Bease Dewitt followed the spotlight on a victory lap around the stadium track, returning to and ending at the stage, where he slipped on his warm-ups, once again.

The crowd was really turned on now, getting readier and readier. But instead of whipping them to an even higher pitch, Bease Dewitt now brought them down a little, getting them to stretch out on their backs and listen to the sounds of gently breaking waves, cows mooing in a pasture, pleasant unpolluted breezes soughing through some healthy pines, the sound of pH-perfect rain upon a cozy cabin roof. He talked to them in soothing tones about the things that they were put on earth for, reminded them of times that they'd felt proud and hopeful, challenged them to just . . . *believe*. Simon (later on) remembered little snatches of the guy's reminders, like for instance:

> ". . . and there it was, your painting on the fridge. . . ."

> ". . . your parents would be out of town until sometime tomorrow. . . ."

> ". . . you jammed the key into the ignition and. . . ."

> ". . . saw the country club, just as you'd imagined it. . . ."

292

They didn't work at all for him, of course, so he simply turned his head and looked at Kate, lying on the tarp beside him. That did the trick and made him feel, like, deep-down *lucky*-tingly-relaxed. He figured Beasely wouldn't mind.

Just when he'd gotten really mellow, Bease and Rob and Niki changed the mood again, got them all up clapping, for a visit to the fire. The speakers blared "The Heat Is On," while people danced around it three-four times. That was the pure, plain truth. Simon knew he'd never seen a hotter, *meaner-looking* fire than the one they had inside that broad-jump pit. People kept their distance when they passed it, pressed against the chainlink fence and picking up the pace a little. Simon saw Phil Hedd, Grant Kahn, and Jeffrey Bung go by ahead of him. Phil was actually trotting along backward, playing a game of pease-porridge-hot with Grant, while Jeffrey, right behind Grant, would occasionally slap him on the back in the tempo of the game. Just so it'd be clear to anyone who might be watching that he was part of their group, apparently. Simon saw Grant Kahn turn his head toward Jeff a time or two; it *looked* as if he might be saying, Will you cut that (something) out, you (something) little simpleton? But Bung just grinned and caroled something back that Simon heard as, "Go, Grant, buddy-baybee!"

When everyone had boogied back onto the tarp again, and Bease had hopped back on the stage, he told them he had something else he had to show them. Another piece of evidence of how he'd been transformed — in almost no time flat — by following the principles he'd talked about before.

"I shouldn't want you to believe," he said, "that

293

it's only physical puhformance that a puhson can improve, by way of these techniques. Though — speaking of that kind of thing — Rob and Niki have some videos of . . . well, themselves, *puhforming*. And while I'm sure that none of *you*, specifically, need any help at *all* in that puhticular *endeavor* — shall we say? — it's possible you *do* have friends whose lives would be just infinitely enriched — and *satisfied* — if they could only *cope* a little better. You do take my meaning, don't you? In any case, they're $69.95, Visa and MasterCard accepted, satisfaction guaranteed, and" — Beasely chuckled — "dem near unforgettable."

Of course there was another bit of rustle, after that announcement — a general shifting around as guys checked to be sure they brought their wallets. Niki on a video? Hey, it wasn't *that* much bread — and this group had a lot of hungry friends.

"But anyway, as I was saying," Beasely said, "the power you can have, by way of these techniques, can be in other realms — in the field of literature, for instance, or the arts. Both of which, I'm sure I needn't add, can mean a marketplace success as well, these days. Anyone who's priced a Renoir lately — or done a first-class romance novel — knows whereof I speak."

There was a general nod and mutter of assent among the Riddle cognoscenti.

"Of course I plan to give you proof of this, as well," said Bease. "Must and shall, in just two minutes, from this stage. The background tale is shorter in the telling, this time." People settled back to listen.

"Just last week," he said, "I undertook to spend

an hour at the New York Public Library, reading all I could about the style and habits, form and implements, beliefs and background of those two great masters of the sonnet, William Shakespeare and Francesco Petrarch. So what I plan to do, right now, before your very eyes and on my first attempt, is write a world-class sonnet. You, as cultured college people, are surely competent to judge my little effort, and say if it belongs in an anthology, or what. Agreed?" Of course there was a murmur of assent. "So, Rob — a sheet of foolscap, one fresh quill, and ink, it please you, sir. I shall begin at once."

Rob did as he was bade. The maiden Niki carried in (*un*-bade) a high, old-fashioned writing table, and Beasely took his stance behind it, elbow on the table, forehead resting on one white and slender hand. And started in to write!

41

Getting Warmer

Professor Greg Holt had always wanted to "make it" with a nurse. First of all, he was the type of guy who (like many doctors) has always *known* that nurses are on earth to serve . . . well, mostly *guys*, in different ways. And secondly, he was also a man who (as is the case with certain members of the medical profession) had secretly wondered, off and on, if nurses knew more stuff than *he* did. In his case, about what felt good, to guys, and how to make such feelings happen.

But, in the absence of a nurse, he was more than willing to "make do" with a medical student. She'd done *dissections*, after all; you couldn't know a whole lot more about anatomy, and this and that, than someone who had done dissections. And, lacking a degree, she couldn't be too uppity about it.

Before anything took place between the two of *them*, however, Professor Holt still had to sell Amanda on the idea of her and Clee affecting Hansen Grebe in ways a camera, hand-held by him, could capture on some film, or tape, in gorgeous living color. Which film, or tape, could later be employed, of course, to guarantee Grebe's nonobstruction of the Grand Design for Riddle. What Holt had figured was: Once he had struck a deal with fair Amanda, then the two of them — though lacking Clee — might have themselves a nice *un*-dress rehearsal, using he himself as stand-in for H. Grebe.

When Amanda, sitting right there in his basement study, heard what Holt was asking her to do with Grebe, she didn't exactly jump up and down with delight, but neither did she tell him to go fish. What she turned out to be (earning, for the first time, real respect from Holt) was one first-class, hard-line negotiator. In fact, it was only by making an all-out effort to fight off the effects of the gin now coursing through his system that Holt was able to salvage what seemed to be a reasonable compromise. By its terms, once the necessary scenes had been played out and photographed, Amanda would receive the following:

1. A letter, suitable for framing, thanking her for "service to her nation's needs" and signed by you-know-who. (This was Holt's idea.)

2. A "symbolic" cash award, sufficient to put both her and Clee behind the wheels of the status symbols of their choices. (Supposedly, the Goddess was on record: "Fiero needs a friend.")

3. The sole existing copy of Simon's confession *and* Holt's written appointment of Simon to membership in A-CHOIR (if all else failed, the least Amanda felt that she could do for him).

Talking about number three had been a bit of an embarrassment for Holt. He'd been forced to admit that "the boys" had been a little "overzealous" in their attempt to keep Simon out of A-CHOIR. And that, yes, he *had* known about the frame (though not until *after* it had happened) and did, in fact, possess the "innocent young lad's confession," having it in his own files that very moment. He claimed, of course, that he wouldn't *ever* have sent the thing to the honor committee, and that he'd given the boys "all sorts of hell" for involving Amanda in their "silly joke" at all. He also told her if her "little friend" felt wronged at all, she should extend Holt's "personal regret" to him — without including mention of his name, of course.

The self-control it took to get himself through that last piece of polluted ethical marshland was so exhausting, as a matter of fact, that when Amanda finally smiled and proposed a toast to their "deal," Holt was near collapse. But also ready. ("Anything you get, you've earned," the economics chairman told himself.)

"And to make it . . . well, more *personal*," Amanda purred, "suppose *I* drink from *your* glass" — blushing — "Greggy. And you can use my . . . *slipper!*" With which she giggled wildly (Dear gracious goodness, Holt thought happily, the girl is higher than a space capsule.), seized the nearly empty shaker, poured a bit into his glass, and the rest into her cunning little boot.

"Bottoms up!" she cried, when both of them were ready, vessels in their hands. With smiling eyes that never left his face, she brought hers to her mouth — *his* glass — *licked* the rim of it, and slowly drained the thing of every drop.

Holt tilted up the boot, in turn, and drank. And drank and drank and drank; it hadn't *looked* as if she'd poured that much, but what the hell — he *was* the guy. And as just an extra little bit of chivalry when he was done, he kissed (as if in ecstasy) the toe of this peculiar stirrup cup.

Amanda smiled — approvingly, he thought.

"And now," she said, "to *seal* our little bargain. . . ." She rose up on her knees, wrapped her arms around Holt's neck, and kissed him on . . . the forehead. And then sat back on her heels and smiled at him some more.

Holt figured: Ho-ho-ho, my turn.

He, too, kneeled up and lunged at her. But, whoops! she must have moved abruptly, just *before* he (would have) seized her shoulders, kissed her squarely on her luscious, wet-lipped mouth. The next thing that he knew, his lips were tasting cushion-of-the-sofa-seat.

He turned his head so he could breathe, and once his eyes had focused and the room had settled down again, he saw, to his amazement and delight, that she was *voluntarily* — before he'd even mentioned it — starting to unbutton her chemise. Wo! Reflexively, he reached to . . . welcome the development. But before his hands could find their latest targets, she had captured both his wrists (in not a girlish grip *at all*) and was leaning toward his ear and whispering.

"Now, you just wait, you naughty boy," she said. (She couldn't know this, Holt believed, but pressing on the insides of a person's wrists like that could really, really *hurt* that person.) "Amanda's got to make a visit to the little girl's room, first. She remembers where it is, upstairs. Better to be safe than sorry, bubba-loo."

Holt nodded rapidly, too flustered and in too much pain to tell her he had had the operation. The nodding made his head begin to spin again, but — ah! — at least she'd finally loosed her viselike grip. In fact she now was — nurselike — sliding some small pillow underneath his head.

"You just stay comfy there," she said. She grabbed her shoulder bag and stood. "Maybe you should even take a tiny nap, so you'll be big and strong" — she winked — "Your Highness."

Holt struggled to produce a lord-and-master smile; he got a sickly simper.

"I'll be back directly, sugar plum," she said. Holt nodded, and the effort closed his eyes.

Before Amanda'd even gotten to the stairs, she heard Holt's breathing change, but still she climbed them halfway up, then sat and waited for a count of fifty before she came back down and headed for the filing cabinet.

Her luck was good, right from the start. The first thing in the first drawer she opened (OPERATION METAMORPHOSIS) was a dark blue plastic folder (with the look and smell of real Moroccan leather). She opened it and found it held not only Si's "confession" and the "witness's report" by Jeffrey Bung, but also other most surprising items, which she very quickly scanned: the Kate Portcullis sweat lodge piece, the carbon of the anonymous letter to Kate's father demanding that he send his resignation, and — good lord! — that very resignation.

"Hmmm," Amanda Dollop mused, out loud.

She went back to the couch, looked down at the recumbent Holt (now snoring loudly, grossly); she bit her lower lip and mused some more. Then she bent over and put on the boot he'd emptied (Yuk, she thought) and picked up the other one. She considered pouring it right down his nose, just as he inhaled. But after further thought she took it to the little sink behind the bar and emptied it, then put *it* on and went back to the files. Maybe there were other treasures there.

The folder that she took out next was red, but otherwise the same (in scent and texture) as the blue one. Inside, there was the carbon of another letter to the college president, this one signed *Doctors A. and B.* and saying that Prof Mowbray was a fake-credentialed fraud. Behind that was an envelope on which someone had written this: THE MAKING OF A MARTYR. It contained a lot of clippings from the *Riddle News*, announcing Mowbray's firing and his reaction to it, outraged student letters to the editor, and stories that described the protest demonstrations that the firing had caused.

"Well, double hmmm," Amanda Dollop now said softly. She put the red folder down on top of the blue one and reached inside the drawer again.

But at that very moment, she heard an unexpected sound, the one a large commando knife is apt to make when it's being used to jimmy open a basement window (that turns out to be unlocked, anyway). Amanda grabbed her folders, bent, and scuttled to the nearest hiding place, behind the little bar.

When she peered around the edge of it, she saw

the window open and a sneakered foot come in the room, followed (awkwardly, eventually) by other parts that, taken altogether, added up to this: Brad Hammond.

They didn't start the digital clock on the back of the stage when Bease Dewitt began to write his sonnet, but Simon, just out of curiosity, did take a peek at his watch (which — did I say? — he'd found inside a slipper in his closet). He did the same thing, slightly later on, when Bease looked up, and smiled and said, "It's finished."

How much later on? (You probably can't wait to know.)

Seven and a half minutes exactly — world-class sonnet-writing time (Si thought), by anybody's standard.

"So, read it to us, bard-o," cried a voice from over near the sideline. And Bease Dewitt came 'round the writing table, with his foolscap in his hand and (if Kate's and Simon's eyes were serious, not playing tricks) a large silk handkerchief now tucked inside one sleeve.

"It's called . . . 'Right-Mindedness,'" he said, with maybe just the faintest lisp. He cleared his throat and laid one hand, its fingers open, on his breast. And started.

> *"The same as when the clouds go chasing by,*
> *That's how my lifetime races to its close,*
> *Both quickly gone, like an ambrosia pie*
> *On Mount Olympus, or last summer's rose.*
> *The first word that I ever heard was 'sales,'*

The next ones were 'You always should buy
  low.'
At ten, I learned you don't promote the
  females;
By twenty, I had split, so as to grow.
And though I'm now a man of middle age,
And drive a car that cost me fifty grand,
I still pay just the lowest legal wage,
And keep my kid from playing in a band.
  When I am gone, let them say this of me:
  He never missed a boat, or split a fee."

When he had finished, there was only silence for
a moment. It was the sort of silence that Jeffrey
Bung would have imagined taking place after Leo-
nardo first showed the "Madonna of the Rocks"
to his patrons at the court of Ludovico Sforza in
Milan — if Bung had ever heard of him, it, them,
or such a place, that is. And it was broken by a
kind of bedlam.

People hollered, whistled, clapped, jumped up and
down. There was moaning, shrieking, panting, gal-
livanting, shouts of, "Send for Louis Untermyer,"
"Get me Bennett Cerf" (both from the same ex-
English major who'd tried to hit that squirrel with
a medieval masterpiece, and still was into tossing
literary names around). Beasely Dewitt just stood
there, smiling, then steepled up his hands, together
by his chest, and bowed and bowed.

Eventually and gradually, this standing-o shrank
down until it turned into a buzz of eager conversation. It seemed the crowd had been completely
sold, and now it wanted nothing more than . . .

power/action/miracles, for and by itself. As the theme from *Rocky* boomed into the autumn air, this (almost) captive audience turned toward the fire, started up its chant again:

"Yes! Yes! Yes! Yes! Yes! Yes! Yes!"

The leaping flames that once had risen from the wood piled in the pit had mostly done their job; the fire had burned down to chunks and gobs of red-hot stuff, and Rob and Niki went and took long-handled rakes and spread the embers so's to make them like a nice thick *quilt* of glowing coals. You could see the "helpers" blinking, flinching from the heat each time they leaned and reached out with their rakes. Twelve hundred Fahrenheit degrees (or more) was what was being moved around down there; time to bring the steaks out, Dad.

Now Bease Dewitt took off his running shoes and rolled his warm-up pants legs up; his feet looked very white and tender (never mind the Adolph's, Ma). Now Bease Dewitt jumped off the stage and marched across the tarpaulin, heading bravely toward the goalpost. (As he walked, the sea of people opened up to let him through, some holding hands, but others clapping still, and chanting.) Now Bease Dewitt swung to the right (of course), so as to get around the chainlink fence and funnel toward the pit from that direction.

Behind him came the crowd: a solid mass of bare-foot Yeses, amongst whom were some (also) bare-foot, panic-stricken Noes, who figured if they *looked* like they were going to do it, there might just be a moment when, with everyone distracted, they could make an unexpected break for freedom. The handful of cautious Undecideds were scattered here and there, still mostly on the tarp. By and large, they'd gone down on one knee; the laces on their sneakers, boots, or shoes had somehow sprouted knots of Gordian proportions. They tried to look regretful — even angry — as they struggled. "No, please go right ahead," they told the barefoot braves. "We'll be there in a minute."

Kate and Simon lagged along, in more or less the middle of the solid mass at first, then farther back. So far, they hadn't shed a shoe or sock, or any of the doubts they'd smuggled in, inside their hearts. But up to that point, neither one had made a single negative remark. And for the same peculiar, all-too-human reason. They both assumed the other one was totally committed, part of this gigantic "everybody else"; so both of them were (semi-)thinking: *I* must be the one who's crazy!

Simon (sort of) kept on saying to himself he really *couldn't* trust his judgment — his opinion — of the firewalk, and Bease Dewitt, and Bease's methods. If he was immature, which he *guessed* had been the way that he'd been feeling, frequently, at Riddle, what was the likelihood that he'd be right and all these older guys, like Phil and Grant and Jeffrey Bung, be wrong? Sure, they weren't very *nice*, but that was probably a sign of their maturity.

And then, of course, there was Amanda. *She* had said this kind of thing was good for people and might be *great* for him — and she was going to be a doctor, had to *know* about this sort of stuff. Plus Grebe, a big psychologist — he hadn't told him *not* to. Nor had K.P.'s parents (he supposed).

This isn't bullshit, gross manipulation (Simon told himself); it only *seems* that way.

Kate (for her part) hid behind the fact that Simon was the smartest kid — the smartest *anyone* — she'd ever known. He was buying this, so who was she to *not* stick SOLD signs on her lawn? Besides, she had a reputation to uphold, for doing crazy things. People who do sweat lodge *never* chicken out.

By standing on his tiptoes and then jumping up and down, Simon could see that Bease Dewitt had almost reached the edge of the pit, that he was close to . . . doing it.

"Come on, you watch," he said to Kate, and gestured, bent way over. She got her thighs around his head, and he stood up, his girl friend squarely on his shoulders. At least one of them'd be able to see, and he could *smell* from there (if other senses got to be important).

So while Simon read the words on the jacket-back in front of him (NATES AMOCO — LIVE MUSIC NITELY — THE STUCKS BOP HERE), Kate sucked in a breath and watched this skinny, barefoot Englishman raise first his right hand (as if he had to leave the room) and then his eyes (as if he hoped he'd make it), and afterward step forward, taking rapid, gliding strides, right across that crunchy red inferno.

As one, the crowd let out the breath that *all* of them had taken in together (it turned out); the coals flamed briefly in the wind from all those pipes. Rob and Niki followed Bease, mimicking his form exactly; then the three of them came back, not walking on the coals this time but squeezing in between the pit edge and the fence.

It was time now for the rest of them to go. Bease took his place at the head of the pit, like a stewardess at the entrance of an airplane; the "helpers" stood on either side, possibly (Kate thought) to serve as escorts for each walker.

The music changed. Simon recognized the song: "First Light," by Richard Thompson: "Give me what I ask for, give me what I long for . . ." Linda sang.

Wild-eyed barefoot people queued up in a line to . . . everything (and every*one* and even every*where*) they'd ever wanted in their lives.

42

Checkers

Following the conclusion of the Riddle-Walden game, Betsy and Henry ("Gates") Portcullis received at home, as was their habit, the president of Walden College, Basil ("Choo-choo") Train and his wife Missy, and about twenty-five Riddle graduates and *their* wives, all of whom President Train dearly wished were Walden grads. Guess why. It is, perhaps, significant that no Riddle alumnae and their *husbands* were known to have attended the game.

Several 1.75 liters of J&B Scotch, Smirnoff Vodka, and Beefeaters Gin later, all the guests had departed and the Portcullises had turned down no fewer than eight dinner invitations by pleading a previous engagement. In actual fact, they liked to sit around their own kitchen after such a "party," and knock back a few combination sandwiches of their own devising (often topped with melted Swiss and washed down by a cold ale or two) and talk about what *they'd* do (sometime) if they ever had the kind of money any of their guests had (other than the Trains) — instead of going to Riddle football games.

But on this particular night, Gates happened to mention the firewalk that was scheduled for the stadium (and subsidized by the Lucretia Hepple-white Foundation) and Betsy said she'd seen a fire-walk on TV once, that had been filmed in some place like Borneo, or possibly New Guinea, or Sri Lanka. And that whoever'd done the film had said — insisted — that it was completely on the up-and-up: that folks with feet "the same as you or me" could *do* this without suffering a quarter-pounder's fate.

"I'd like to check that out for myself," she said.

"Okay," her husband said, "let's go. We can hike on down there — keeping to the shadows — and sit up in the stands. No one'll ever know."

"Just let me pick up my binoculars," she said.

43

Getting There

Amanda was extremely surprised to see Brad Hammond B-and-E-ing into Greg Holt's study, probably with L in mind. Why hadn't he just walked right up and rung the doorbell and asked if he could *have* . . . whatever it might be? A drink, a market tip, a cashmere sweater — anything that figured to be there. After all, he *was* a guy, a member of A-CHOIR, one of Holt's anointed; you had to say he kind of had a license.

But here he was, a creeper-in-through-basement-window, who, when he (quite suddenly) saw Holt, recumbent on the couch, jumped backward in a perfect "startle pattern." That was a term Amanda'd first encountered in Psych I. It's the body language people speak if, say, you cat-foot up behind them and shout out a line like, "Xerox, down eighteen." Just before they punch you out, or kill themselves, they do this other number. The body bows, fists clenched; the person's head comes forward and his mouth gapes open wide. In a maxi-startle pattern, someone's tongue comes out, as well. Overall, it's not a real attractive pose.

But when Brad Hammond realized that Holt was

fast asleep, he straightened up and smirked — then nodded when he saw the cocktail shaker. There was only one glass visible, because Amanda had taken the one she'd used for toasting Holt over to the bar at the same time she'd emptied her boot. Amanda had been perfectly brought up: She *always* took her glass back to the sink when she was done.

Brad next tiptoed to the files. He opened the same drawer that she'd been into and took out the white folder she'd been reaching for when she first heard him coming. Obviously (Amanda thought) he'd known what he was looking for and this was it, or part of it, at least. She had another thought as well: If Hammond wanted it, she *had to have it*. Amanda was a girl of normal appetites, who'd roomed with Clee and all *her* stuff three years and some, who'd been in Bloomingdale's at least a hundred times. But up until that moment she had never *mega*-coveted a thing. She was damn well going to have that folder.

She watched Brad walk back to the couch, look down at Holt again. He seemed to be taking his time, savoring the moment. Holt now was snoring louder, making noise like this: "ONNK–TSCHIOU." Hammond smiled the contemptuous smile that sobriety reserves for drunkenness, that people who believe they don't make noise at night display to known, recorded snorers, that college students offer to professors' backs.

Amanda's hand settled on the cutting board behind the bar, the small one shaped like a pig that Holt's young daughter Jessica had made for him at private school. She seized it by the snout and came out swinging.

The only shot she needed caught Brad Hammond on the side of his round head, made him see a galaxy or two, and dropped him neatly on the sleeping Holt. The folder fell from fingers whose instructions from Brad's brain were interrupted while it tried to figure out why it was watching stars and feeling panic while lying on a wiggling professor.

Amanda scooped up the white folder and headed for the stairs, but before she'd conquered even ten of them (two at a time), she stopped. She didn't have her other folders; she'd left them on the bar. So down she came again.

By this time, action on the couch was heating up. Holt was flailing with both arms at Hammond, shouting questions and instructions, both.

"Whash goin' on? Get offa me, you ashhole! My god" — his eyes came into focus — "Hammond! What the hell you doin' here? Whersh Amanda, anyway? Wudja do with her?"

Maybe it was hearing that word *Amanda* that tightened up the loose connections in the Hammond brain. In any case, he got the picture — suddenly. Amanda, there, had cold-cocked him and — look! — she now possessed the folders that he simply *had* to have. And — hey! — she also now was charging up the stairs with them.

"Shit!" Brad Hammond cried. "She's got my folders! Get your hands off me, you pervert!" This last to Holt, who in his efforts to push Brad off him and get onto his feet, had grabbed him . . . carelessly, let's say.

By this time, Brad was on his feet, shaking his head to clear it further. A few seconds later he was stumbling up the stairs in hot pursuit of what he had to steal to keep his virtue safe from common criminals, in jail.

Holt's eyes took in the open window and the open file drawer. Two stagger-steps and he was peering into it, seeing what was gone, gone, gone. It didn't make the slightest bit of sense; clearly, Hammond and Amanda, both, had lost what feeble minds they had. Did either of them think that she or he — a woman and a fool — could get away with this? When he got through with Hammond's recommendation, the kid'd be about as welcome in the business community as a reducing salon in central Africa.

But first he had to get his folders back. Those folders were his ticket on a trip that went like this (in his imagination, anyway): department chair to college president to either U.S. Senate or the Cabinet, to . . . well, let's simply say: Who knows? (Remembering that this is still America, where *anyone* . . . et cetera. That's proven fact.)

And so, as Holt ran/staggered up the stairs, he wasn't just pursuing Hammond or Amanda. When he got outside and settled in his stride (such as it was), he clearly heard the music in his head: Da Da DaDa*Da*-Da, Da Da DaDa-*Da* . . . It was the theme from *Chariots of Fire*.

With the time so very near to — so absolutely almost — *now*, Phil Hedd and Grant Kahn were so completely terrified by what they were (theywere, theywere) about to do that they were even being nice to Jeffrey Bung. If, by any chance, there was a god of wimps and nerds (which both of them were very much inclined to doubt), that god would surely notice their good deed and so preserve them from the fire. Bung, though also petrified, took courage from the fact that maybe it appeared, at least, that he was *with* the other two, a member of their team. The coals would not harm Kahn or Hedd or *any of their party*, he believed; certain people just did not get burned, or go to jail, or have their car break down when it was raining.

The three of them had made a small circle, the way a team will do before a game, and they were bent way over with their six hands clenched together, and all of them were talking — jabbering — at once. Basically, their pep talks to themselves and to each other were the same: that this was "it," that "we" are going to do it, that conquering this fear would mean they'd never be afraid again, of anything. Not of their dads, of interviews, of being lousy lovers, of business trips to Athens, of a 700 Dow, of Teddy in the White House, of being slicked and staked out on an anthill by some guys like one another. "I believe," they kept on saying. "I believe."

The sight of these three getting off on hope or greed or one another (or whatever they *were* doing) was almost too much for Simon's gorge. By then, he and Kate had actually taken off their shoes and socks and rolled up their pants legs and, more or less carried along by the crowd, had allowed themselves to be brought to a place where they could see the backs of people walking on the coals, flanked by Rob and Niki, getting to the other side.

So it was working, Simon saw. At least in the sense that no one was going, "Youch, youch, youch," the way they would have on a sunny, sandy beach

July the Fourth on Fire Island. Nor were they sitting down and moaning on the other side. Nor was there any . . . walking-by-a-steakhouse smell.

They got a little closer to the pit, to being first in line. And that was when Si realized it was "working" other ways, as well.

He'd focused on the people on the other side, the one's who'd done it, and who now included Bung and Hedd and Kahn. The ones who now had "conquered" fear, who thought they now could go beyond their (former) limitations and do anything they wanted to. Simon watched them talking to each other, watched their faces closely, saw the looks way deep inside their eyes.

And hated what he saw.

"I'm not going to do it," Simon said to Kate. "Forget it. I don't want to feel that way."

"So confident, confident, right, and secure?" Kate said. "You're not going to raise your hand, *champero*? You maybe want to go to heaven, but not with that bunch, are you saying?"

"Yeah, I guess so," Simon said. He smiled. "Something like that." He now knew that somehow — for some reason — it was possible for a person to walk across hot coals, as long as they moved fast enough. Maybe it was the thin film of sweat on the soles of any normal foot (plus calluses), or the fact that there wasn't any clutching action involved — of course there was some explanation. But he also knew the fact of having done it didn't make you special — the way those bozos clearly thought it did. It didn't *change* a person for the better. In fact, in certain cases (far as he could see), the opposite was true.

"Well, I'm not going to, either," Kate said, smiling back. She'd already recognized among the firewalkers a guy (Jeff Bung) who once had made *extremely* gross remarks to her and Pam, in town. They'd yelled right back at him, saying that they'd tell their brothers, who would come and break his kneecaps for him. The guy had looked afraid (back then), but now, perhaps, he never would again.

"But I'd like to watch some more," said Simon. "You know what I think these people look like? They look like they're having some kind of religious experience, almost."

"Absolutely," Kate replied. "One up from born-again. Jesus walked on water? Hey, big deal. *They* just walked on fire, babe."

At twenty-five to nine, Hansen Grebe still hadn't seen hide nor hair of Brad Hammond — or even heard from him — and he was slightly irked. "Whitemail" ought to go without a hitch, and Brad had specifically said that he'd be "getting into" Holt's place shortly after nightfall, and would head right over to Grebe's directly afterward. And night — or darkness — had been going on for, well, three hours, anyway. Of course what Grebe *didn't* know was that to an idiot like Brad Hammond, "nightfall" was a *time*: exactly eight o'clock, the year around. So, bathed in anxious sweat but doing what he thought he said he would, he'd started getting into Holt's at 8:15.

Grebe, without those facts (of course), now had a problem. He'd promised Simon Storm he'd see *him* at the stadium at nine o'clock. Should he wait some more for Brad, or what?

316

He didn't ponder long; a Grebe is not a Hammond, promises-to-keep-wise. At 8:40 he headed out of his apartment door and started strolling toward Riddle Stadium, a walk that always took some twenty minutes' time.

Because Grebe's place was in that part of town where lots of gownies lived, his route went by the Holts' Victorian. He peered at it and also listened, as he passed; the silence made him think that Hammond wasn't there. He saw a dim light glowing in a basement window, but Hansen Grebe assumed the Holts had left it on by accident.

"Cellar bulbs are made to be burned out," he muttered to himself. "It is a law of nature," he continued, thinking of all the times he'd flicked a switch at the top of some dark stairs or stood on musty concrete floors and pulled a cord, and nothing happened. He wondered where on earth Brad Hammond *was*.

A little farther on he took a left and started down a lighted campus walk. He hadn't gone a hundred yards when he heard footsteps, rapid footsteps, coming up behind him. Turning his head, he saw a girl approach and then whiz by him — an attractive girl who made him think of someone (not a bishop). She was sprinting pretty rapidly in spite of boots and also, yes, an arm quite full of folders.

" 'It's Saturday night . . .' " Grebe sang softly to himself, starting an old Donovan song, but stopping it again almost at once. Now, in the eighties, girls like that were going places: to a meeting, a discussion, maybe to the library. Grebe believed that women — *maybe* — might obliquely change the world by helping men to develop a new consciousness, "to shake off our ancient prejudices and to build the earth," as wise old Teilhard put it.

He'd barely run that thought along the edges of his mind before he heard more footsteps back of him, twice as many as before, it seemed. This time, though, he didn't turn his head. Just a few more pretty girls a-galloping toward the library (he kind of hoped).

But the person who sped by him next was neither pretty nor a girl. He was Brad Hammond. And before Grebe could get his mouth into the shape that it'd need to call Brad's name (and ask him where the hell he'd been), here *also* came his colleague, Mr. Holt, bathed in quite a little cloud of gin-smell.

Holey-moley (figured Hansen Grebe), Holt's not only here in town, the guy's been partying. *And* he's after Brad-the-bare-but-crimson-handed, who (he, himself) is chasing pretty-girl-with-folders!

It didn't take a PhD (though Grebe had earned one, honestly, at Princeton) to figure out that she was holding Riddle's future in her hands and that he had better join the party, see where it was going, maybe crash it at the end.

Grebe's running stride was fluid and relaxed. He had his Celtics high-topped sneakers on, and he jogged five miles most every day, the year around. He only wished he had his Batman mask to wear. This job might really need the Caped Crusader.

44

A Great Blue Ball of Fire

By the time Amanda reached the stadium, she was pretty well exhausted. At first, she'd felt the one martini she had actually consumed was giving her some extra bounce and energy, but pretty soon an opposite effect was clear to her; she wasn't feeling all that great at all.

Those boots were no help, either. Cunning as they were to look at, they weren't made for running in — except, perhaps, from curb to cab. And with their insides still martini-moist, the things were heavier than usual, and also blister-city. Groan.

But still the brave girl held her pace and even tried to go a little faster. There was so much at stake, starting with her own self-image and working out from there. When she'd signed on as R.A., she'd accepted a responsibility for younger kids like Simon Storm — that little cutie — and if she didn't get back the fake confession that he'd made to save *her* reputation, she'd . . . just *die*!

But even if she could survive that blow, she couldn't stand the thought that Holt — the lecher-prince of sexual harassment (as she now could think of him) — and all his sneaky MCP's in stinky old A-CHOIR could calmly dispose of not only sweet little Simon but also that *nice* President Portcullis. Who did they think they were, anyway?

Amanda hadn't bothered to figure out what Simon would *do* with all the stuff she was clutching, once she'd handed it over to him. But she was sure he'd think of something — *he* was the genius, after all — and she would have done her part to make everything okay. So what if she dropped dead right afterward, just like whoever it was who brought back the good news (wasn't it?) from somewhere to someplace else, back in Greece? Zidippides, was that? Zippitocles? She thought the Greeks had funny names. Hippocrates — did hypocrite come from that? And Play-Doh.

As she ran through the tunnel that led to the floor of the stadium, Amanda's heart was pounding in her chest. The front parts of her thighs were cramping up, and she was having trouble going in a real straight line. Every breath she drew came with a sobbing sound; her head felt light and wobbled on her shoulders. But as she reached the floodlit running track, she'd stretched her lead to eighty yards ahead of Hammond, who in turn led Holt by thirty-five. (Grebe, now merely trotting, trailed his colleague by another twenty.)

This was a tribute to Amanda's character and life-style, and to the fact that just to *get in* med school a woman has to be much fitter than a man. That Hammond was a spineless, under-egoed lounge lizard, and that Holt had started to sing "Boomer Sooner," the University of Oklahoma fight song, as he ran, hadn't hurt her in this contest, either.

* * *

It was Betsy Portcullis who spotted Kate and Simon first, through her binoculars. She and Gates had been sitting high up in the end zone stands for twenty minutes, watching people walk across the coals, singly and in pairs. The trip itself did not take long, but by and large the walkers didn't follow one another closely. This was their moment, after all — almost their epiphany; a person wouldn't want to rush an almost sacred time, like that. And besides, those coals (from right up close) were *sort of* BLAZING hot, you know.

Checking out the ones who'd walked already, Betsy found a face she recognized. He was a member of the anthropology department, and she'd met him at a faculty reception. As she recalled, he came from California, drove a small two-seater Triumph, and once had been a devotee of the Maharaj-ji. Now, he looked ecstatic. But come to think of it, he'd looked that way at the reception, eating cheese puffs.

"D'you realize that under ordinary circumstances," Gates was now saying, "it'd be costing those people something like a hundred and fifty bucks to take their trip across the great hibachi, there? Can you believe it, Bets? That anyone would pay real money of their own for that? It's gotta make you wonder. *I* wonder things like: Is this covered by Blue Cross? Could it be a tax deduction, maybe? I wonder why the Hepple — Hey! What's that?" He pointed. "Oh-oh, looks like someone's trying to get a better place in line. And here comes someone else. . . ."

Betsy had been following the same events through her binoculars. In fact, she'd chanced to spot Amanda

321

just when she had staggered in the stadium, and she'd been struck by (1) how wasted she appeared to be, and (2) how very much intent she seemed to be on finding someone in the crowd. She'd run this way and that, stopping, peering, craning for a better view. Then, all of a sudden, she made a beeline straight into the mass of people (sort of in a big fat line) headed for the "start" end of the firepit.

Betsy aimed her glasses where she thought Amanda might be struggling to get to — and there were Kate and Simon.

"Shit," said Betsy P. "I don't believe it." But she didn't blanch or cry or get the vapors; she was just surprised. She knew those two were curious, but still.

They were looking backward at that moment, toward Amanda; obviously, they'd seen her, seemed to know her. Okay — Betsy switched to *her*. She was certainly a *pretty* girl, looked nice — though pooped; her mouth was open, shouting. She had something in her hands that she held up; it looked like notebooks, folders, two or three of them, the colors of the flag.

"What's going on down there?" the president of Riddle asked.

"Hard to tell," his wife replied. "Could be Federal Express."

She didn't see the point in getting Gates excited, and the news that Kate was down there in that throng and possibly still planned to put her little piggies (the ten that Gates had often counted, not that long ago) atop the giant barbecue would certainly produce excitement. Whatever was going to

322

happen would happen long before they possibly could reach the scene.

Betsy now could see a new disturbance in the crowd; someone else was trying to make *his* way toward her daughter (and the others). Simon was now holding the folders, or the notebooks, and appeared to be leafing through them rapidly. Betsy knew that, at that pace, the guy was reading every word. The crowd seemed more resistant to this new one's progress (of course it was Brad Hammond), and as he moved extremely slowly through it, his head kept turning back, as if he thought *another* someone else was on his trail.

And sure enough, when Betsy checked, she found . . . Professor Holt of economics, looking rather bullish (Betsy thought): in shirtsleeves, tieless, arms both waving wildly, mouth wide open as if shouting "Tally-ho" or "View Halloo" (or "Boomer Sooner"). Just for the hell of it, she checked to see if . . . sure enough! Coming after Holt and almost close enough to grab the guy was Doctor Hansen Grebe!

"Peculiar," Betsy said. Her eyes came back to Kate and Simon. Hmmm. They both looked agitated, *goosey* (you could say). The pretty girl who'd handed off the folders had collapsed, it seemed. The young man coming after her was getting very close to K. and S. The only way for them to run was toward —

"My god," her husband shouted. "Look! There's Kate and Simon — *on the coals*! And — hey! — d'you see what she just did? What's going on? Who's that? Oh, wowie, did you see that shot? Just *look*!"

B. Portcullis *had* been looking, naturally. Or even

*un*naturally, you could say, seeing that her vision was assisted by binoculars. But she understood her husband's wonderment/confusion. Even she would have had trouble filling out a witness report with any degree of certainty. But here's the way it *seemed*, to her:

She'd definitely seen Simon and Kate, both barefoot, dart to the very edge of the fiery pit and . . . stop, looking like two people standing by an outdoor pool, but *very* early in the swimming season. The man who was in charge — the starter, so to speak — was talking to them; his assistants, one on either side, were making it impossible for Si and Kate to go around the firepit.

"Raise your right hand and look up," said Bease Dewitt. *"That's very good. Now imagine you are stepping onto nice wet sand. Say it with me, now: 'Wet sand.' "*

" 'Wet sand,' " said Kate.

" 'Wet sand,' " said Simon. Then, to her: "Here. *You take the blue one. Throw it on the coals behind us, right? Let's go."*

A moment later they'd stepped onto it, both of them together. They started walking rapidly, Rob and Niki keeping pace on either side of them.

It was more like walking on . . . say, broken pine cones, than wet sand. The heat from off the coals was quite intense but yet, and strangely, none of their four feet felt more than just a slightly stinging feeling.

Betsy saw Kate turn to Simon.

"Now?" she asked. *She'd balanced the blue folder on her head, like in that posture exercise.*

"Yes," he said. *"And quick."* They were almost

at the other side. She flipped it off behind her, the way a baseball catcher does a mask.

It landed flat upon the coals, just as (1) Brad Hammond, (2) Professor Holt, and (3) Professor Grebe arrived at the (or their) pit's end, where all of them stood blinking in the sudden heat.

Before their very eyes that folder just about *exploded* into flame — a great blue ball of fire. Brad Hammond looked at Holt and then at Grebe. Holt was almost apoplectic, waving both his arms and shouting orders to . . . whoever: "Get 'em! Grab 'em! Get the other folders!" Grebe was simply smiling broadly, nodding.

Hammond snuck behind Holt's back, maneuvered to the other side of Grebe, where he would have a full professor's width between himself and Holt. He even went so far as to lay down a tentative but friendly palm on Hanson Grebe's right shoulder. His lips, unbade, formed two familiar words.

Betsy, high above the field, couldn't hear what Holt was shouting, but she could see what those shouts' effects were. Just as Kate and Si stepped off the coals, three *most* obnoxious-looking student sorts reached out to grab them. Them *and* the folders Simon still was clutching, colored red and white.

It was then that the "shot" her husband had exclaimed about took place. It "came from nowhere," as the saying goes, and bowled that trio over — as neatly as a cricket ball takes down a wicket. In spite of its wholeheartedness and really awesome power, it was not delivered by a man named Lawrence Taylor (Betsy P. was sure). Though *this* man was also black, he was a great deal smaller; and he wore a double-breasted blazer, blue, instead of jersey number 56. Hedd and Bung and Kahn, who should have been the ones to know, all swore (much later on) they never saw the the guy who hit them.

Si and Kate just scurried off and disappeared into the darkness, laughing.

They never were afraid to be themselves again.

Author's Postscript

Readers who are in the midst of filling out and sending college applications (and also their parents) will probably want to know a good deal more about the situation down at Riddle, nowadays. Whether it's at all the kind of place they'd want to go to, if they could; what's happened to the people in this book. In sum, the kind of dirt you never find in Barron's, or the other so-called "guides."

Well, first of all (alums, relax, undo those money belts), Riddle University *isn't* FATCAT College (any more than it ever was). It's still what's known as "a good little liberal arts school," and its econ department is no bigger than the next place's — though *it* might drop its eyes and say "a little better, maybe." A lot of the kids who go there *do* hope to make a very great deal of money after they graduate, but so do a lot of kids at the University of Leningrad, if you want to know the absolute truth.

Henry ("Gates") Portcullis — not his real name, remember — is still the president of Riddle, still happily married to Betsy, and still wild about his daughter Kate, who he thinks is turning into quite the young lady (though she's still wild about — and with — S. Storm, and vice versa). Gates didn't have to ever "take back" his resignation because it never did get to the board of trustees before it went down in flames. The only people who know that he wrote that letter, and why, are either much too nice to bring it up or would just as soon forget the whole thing.

Professor Greg Holt resigned his position as chairman/professor of the department of economics on the day after the firewalk. Two weeks later, his wife Renée filed for divorce (she got the children and everything else except that junk on the wall of his study and his Bentley, which broke down that same month on a rainy day in west Texas). He is currently believed to be in private business, somewhere in the Caribbean.

Professor Hansen Grebe closed down his adolescent study, but had enough to do a book: *Bummed-Out: The Zits and Zest and Zaniness of Normal Adolescence*, which he published under the pseudonym D. Bishop. There are reports that he's been seen from time to time in restaurants and nightclubs with a certain well-known actress.

Grant Kahn, Philips Hedd, Jeffrey Bung, and Brad Hammond have all graduated from Riddle and now hold jobs out there in the real world. Because all of them (in happier days) had listed Professor Greg Holt as their main reference on their various applications, Hedd, Bung, and Hammond are all "nutrition enhancement" trainees at a well-known chain; this gives them first shot at any counter jobs that open up, supposedly. Kahn is executive vice-president of a major corporation owned by guess-who.

Amanda Dollop is still in med school, has bagged

being an R.A., moved off campus, and has lost interest in all investments other than U.S. treasury bonds. Like most soon-to-be doctors, she now believes all confidence-building find-yourself therapies to be utter bullshit. She's said to be dating an older man.

Clee Clymer has discovered — and currently resides at — the best place for tanning in the world: four fifths of the way up Mount Ichibamba, in the Ecuadorian Andes (she thinks) — not far from the equator. Indigenes, from many hectares around, just (absolutely) worship her.

Asmussen is believed to be a member of the senior class, though nobody seems sure. His salesman's badge has been revoked, and The Last Resort was closed by the local board of health.

For the past two years, there has been no answer at the telephone number printed on the PREVIOUSLY OWNED PAPERS business card. Some people at Riddle still cheat, but mostly just to get into medical school.

Ex-professor Vincent Mowbray now lives on Maui and has bought (which makes him president of) Western Hawaii A&T.

Clovis St. James has disappeared — for good. As you'd expect he would. Everything he does, he does "for good," of course. And the best part is: He could show up again at any place, at any time, for any (darn good) reason.

Bease Dewitt was seen fooling around with quicksand as a possible therapeutic tool of the future, but not recently. Or, actually, at all, since then.

Simon Storm took two years off from school to write a novel.

ABOUT THE AUTHOR

Julian F. Thompson insists that *Simon Pure* is *not* an autobiographical novel. But consider the facts: He was one of the youngest people in his college class, he lives in Vermont, and he often loses games of badminton to a woman he's mad about (and who just *happens* to have the letter "P" as one initial, too).

It is also a fact that he is the author of *The Grounding of Group 6, A Question of Survival, Facing It, Discontinued,* and *A Band of Angels,* as well as the husband of the aforementioned Polly Thompson, who makes paintings when she isn't taming pigeons.